THE SCOTTISH]

Incorpora

THE WUHAN AFFAIR

By James Dalby

This is "A BEHIND THE NEWS SERIES" of Books.

My thanks to my Editors Elizabeth Dawson

THE SCOTTISH PREROGATIVE
Incorporating
THE WUHAN AFFAIR

By James Dalby
THE STORY

This story deals with the fact that Scotland was moving closer to home rule, supported by Russian money. Such a move by Putin would create the ultimate pincer movement in history, but has the Saudi decision to flood the world with cheap oil spoiled their plans? Russia depends on oil sales for the greater part of their income, in one stroke they have lost almost half, and the Russian people will feel the economic downturn, just as Putin was about to gain total control of the country for the rest of his life. Has the Corvid-19 virus made it impossible for Scotland to even consider moving from the Union?

Was China complicit in spreading the Corona Virus? One fact is true, and that is Wuhan is the centre of China's biological weapons research facility for the Peoples Liberation Army. Is it a coincidence? There are reports that Donald Trump's sanctions against China were biting. Is this their method of hitting back at the Western World and the USA in particular? Would the Chinese government risk many deaths of their own people? Chairman Mao did. Why has China only suffered 5,000 fatalities? Is it because they were prepared for it? Why has no senior member of the Chinese government become infected with the virus? Would China have produced such a virus without manufacturing a vaccine? It seems doubtful. What country will profit hugely from the collapse of the Western economies, is it China? Food for thought?

This book is **fiction** but like all the James Dalby's "Behind the News," novels, there are a substantial number of facts added to the stories.

NOTES:

The villa in Crete and the details surrounding it all are factual, the author and his wife lived there for several years.

The story about a small Caribbean airline used for anti-terrorist purposes by the CIA is true. The chairman of the airline was a business partner of the author.

The story of Operation PB success was a true CIA operation to change a democratically elected president of Guatemala, by a right-wing military man.

The author is a qualified helicopter pilot.

Other books written by the author

Sailing on Silver

The Crowley Affair

I Am Who I Am

The Gorazde Incident ***

Don't Stop the Eating

Moscow Assassin ***

The Castrators ***

A Shitty Day in Paradise

The Shanghai Incident ***

*** A BEHIND THE NEWS STORY

Want to know more about James Dalby:

www.goodnessmepublishing.co.uk

Note: At the end of this book there is an Appendix with some detailed comments on China and the countries surrounding it.

TABLE OF CONTENTS

THE CHINESE VIROLOGIST WHO BLEW THE
WHISTLE ON COVID IS NOT FINISHED YET

SHE WAS TOLD SHE WAS IN DANGER OF BEING
'DISAPPEARED' BY THE PARTY.

Family

COVID-19

THE BEGINNING

Chapter 1

It was a bright sunny day. Ian McLeod, an oil employee decided to take his pretty wife Martha and their two young children camping for the weekend. The forecast was set to be sunny and dry, perfect conditions for a great weekend. They enjoyed the freedom that camping gave them and the children of three and five years old loved playing in the fields and nearby woods with their old English sheep dog Rusty. They set off from their home in their second-hand 4x4 towing a trailer tent. Martha preferred a trailer tent as it meant they did not actually have to sleep on the ground. Although there were many areas they had been to before, Ian decided that they should strike out a little further from home. After driving for about thirty miles, they came to an area that looked perfect. They turned off the main road onto an unmade track and after about half a mile they came across a wood. There was a small track in the wood which was no problem for the 4 x 4 to traverse. It was some surprise to them that at the end of the wood was a large security fence, but it had been cut allowing them to drive through down to a small stream nestled between two small mounds with a covering of trees. It was private and perfect for a quiet weekend. As Martha was climbing out of the vehicle, she commented that it may be private land and she worried they should not stay there. Ian shrugged his shoulders and said there seemed to be no one around, and if someone came, they could always leave. He unhooked the camper trailer from the 4 x 4 and it took them less than half an hour to assemble the tent which also had a large canopy. Walking down to the stream, Ian was surprised to see many caterpillar types of tracks that had crossed the stream recently, but he took the view that no one would be working during the weekend. They had a picnic lunch and played French cricket with the kids in the afternoon, when tiring of that they threw the ball for Rusty. Martha sunbathed for a time, and once the sun went down, she prepared dinner. Afterwards the children were put to bed, and both Ian and Martha read their latest novels by the light of gas lamps, Martha 'The Island' by Victoria Hislop and Ian 'The Shanghai Incident' by James Dalby. It was not long before eyes started to droop, and they both turned in after checking the children were asleep.

They had all been sound asleep when Ian woke to the sound of some heavy machinery. He looked at the luminous dial on his wristwatch and noted the time; it was just after 2 am. It was the last thing he did on earth. The sound had risen to a crescendo and suddenly a huge, tracked machine burst through the tent killing all inside except for Rusty the dog who managed to move out of the way in time. The machine was a Russian Battle Tank the revolutionary Armata T-14 and this was in an area north west of Berwick on Tweed just over the Scottish border.

THE SCOTTISH PREROGATIVE

Incorporating

THE WUHAN AFFAIR

WUHAN

Chapter 2

There was some excitement in the Wuhan Biological Weapons Facility, this was the day that The Minister in charge came for his annual visit. The reason for the excitement was that a new virus discovery that could change the economies of the world in China's favour.

It was 10 am when the cavalcade drew up outside the facilities building, having driven through the heavily guarded gates. One of the staff quickly went to open the rear door of the large Mercedes limousine but was shoved aside by a man who had climbed out of the front door. The Minister appeared; impeccably dressed. He was a small overweight man. He smiled, his expensive implants glinting in the sun. He had a wisp of a moustache. Following him was a good-looking young woman who carried his briefcase.

The manager of the facility stepped forward with a bow, they did not shake hands. The Minister ignored the senior staff lined up in front of the entrance as he was led into the Manager's office via an elevator to the sixth floor.

'Well Mao, what have you got for me?' He asked, as he sat down at the head of a large boardroom table in the centre of the room. He appeared to be slightly out of breath.

Sitting down next to the Minister, the manager produced a folder marked SECRET. Three other people had entered the room and by invitation sat down at the table. The pretty woman sat opposite the manager. The Minister was handed a folder. He took it and threw it on the table. 'I will read it later Mao, now tell me what is so wonderful about this new virus you have developed?'

Mao coughed, 'Well as you know Minister, we experiment with all types of virus's here, we have two laboratories particularly set up to investigate within the terms of our covert biological weapons programme. The Wuhan institute has studied corona viruses in the past, including the strain that causes Severe Acute Respiratory Syndrome, or SARS, H5N1 influenza virus, Japanese encephalitis, dengue, and Ebola. Researchers at the institute have also studied the germ that causes anthrax – a biological agent once developed in Russia.

'You will also be aware that the P4 lab in Wuhan has connections to the Chinese military, the People's Liberation Army. We were tasked to produce something even more infectious and deadly. We have succeeded in doing so. The beauty of this virus is it is dangerous for older people and particularly for those with underlying health problems.

'The answer to our continuing prosperity used to be cyber warfare it not only to ensure our military goals we have been able to copy many secrets from computers around the world.

'The problem now, however, is that our enemies can detect where the hacks come from, and they are using methods to block our efforts by utilising the Quantum computers and new ways of encryption using photon technology.

'With this Corona Virus, Covid-19, we can bring the Western Democracies to financial ruin within a few weeks and the United States, our prime target, is particularly susceptible due to their health system.'

'So, what is the difference between the ordinary Corona Virus and Covid-19?' Asked the Minister.

'It is hugely infectious and is carried on the air, so anyone infected can pass it on without touching. It can live for at least 72 hours on an immobile product, such as a shopping trolley. The first symptoms are like flu, but it attacks the respiratory system and so is extremely dangerous to those that smoke or have smoked. Most of those affected get pneumonia and it can therefore be fatal. The beauty of this, used as a weapon, is that it can spread without trace from any area.'

He laughed, 'indeed, we could create fake news once a breakout was instigated, that the virus is a part of a U.S. conspiracy to spread germ weapons.'

The Minister smiled. 'You and your team have done well Mao.' He looked around the table and all felt a warm glow of the congratulations proffered by the Minister.

'I have two questions, however, how do you know what result can a human expect from the virus and what benefit could we achieve by spreading it, surely it could create havoc in China too?'

Mao nodded, 'we tested it on the Uighur people who are contained in the re-education camps in Xinjiang Province. Most of the new incumbents survived, but for those that had been in the facility for some time, the death rate was high'

'How high?'

'About 33% Minister.'

'Very well, have you created a vaccine for this?'

'Yes, we tested that out on the Uighur people as well, there were a few fatalities, but we got it right in the end. There are no vaccines in the rest of the world though.'

'You have done well Mao; I will take this folder back to Beijing with me now and discuss it with my colleagues. Depending on their view, I will give you, our instructions.'

THE SCOTTISH PREROGATIVE

Incorporating

THE WUHAN AFFAIR

MEETING OF COBRA

Chapter 3

It was some months earlier when Adrian Bradley, the current head of MI6, asked for an extraordinary meeting of Cobra. Present were the Prime Minister, the National Security Advisor Sir George Pemberton, the head of MI5 Sir Ian Crowley, The Chief of Staff of the Armed Forces, Admiral John Scott-Jones, and the head of the Metropolitan Police Sir Harry Booth.

Only heads of departments were invited, so secret was the information he had to discuss. He knew both the Foreign and Defence Secretaries were overseas, otherwise they too would have been included.

The Prime Minister formally opened the meeting and then handed the floor to Adrian Bradley.

'Thank you, Prime Minister, the reason I asked for this special meeting is because we've received information from an important asset inside the Kremlin. Some of you are already aware of this significant person, but for obvious reasons we do not want it to be known that we have such an asset, not even to your number two and certainly not to any of your assistants, however trustworthy they may be.

'We've received information that Russia is instigating a new operation called "Open Door".'

The Chief of Staff leaned forward, 'but surely Adrian, we get these coded operations from time to time, why is this one so special?'

Adrian looked round the large conference table where they were all sitting, he paused deliberately for effect. 'The reason we are taking this extremely seriously is two-fold. One, our asset is connected to the military and although extremely senior in the Kremlin hierarchy, he is not in the loop, so it appears the operation in question is being kept to a very few people. This suggests to us that it may initially be a political matter leading to a military incursion at a later stage when more people become involved. The second point is more serious however, and that is fifteen billion dollars have been appropriated for the success of this operation, with a further ten billion in reserve.'

The Chief of Staff whistled, 'that is an extraordinary figure, we could build four aircraft carriers for that amount.'

The Prime Minister intervened. 'All we know so far is what Adrian has told us. "Open Door" suggests that there could be a specific target where the President of Russia sees an opportunity from which he can gain a major advantage.'

'Well, he is certainly an opportunist,' said Sir George Pemberton, but we need to start looking at the various parts of the world where there may be a political or an obvious area where he can create mischief.'

'Hmm, well we know what he's already achieved in Syria,' said Admiral Scott-Jones, 'and it's doubtful that he can gain more influence or territory in that area.'

'Don't forget that he's cosying up to Turkey though,' answered Sir Ian Crowley.

14

'Yes, good point Ian, and that is one area to watch as it would be a great coup for Russia to ally itself to Turkey, a NATO member,' said the Prime Minister.

'Doubtful,' answered Adrian, 'Turkey may make collaborative noises, and indeed they have recently signed a deal to buy S-400 air defence missiles from Russia after the US objected to them buying from China, but the President of Turkey knows very well it was Russia that was behind the latest coup there. While it's in his interests to frighten the West into a belief that rapprochement between the two countries is a possibility, it is extremely unlikely he will get any closer to Russia, which is after all, their traditional enemy.'

'What about Iran?' Sir George Pemberton asked.

Adrian shook his head, 'no, they may have become temporary allies against the Islamic State, but their ideologies are too far apart, in any case, what would Russia have to gain from such a partnership?'

'Well, where else in the world is there an opportunity?' Sir Harry Booth asked.

'We can forget the far-east,' said Adrian, 'as that is in China's sphere of influence, which is another problem pending, we are very concerned at what is going on at their biological weapons facility in Wuhan. It is my opinion we can forget India, Africa, and the United States too. My feeling is, that it is nearer to home, in other words Europe where he has already moved against Armenia, Monrovia, Montenegro, Georgia and the Ukraine. Obviously states that contain Russian speakers are more likely to be in Russia's sights.

The one factor that stands out in all of those instances is either a weak political situation or a complete political breakdown such as happened in the Ukraine.'

15

'There are Russian citizens living in Ukraine, Poland, Lithuania, Latvia, Estonia and Finland, they could all be made to feel insecure due to fake news and media propaganda,' said Admiral Scott-Jones. 'It is all too easy to create instability within those communities, giving Russia an excuse to invade. Remember Hitler used a similar excuse when invading Czechoslovakia.'

'True,' answered Adrian, 'but Russia already have a state on the Baltic which they named Kaliningrad, this is the land they annexed from Germany at the end of World War 2, so they have a strong presence there. In any case, most of those mentioned are part of NATO, apart from the Ukraine and Finland, so the President of Russia is not stupid enough to start a third world war over relatively small pickings.'

'I agree,' replied Scott-Jones, 'but we must remember that they have recently updated their missiles in the Kaliningrad area, replacing their obsolete OTR-21's with the SK720 Iskandar multi-purpose missiles, which almost certainly contravene the INF treaty. We suspect they have the capability of reaching targets well beyond 500 kilometres, which is the agreed distance of travel within the treaty.'

Scott-Jones continued, 'for those of you who are not familiar with this updated weapon, the Iskandar mobile missile system is equipped with two short-range ballistic missiles which substantially increases the fire-power of the missile units, as each can be targeted independently. Even while these weapons are in flight, the target coordination can change. It has several different conventional warheads, including cluster, fuel-air explosive, bunker-busting and electro-magnetic pulse. They are also capable of carrying nuclear warheads. Although principally designed as an anti-aircraft missile, they are capable of much more.

'For instance, the magnetic pulse capability is the one that fries digital operations on the ground, in other words it puts the lights out. Now most of Poland, Germany and all the Baltic States are under their umbrella, and you can be sure that their distance capability can increase, even to threaten our shores.

'We should also consider that Russia has developed a warhead that may make our defence system obsolete, in that they have built in an avoidance system to their ballistic missiles. They have also recently developed underwater drones that can look for and destroy submarines. The fact that our Chancellor wants to cut our defence budget is not just a concern, but dangerous.' He concluded, eyeing the Prime Minister.

'They have a northern land connection with Norway,' mused Sir George. 'If they went into Norway, they could effectively create a pincer movement that could threaten the whole of the Baltic and that would be a pincer movement of all pincer movements.'

Adrian nodded, 'but again, Norway is part of NATO and thus it would almost certainly start a major conflagration,' he answered.

'For those of us who read our history,' said Scott-Jones, 'it is not new for Russia to use creeping expansion tactics, it's called "maskirouka". They did so from 1836 to 1899 when they effectively moved south from the northern end of the Caspian Sea to the south, only stopping at the north east end of what was then India, now Pakistan. It was where the British Empire stopped them moving any further.

'In the nineteenth century when we had grown tired of war after defeating Napoleon, we allowed our military to be run down. The result was Kaiser Wilhelm 2.

'After the horrendous conflict of World War 1, we embarked on another reduction of arms and so another opportunist called Hitler annexed Austria and invaded Czechoslovakia on the excuse that there were Germans living in the northern end and then carried on to Poland. He took our first reaction as a sign of weakness. Using the assets of those countries, he then took Norway, Denmark, the Netherlands, Belgium, and France. At this stage Italy joined the Axis as they thought they were on the winning side. It was not long before Yugoslavia and Greece fell too.

'Can you see the connection? We take our eye off the ball and allow ambitious dictators to consolidate their gains and then we appear surprised when we suddenly find that our State is perilously under threat.'

'That's certainly true,' answered George Pemberton. 'But in recent times we made an error in going into Iraq, which understandably turned the democracies against using military might as an answer to a problem. In that case there was no clear threat, although we were initially led to believe there was.'

'The true story of that war is still to be made public,' answered John Scott-Jones. 'There were certainly no WMD found, but the sign given to us by the Israelis was that they were there. We suspect that they were moved into Syria and had we not gone in, the Israelis might have done, thus causing a Middle East catastrophe.

'More seriously, when Obama gave up on his red line on chemical weapons used in Syria against its own people, it was taken as a sign of weakness. However, what I have shown is there are disturbing similarities with prior events in history. Germany, humiliated after the First World War, looked for a saviour, any saviour, and they got Hitler.

'The Soviet Union was humiliated by Reagan's administration, which brought about their economic collapse. The result was a loss of a substantial amount of territory which they had subjugated during the 18th and 19th century and subsequently during World War 2. Humiliation of a State brings repercussions where the people are eager to accept a stronger leader. What they do not realise is that strong leaders often exceed their initial brief, believing that democracy equals weakness.

'China is a good example, where the populace now has little or no say in how their country is run due to humiliating defeats in the 20th century. Now their leader has been voted in for life. In countries like this, the law is ignored or changed to suit the ruling clique and dissenters are either murdered or disappear and this is also happening in Russia and North Korea. To ensure the rulers continuity of power, they must have enemies and the quickest way to create enemies is to subjugate other sovereign states.' Scott-Jones sat back in his chair.

'Now we have a situation where President Trump has created sanctions against China,' said Adrian, 'which is causing problems to their economy. He may be right in principle, China has always guarded their own market while flooding others with their goods, most created from stolen technology, but now the Chinese leaders will lose face. My concern is what they might do to overcome their humiliation.

'We never take lessons from history, only acting when things have reached a pitch that is only solved by a huge conflagration. Prevention is better than cure, Churchill said "jaw-jaw was better than war-war." we should "draw a line in the sand" and be prepared to back it up. Of course, the forming of United Nations formation was to ensure peaceable solutions to disagreements between States, but when you have countries with vetoes, it simply turns into a

19

talking shop, just as the League of Nations was. Unfortunately, there are now ways of waging war without declaring it, and we are dealing with a multitude of leaders who have no concern with human life, whether it be their own people or others. Power is their aphrodisiac.'

George Pemberton leaned across the conference table. 'You're right of course, democracy is undeniably weak when faced with leaders that are totally ruthless and have no purpose other than to expand their own personal power, usually at the expense of their own people. The problem we face is even greater than 1876, arguably the beginning of modern warfare. (The Franco Prussian war). Our populace is better educated but still inward looking, their main concern being what is the country doing for me, not what can I do for my country. Things are changing, the cry now is why are a small number of people getting rich while we foot the bill for their comfortable existence, which still focuses the electorate's eye on what is happening in their own backyard.'

The Prime Minister held up her hand, 'I think political philosophy is a great thing to discuss,' she said, 'but we are straying from the point of this meeting, which is to discuss how we deal with what may be a serious threat to world peace.'

Scott Jones nodded, 'could it be that we are going down the wrong track, is it possible that Russia have developed an advanced weapon that we are not aware of, the threat of which could "Open a Door"?'

'We already know that they have a powerful nuclear capability,' answered the Prime Minister, 'but no-one in their right mind would use those weapons except in extreme circumstances, and the use of them would trigger immediate repercussions.'

'You're quite right Prime Minister,' answered Adrian, 'the current President of Russia is no Khrushchev, but we can be reasonably sure that he will take advantage of a political situation, just as he did in the Ukraine and elsewhere.'

'Perhaps then we should be looking at a weak political situation emerging,' said Harry Booth.

The Prime Minister smiled, 'in that case, the "door" is truly open in the USA, South America, Africa, Europe and the Middle East. Elections in Germany have created a moribund and a divided nation and France, although electing a strong President, they have many in their population following a far-right party, financed by Russia. Italy is also divided and could even have their own ITEXIT, and we have Brexit. Greece is closer to Russia than we are comfortable with. I would remind you that if we lose the election, your new proposed Prime Minister has already indicated that he would cancel Trident and would not under any circumstances press the nuclear button, thus negating our main area of defence.'

Scott-Jones nodded. 'That would be disastrous as we would then effectively have no defence. Our armed forces, such as they are, have worked on the nuclear deterrent policy for the last fifty years and we would be totally naked from a military point of view, if our enemies were the only ones that had nuclear weapons.'

'We also have to consider that Russia would have certain advantages in a nuclear exchange,' said George Pemberton. 'They have about the same number of nuclear weapons as are available to NATO, i.e., about 7,300 but their main advantage is their land mass.'

'Hmm, but NATO arguably have currently better technology regarding defence of nuclear ballistic missiles by destroying them in outer space via the N.M.D. system. The

Russians only have a defence system around Moscow. Of course, technology changes quite quickly in this business and the only way to see which country has the edge, is to try them out,' said Scott-Jones.

Adrian looked sober. 'God forbid we ever get to that stage but there is another fact to consider. President Trump has warned that the USA may turn their back on their penny-pinching allies in Europe, where only five out of 27 spend the amount, they are legally committed to within the NATO agreement. This is not a payment we make to a bureaucratic body such as the European Union it is based on how much we spend on our own defence, the bottom line being 2% of GDP. The countries who adhere to the agreement are the USA, UK, Lithuania, and Greece. It is interesting that Greece has more tanks available than the United Kingdom and France together, but not enough money to support them never mind training the crews to run them. My understanding is that Poland and Estonia have already agreed to up their expenditure to meet the NATO criteria but if Britain cancelled Trident, the States may well say "you're on your bike buddy".'

'The more I listen to this discussion,' said Sir Ian Crowley, 'the more I think it would not be in the interests of Russia or China to start a nuclear exchange as they certainly couldn't be sure of winning. Indeed, why risk everything when they can achieve their aims without using military power? It seems to me that it points to a political "Open Door," perhaps followed up with a military threat once secured.'

Adrian nodded. 'Yes, that is our conclusion now, considering the rather tumultuous political and financial situation in the Western World. We feel that it may give Russia several "Open Doors" and perhaps they don't even have a specific plan, simply the funds appropriated to take advantage of any situation that may arise.'

'That could certainly be the case,' answered Scott-Jones, 'but the appropriation of such large funding suggests it's targeted for a particular situation. Let us not forget that Russia has allegedly put funds into trying to change the election in the USA to someone who they believed would be either more compliant or isolationist.'

The Prime Minister looked at her watch. 'Well gentlemen, I don't think we can go any further at this stage,' As she stood up, she put her papers back into the folder she had in front of her. 'Adrian, I suggest you find a way of obtaining more information from your asset in Russia. We urgently need more details, although there may not be any specific areas as you have shown. As far as the rest of us are concerned it is a matter of a watching brief. You've got the background; all you can do at this stage is to alert this committee if you spot an "Open Door" situation arising.'

'Thank you, Prime Minister,' said Adrian also putting his papers into his brief case, 'I am going to follow up with the Russian asset as you suggest, but to do so I am going to need someone who I believe is capable of helping us with this matter, I'll keep you all informed.'

THE SCOTTISH PREROGATIVE

Incorporating

THE WUHAN AFFAIR

THE PLAN TAKES SHAPE

Chapter 4

When Adrian, known as C, returned to his office at 85 Albert Embankment in Vauxhall, he picked up his internal phone. 'Geoffrey, could you pop up to my office? I have a query on Goldilocks. Bring his file up with you please.'

Geoffrey Williamson was an old hand having previously served as "the political man" (a euphemism for spy), in many embassies throughout Eastern Europe. The last country, before moving to MI6 headquarters was Moscow; he spoke Russian fluently. He phoned through to his assistant Mary Armstrong and asked her to retrieve the Goldilocks file from the secret archives and meet him outside C's office. As he was walking out, he handed her a request signed by him, which would be kept by the archive section until the file was returned. Only very few senior officers can authorise the retrieval of files of overseas agents.

He waited a few minutes before entering C's office suite to enable Mary to obtain the file and bring it to him. He checked it with a cursory glance, ensuring it had been correctly updated and then entered the office next to Adrian Bradley. Adrian's secretary told Geoffrey to go straight in.

'Ah Geoffrey, have a seat.' Adrian pointed to a comfortable armchair situated in a corner of his office. As he was sitting down, the telephone rang, and Adrian took the call. While in conversation C's secretary came in with two cups of coffee and some chocolate biscuits. C' was known for his "sweet tooth." It was rare that Geoffrey was called to Adrian's office, he usually met him instead, in a conference room two floors below. As a result, he assumed that this request was important. After taking a sip of the excellent coffee, he looked around the room that had only one window which was facing the Thames. The office was spacious with a large desk having several telephones and an intercom. There were two chairs in front of his desk, and a leather topped boardroom table with eight chairs. Where he was sitting, there were another four chairs spaced around a polished coffee table. The office had a few pictures dotted around the room, which Geoffrey assumed belonged to Adrian and his desk was clear of paperwork but supported two small pictures of his wife. He knew they had no children.

Adrian had experienced a meteoric career; he had joined the security service as a courier twenty years before. He had spent some time in the field before returning to London as a section head and had scored some spectacular successes, particularly against the Islamic State. He was an expert on the Middle East, and he was fluent with Arabic.

He finished his conversation and put the phone down pressing the internal intercom to his secretary. 'No more calls Joan, until Geoffrey and I are through.'

He walked over and sat down. 'Now, I want you to know that I relayed the information you gave me to the COBRA meeting, but I need much more information. Firstly, tell me about Goldilocks, his background, how we currently contact him and if it is possible for us to get a private meeting with him to discuss the matter further.'

Geoffrey did not look at the file, he knew the answers. 'Goldilocks is Peter Validich who was a Major General in charge of the Soviet Air Force in an area covering Orel to the Belarus border.'

'A large area...'

'Very and extremely sensitive too, he was instrumental in supporting an asset of ours over the Belarus border, her name incidentally was Ladvia Patricia Silonovic. He did not know at the time that she was one of ours, but she was an accomplished pilot originally trained by him when he headed the training section of Debrenic, the KGB's covert training centre. It was there she learned to fly the Hind helicopter. She was flying such an aircraft out of Russia when ordered to land at an air force station within the State boundary before crossing the border to Belarus. To cut a long story short, she had to pay a large sum of money to the local Commandant for clearance and in addition to stay the night in his house. While there, the Commandant became drunk and tried to rape her and, in the scuffle, he was killed, setting off all sorts of alarms as he was the brother of a member of the original Politburo in the Soviet Union. As you know, this was disbanded in 1990 but some of those members were transferred to Putin's new Ministerial set up, which included the brother. He used his power to force Validich's resignation and tried to get him arrested for treason. Fortunately, caught with his hands in the till, he was removed from power and disappeared. We understand murdered by the State, not an unusual occurrence in Russia today.

Due to Peter Validich's experience and background, he accepted a senior post in the Kremlin as an official advisor on Air Force matters. His cancelled pension reinstated.

'It didn't take long for him to realise that the Putin government was not the democratic force he thought it was, and when a friend of his, a man called Boris Nemtsov was murdered in cold blood, he realised that he had joined a government that ignored the law, justice being decided at the whim of only a few. When he discovered other state murders, particularly of journalists, he became thoroughly alarmed, and even more so when Russia invaded the Ukraine.

'When his eldest daughter returned to their home in Russia on holiday; she is studying archaeology and history at Oxford, he discussed the problem with her as he was thinking of resigning. She suggested that was exactly what he should not do, but as an honest man he could help her to stop the worst excesses of the politburo.

'She returned to Oxford and sought the advice of a senior lecturer who was her mentor, and she explained her father's position. The Lecturer Gordon Strachan is one of us, and he suggested that she persuade her father to inform her of problems or new policies that could be damaging to Russia or the free world. He made it clear that we were not asking for secrets of military equipment,' Geoffrey looked up, 'we have that area covered from other assets anyway. We told Gordon what we needed was simply a coded message giving us top secret intentions. Validich had stressed that under no circumstances was any sort of code table such as RSA or PGP to be used, so if he were ever suspected, a search would not in any way compromise him or her. I suspect he knew that our encryption on which we base all our financial dealing and much more, was already compromised.'

'And what sort of code did he suggest?' asked Adrian.

'Both father and daughter correspond often in English with each other, so it was suggested they simply continued their letters and the code to be based on the date the letter was written. So, if a letter were written on the 5th February, the code would indicate that the first seventh word to be a code word which would end in a full stop and each seventh word thereafter would be a code word, i.e., 5 + 2 = 7, and so on. Obviously if the date were larger such as 25 December the thirty seventh word would be used. Once the message had become part of the text, then a full stop would follow before the next coded word. If an amount was to be in billions a dollar sign used next to two or three numerical figures. The end of the message was indicated by the next paragraph starting with the letter "I".

'Here is a typed copy of the letter written in the last communication.

Date: 31 December

My Darling Aleski.

Mummy sends all her love to you, and we are both delighted at your progress at Oxford and the hard work you have done.

I have not been well lately, and it may be that I may have to endure an <u>operation</u>. I am hoping that this is not a serious matter, but I am going to have to consult a surgeon and have some tests carried out to decide whether I may have to go into hospital here and undergo procedures that includes <u>open</u> surgery.

Anyway, don't worry I trust all will be well.

Your mother is fine but had a minor accident the other day when her car had a slight confrontation with another car, your mother's car was lightly damaged, but only the back <u>door</u>.

I don't think it will be a large bill though, although the garage suggested <u>$15 at most $25.</u>

I would be interested to know how your archaeology studies are progressing (the letter went on to other subjects)

Love from us both and hope to see you soon.

XXX

'I've underlined the relevant words but take the underlining out and it's fairly innocuous. The problem with such a code is it is very restrictive and thus there is never any further explanation.'

Adrian grimaced, 'I trust that code was not suggested by us, if he came under suspicion, it would not take long for it to be penetrated.'

'It wasn't but contacting him to create a safe method has not been possible.'

'Can we persuade him to visit the United Kingdom?'

'No, not even to visit his daughter, we tried through her to get him to go to Oxford, but his view is that such a visit would arouse suspicions. He is incredibly careful, particularly so as he remembers the Philby affair and does not entirely trust us as a body. As you know, he has already indicated that he thinks that there is a mole within the firm although not yet at a very senior level.'

Adrian frowned, 'You've mentioned that before, and we carried out a security sweep, but found nothing untoward.' Adrian stood up and walked to the window staring at the traffic far below. 'We have to get him to a secure environment where he feels completely safe. What about the asset he helped to escape, he must have trusted her otherwise he would not have become involved, could we use her?'

Geoffrey grimaced, 'unfortunately she was killed, apparently shot by Jeremy Kirkham, the reasons are not known, but shortly afterwards Jeremy resigned, and he now lives in Chile.'

'Ah yes, I remember Jeremy well, he was the liaison between all the security services at the time, he would almost certainly have been in my position had he remained in the firm as he was an extremely talented operator. You probably don't know this, but he was mainly responsible for the ending of the Bosnian situation, quite a coup at the time.' Adrian paused, 'I wonder if he could help us with this problem, perhaps we could persuade our asset to have a holiday in Chile?'

Geoffrey shook his head, 'doubtful on two counts, Validich's friendship was with Ladvia Silonovic not Jeremy Kirkham and he was not aware of Jeremy nor have the two ever met. In any case, I have a feeling that Chile would be a step too far and what excuse could he give for travelling there?'

Adrian walked back from the bullet proof window that had splinter proof drapes and sat down looking thoughtful. He turned to Geoffrey, 'where do Russians generally go on holiday out of Russia?

Geoffrey pursed his lips and laughed. 'Well Cyprus is one that was well frequented by those wanting to squirrel funds away, but since the financial situation, it is not quite so popular.' He stopped, 'Crete is quite popular,' he mused, 'I happen to know that because we have a senior retired operative there who owns a luxury guest house in western Crete.' Geoffrey put his chin into his hand. 'In fact,' he said with some excitement entering his voice, 'that would be a perfect place, as the villa is super secure and they only take one party at a time, which would mean that Peter Validich would not need to travel outside the villa once there.'

'Then why don't we suggest to Oxford University that they grant Validich's daughter a special endowment for her to travel to Crete to study the archaeological remains on the island of which there is a considerable amount, it being the earliest recorded civilization in Europe?' Adrian smiled.

Geoffrey looked surprised, 'I didn't know that, or are you referring to Greece?'

'No, the Cretans had an advanced civilization over 5,000 years ago, long before the Egyptians, Greeks or Romans. Indeed, it is suggested that Cleopatra was of Cretan stock. The Minoans ruled the country, they were an ancient breed from which the Greek civilization grew. From an archaeological point of view the island was later populated or occupied by the Minoans, Mycenaean's, Dorian Greeks, Pirates, Romans, Byzantium's, Venetians, Turks and eventually became part of Greece in 1913. In May 1941, the Germans occupied Crete until the end of 1945 when they surrendered to the British forces in the area and the island returned once again to Greece. There is also some considerable evidence of an advanced pre-Minoan settlement at Phalasana on the west coast, where a sunken harbour has miraculously re appeared.'

Geoffrey was impressed, 'how on earth do you know all this?'

Adrian smiled, 'I spent over three months on the island after the Turks invaded Cyprus in 1974. I had just joined the service and went with a senior colleague to report on the possibility of Turkey expanding their interests in the area.

'The US Naval Detachment was established in May 1969 with a staff of 13 members. It was a detachment of the Naval

31

Air Facility at Sigonella, in Sicily. The detachment accommodated 93 enlisted personnel and three officers by August 1972.

'Due to our report, the base in Crete was substantially expanded to include a major military air facility and is now used by all NATO ships as a supply centre. I was lucky, because of my interest in history, I was able to thoroughly explore the island.'

Geoffrey nodded, 'it's clear from what you say that Crete is a secure place and would be perfect for all parties to meet there, and it appears that Validich and his wife holidaying there with his daughter, could not in any way arouse suspicion in Moscow. My feeling is that getting him and his wife there should not be a problem, but if he realises that he and his family have been drawn into an SIS enclave he may react negatively, we need something else to persuade him.'

'What about security....'

Geoffrey predicted what Adrian was about to ask. 'The man and his wife who own the villa are completely safe, no one in Crete knows their background, except that they have run their own businesses in various parts of the world, which is true as both have been under cover most of their working life.'

'Their names?' Asked Adrian

'They go under the name of James and Kate Alexander, not their real names of course. Both retired some years ago, but it suited us to persuade them to go and live in Crete which is becoming an even more strategically important area.'

'So, James and Kate essentially work for 'Q' section?'

'Correct, sleepers,' answered Geoffrey. 'The fact that James is now well over seventy years of age is an excellent cover, as what spy agency would employ someone of over sixty-five?'

Adrian nodded, 'that sounds perfect, but we somehow have to put Validich in the picture to persuade him to go there.'

'That is probably not possible given our communication system, but he may guess there is something else behind it,' answered Geoffrey.

Adrian bit his lip, 'this is probably a one-time operation, we have to be sure that he will go. Who do you suggest should meet him there?'

'Oh, that's easy, you should. You could fly in on an American C130 and thus avoid any prying eyes at the International airport. The villa is only 35 minutes from the NATO base by car.'

'Well, I could do with a short holiday,' Adrian smiled. 'What I need from you is a complete report on what this man has done for us in the past, in the meantime I have niggle in the back of my mind regarding Jeremy Kirkham, I have a feeling there was more to that story than meets the eye.'

Geoffrey stood up and headed for the door. As he opened it, he turned. 'You may be right; I happen to know that his file is marked the Gorazde Incident and is for the eyes of C only. It's in your safe in the archive department and only you have the combination.'

When Geoffrey had left the office, Adrian picked up the internal phone to the archive department. The phone was answered by Justin Morton who handled all MI6 archives, including the most secret files.

'Justin, C here, just to let you know I shall be coming down shortly to open the vault and I will be taking out the Gorazde Incident file.'

Twenty minutes later Adrian was back in his office flipping through the pages of the retrieved file. What he read surprised him. After reading and assimilating the data, he picked up a direct secure line and punched in a number.

A man answered: 'Jeremy Kirkham here, who is that?'

'Jeremy, you don't know me, how secure is your line?'

'It isn't.'

'Okay, I'll be brief, my name is Adrian Bradley...'

Jeremy's hair prickled at the back of his neck. 'Hello Adrian, I know who you are, and the answer is no.'

Adrian laughed, 'yes I can understand that, however something has arisen that you could help us with, it's so important that I'm travelling to Santiago tomorrow and would like to meet.'

There was a moment's silence, 'where, at the Embassy?'

'No, they are not aware of my trip.'

'I see,' Jeremy paused, 'okay, we'll pick you up in our Jet Ranger, what's your flight number?'

'BA0251 arriving at 09:40. I have your wife's photograph, so if she meets me ...'

'No, she'll fly the chopper, but it'll be me who meets you.'

'Okay, I have your photograph too, so no problem, I trust you haven't changed too much in the last fifteen years or so?'

Jeremy just laughed, 'I think you'll recognise me.'

THE SCOTTISH PREROGATIVE

Incorporating

THE WUHAN AFFAIR

SANTIAGO

Chapter 5

Adrian caught the British Airways flight to Santiago. The flight had been full, but he had used his authority to ensure he received a seat in the first-class cabin. He was pleased with his company as the passenger in the next seat was an attractive and famous American actress. Fortunately, the fourteen-hour flight gave him plenty of time to discuss the world at large and the election of Donald Trump who she knew. He had brought the secret file on board with him, and once his new companion was asleep, he studied its contents in detail.

File 1043824. The Gorazde Incident

For the eyes of 'C' only

The beginning of the file traced the story of the Balkans War and the horrific genocide that was perpetuated by both sides, but particularly the Serbs. It was realised that unless a stalemate was broken the Serbs would control Bosnia and so Jeremy Kirkham put forward an idea that brought the two sides to the table which essentially stripped the Serbs of their overwhelming military forces. It was a huge success and brought the war to a fair end.

Adrian read a brief description of Jeremy's background

JEREMY KIRKHAM

Jeremy Kirkham, a Yorkshire man by birth, educated at Ampleforth College and Oxford, he was one of the new breed. He had no particular security connections, his father had been a dentist in a busy practice in Leeds and his mother a housewife until his father had died, when she became a legal secretary after a year's training.

Jeremy studied law at Oxford but decided not to practice. His brilliance was such that he had come to the attention of the Foreign Office recruiters, rather than the reverse. Their first offer for him to enter the Diplomatic Service had not been of interest to him, but their later persistence in offering a job in the security service had intrigued him. After joining the service, he experienced a meteoric rise over a period of ten years, and at the time of his resignation he was directly responsible to the Deputy Head for all liaison duties between the other services including the military. This was an unusual responsibility for someone of only 34 years. During his term, terrorism had taken over from the Cold War, and he had instructions to reform all current terrorism policies to consider the current world situation.

He had broken down the possibilities of threat from various factions, and his recommendation of policies were adopted and implemented. During his tenure, he had befriended a young woman who had also had a meteoric career and between them they conceived an idea to break the Bosnian Serb dead lock, near the end of the Balkan Campaign. Her name was Ladvia Patricia Silonovic.

There was much more in file, but Adrian was particularly interested in reading up the details and background of Ladvia. This was a file handed over to the SIS security service by Bosnian authorities, after it became public knowledge that she had been killed in the UK.

LADVIA PATRICIA SILONOVIC.

Ladvia Patricia Silonovic.

36

Date of Birth 27th July 1960.

Place of Birth: London

Father: Patro George Silonovic - Father Serb, Mother Macedonian.

Mother: Dorothy Margaret Frimsby - Father English, Mother Welsh.

Father's Occupation: Diplomat, Ambassador to London for the Tito government, mother and father killed in a suspicious car accident near Sarajevo, August 1985.

Patro Silonovic was instrumental in trying to keep the various factions of Serbia together after the death of Tito, and his notable success caused his death at the hands of the right-wing Serb nationalists. The wreckage of the car and the bodies were at once taken to Belgrade by the secret police They were never returned to their homeland for burial.

Ladvia was educated in London until the age of seventeen, when she entered Belgrade University where she studied Political Science. At the age of 21 she gained a prized scholarship to Moscow University. During her time in Moscow, she came under the influence of the KGB, later to become the FSB under President Yeltsin. She carried out a twelve-month course at Debrenic, the KGB's covert training centre. By the time she was 24 she was fluent in both Russian and English and had undergone a flying course on various assault aircraft including the Mil MI-6 "Hook" a popular assault and lifting helicopter work horse, often used for clandestine missions, and sold to client states around the world. She excelled on the course, coming first out twenty-three men and three women. She still holds an honorary commission of Major in the Spetsnaz, the Russian elite commando unit. The senior training instructor was a Colonel Peter Validich.

At the age of twenty-five she married a Russian air force major, who was posted to Paris as a military attaché shortly afterwards. In 1987, her relationship with her husband broke down, and when he returned to Moscow, she went to live in

London attached to the Bosnian Embassy. In 1988, her husband was killed test flying a new Mil MI-24 Hind-D helicopter. Since that event she was not known to have had any long-term relationships although it is known that an Englishman attached to the Foreign Office called Jeremy Kirkham dated her from time to time. Kirkham's job is that of security liaison and there was an alert in Bosnian security when this fact became known in 1992. The Director of Operations cleared Ladvia of any complicity later that year.

She is known to be in favour of the peaceful reconciliation of the Balkan States, as was her father, and she is very much against extreme national elements, particularly on the Bosnian Serb side, as she believes it was these people who were responsible for the death of both her mother and father. She carried out several covert operations, both within a team structure and individually, between the years 1988 and 1993 including the infiltration into the Bosnian Serb intelligence service.

Ladvia is totally committed to her cause and has no compunction about sleeping with the enemy for information. She has killed twice in the performance of her duties. We consider her to be highly professional, loyal to the Bosnian government and capable of taking difficult decisions. She was promoted Deputy to the Assistant Secretary of the Bosnian government Security Service in March 1994.

Note added 25/5/1994. To facilitate and maintain the Serb contact, Ladvia is still given sensitive material to pass to the other side, implying that she is a highly placed agent for them inside the Bosnian government.

Note added 25/10/1994 In August 1994, on hearing that Ladvia had been promoted, the British MI6 reported to the Head of Security that Ladvia Silonovic was working for the Bosnian Serb Security Service. Acknowledgements were sent without telling the British that this fact was known and encouraged.

SIS note added by "C" 14/02/1995

The scheme which Jeremy and Ladvia hatched between them was controlled by certain senior members of SIS. It was hugely successful. Silonovic was wanted for murder by the Russians, the theft of over one million pounds taken from the Muslim fund set them on her trail, and she was wanted by the Serbs, because she had completely compromised them. The new Bosnian government was aware that she had disappeared with the Muslim funds of around 1 million US dollars and as such branded, they her a traitor. It was recognised that it was only a matter of time before she was assassinated even if she lived permanently in the UK. Jeremy and Ladvia hatched up a plot to ensure several Serbs witnessed her killing. They were later arrested, and after questioning released back to Serbia where they spread the news of her demise. She was not killed of course, although she should have received an Oscar for her performance. Later, Jeremy resigned, and they were secretly married in the UK under her alias of Patricia Johnson. During her time on Operation Gorazde, she had bought a Llama farm north of Santiago which is where they now live. In view of the sensitivity of this matter I decided that the file of The Gorazde Incident should be available to the head of SIS only.

SIS note added by C (Andrew Arnott) on my new appointment as head of SIS. 27/07/2010. I authorised the sending of a case of special champagne to Mrs Kirkham in Chile, to remind her of an event there in which I was involved.

There was a huge amount of detail about the Gorazde Incident some of which Adrian had been aware of before he took over the job when Arnott retired in 2014. Arnott knew that Ms Johnson had not been killed and the file which he had drawn up confirmed this.

The flight of fourteen hours passed more quickly than Adrian had expected, but he was able to get quite a lot of reading completed whilst in the air. He also slept as well as one can on a plane and so felt fresh when the plane arrived about ten minutes late in Santiago.

Treated as a normal passenger, he had to endure the normal immigration and customs facilities, which he was not used to, particularly when his case was searched for drugs. It took an hour to clear and as he walked out, he immediately picked out Jeremy Kirkham grinning at Adrian's obvious frustration of the bureaucratic nonsense one must go through when travelling.

They shook hands and Adrian was surprised at the athletic countenance and obviously fit and tanned person who met him. He was conscious that his own once athletic frame had deteriorated into a portlier figure.

Jeremy passed the time of day as he drove Adrian to the private side of the airport and parked his hire car in the parking lot designed for pilots. They walked to a jet ranger helicopter standing on the tarmac. The rotor was running as they approached, and Adrian noticed the woman pilot who smiled at him and gestured to the rear seats. Jeremy made sure Adrian was fastened into his seat, and then climbed into the front on the right-hand side. Within seconds they were in the air, and only twenty minutes later they landed on a private air strip that was part of their estate.

As they disembarked, Ladvia gave instructions to a young man who came running up. 'Carlos, please put the aircraft into the garage and check the oil leak on the gearbox, it may be that we'll have to take it to get a new seal fitted.'

'Yes ma'am, I'll do that straight away.'

Adrian noticed the large building, obviously built specially for the helicopter. The skids beneath the aircraft had four small wheels controlled by hydraulics, which he had not seen when he climbed into the helicopter in Santiago.

There was a Mercedes 4 x 4 standing by and Ladvia opened the rear door for Adrian to climb in, the small amount of baggage he had brought with him was put in the rear luggage section.

Ladvia's file had a photograph of her, and he had realised that she was a beautiful woman, but that was several years ago. She was still stunning, her long hair obviously dyed blond. He knew she naturally had black hair from her picture, but guessed its natural colour was now grey. She wore designer jeans and a white blouse, so simple, but if you are beautiful, you do not really need any accoutrements Adrian thought. Ladvia climbed into the driving seat and after expertly backing the vehicle out of the parking area, she engaged the automatic gear and the 4x4 shot forward.

The house was on raised ground about a quarter of a mile south of their position. The whole front of the house was white which caught the sun. Adrian guessed that they had added to the structure, as there was a wing on the west side that looked newer than the rest. He would find that it was the guest quarters and had indeed been added since they bought it.

Jeremy told him, that all the land as far as one could see on the south side belonged to the estate. Adrian noted the superb views of the mountains in front of the house about five miles away.

They arrived at the front door covered by a portico with pillars either side. The door, opened by a girl in a white dress was mahogany with brass fittings, making an attractive contrast to the white walls.

As they went through the front door, Jeremy said, 'we've arranged for you to stay with us, as to book you into a hotel could be somewhat of an embarrassment, particularly as the political section of the British Embassy usually shows extreme interest in any Brit arriving in Santiago.' Jeremy smiled, 'if the head of SIS were recognised, it would send them all into a flap.'

Adrian laughed, 'yes you're quite right, in fact I was going to ask you if you could put me up for 24 hours, as I will be returning on the night flight,' he looked at his watch, 'on Wednesday, I think it's now Monday...'

Jeremy nodded. 'I suggest that you have a kip, one never sleeps properly on a night flight, even in first class, so we'll have lunch sent up to you and...'

Adrian held up his hand, 'no, please don't do lunch for me, I'm going to have shower and then bed as you suggest. If you can put up with me at around 16:00 I'll wend my way down to your drawing room.'

'Okay, that's fine by me,' said Jeremy, 'as I have quite a lot to do on the farm, so we'll meet then. We have two children now, they are here on holiday, but we have sent them off to stay with friends while you are here. The girl goes off at four as well. Do you want to speak to me alone or...?'

'Good Lord, no, in fact it's really Ladvia that is crucial to what I want to talk about...'

Jeremy looked surprised but said he would inform her, and they would all meet at 16:00 in the drawing room where a light afternoon tea would be available.

The young girl took Adrian to the guest bedroom and left him to unpack.

At 16:00 Adrian presented himself and professed that he felt much better after a sleep. Tea came and the young girl whose name was Sally asked if there was anything else, otherwise she would leave for the day.

After tea, they chatted about the Llama farm, and the weather in the UK, which was terrible at that time, as was the politics,

Adrian had brought his brief case down with him, and he extracted a thick file and leaned forward. 'I'm most grateful for you allowing me to see you,' he smiled. 'But a situation has occurred, which we believe may have huge consequences, for the UK and Europe generally.' He sat back in his chair looking for a reaction.

Ladvia spoke, 'I know Jeremy told you that we are

42

finished with that sort of life and that we didn't wish to get involved, particularly as we now have two young children.' She smiled. Adrian noticed a steely resolve being shown. Jeremy was looking puzzled and was obviously keen to find out what Adrian had to say. The head of SIS did not fly halfway across the world on a completely secret mission unless there was serious concern.

'Why don't you start by letting us know what the problem is?' Jeremy poured another cup of tea into Adrian's cup.

Adrian nodded, 'okay I assume that you both watch the world news here...?'

'Yes, we have access to Sky News,' answered Jeremy.

'Okay, that's helpful, but as you know the media don't always give the background to what's behind the news and so what I am about to tell you is my opinion of current events.' Adrian looked at them both.

'Russia is now our bogeyman in Europe since the apparent friendliness between Putin and President Bush. Bush was then seen to be supporting the President of Georgia when he declared independence from Russia and around the same time, Tony Blair stopped the extradition of a number of wealthy Russian businessmen who had moved to the UK, which also soured the relations.'

I assume you are talking about people like Gusinsky and Berezovsky?' Jeremy raised his eyebrows.

'Yes, they were the first but there have been many since. The murder of Alexander Litvinenko in London further deteriorated relations, then there was the Novichok affair, when two GRU agents infiltrated the UK and poisoned Sergei and Yulia Skripal on the 24th March 2018. We now know that there was a third man overseeing the operation from London, a Major General Denis Sergeyev also from the GRU. We now have a situation where Russia appears to be moving towards open conflict with the west, Georgia, Moldova,

Abkhazia, and Ukraine just being a start. Putin tried to have the President of Montenegro murdered, fortunately we were able to warn his government in time, and the plot failed. The annexing of the Crimea sent shivers down the spine of the Western world, and many started to wake up to what Putin was doing. Hitler used similar tactics: destabilise the country concerned that have minority factions and then use that as an excuse to invade. You may remember that led to the invasion of Austria, Czechoslovakia and Poland.'

'But he didn't stop there, did he,' answered Jeremy. 'He then went on to invade The Netherlands, Belgium, Norway and France. He could have been stopped by us and France, preventing him breaking the Versailles Treaty by walking into the demilitarised Rhineland with the Wehrmacht.'

'That's right Jeremy, the more he conquered, the more powerful he became, drawing in other countries such as Italy, Hungary and Bulgaria.' Adrian continued.

'Russia is now heavily involved in cyber warfare, fake news and the interference in democratic elections perpetuated by the GRU and this shows us that Putin is upping his involvement in our affairs.

'It will not surprise you to learn that we have assets in Russia from whom we receive regular reports on what's going on, particularly regarding military expansion. Our assets are usually ideological. The Americans usually buy the information, we, like the Jews have Brits in situ in most countries, a throwback from our Empire. However, we now pool our information with the CIA and NASA, and we are receiving confirmation that is alarming, particularly regarding the modernising of the Russian military. The SIS has a very highly placed asset in the Kremlin who has expressed grave concern over the path taken by those in power. He is very senior in the military, but refuses point blank to give us military secrets. He does however forewarn us on political matters that could affect world peace. This person is extremely cautious and will not deal with us directly. He gets his messages to us through his daughter who is studying at Oxford. You will know that we have more than one asset on the staff there, mainly to alert us to any bright spark that we might recruit.'

Jeremy smiled, 'I remember that well, as that's how I was inveigled into the firm.'

'Hmm, well there is a young lecturer who has struck up with this asset's daughter, I believe it's a sexual connection as it happens, but that's not important here. She hands over her father's letters and we receive and de-code them. The problem with this method of contact is the messages we get are necessarily short. For instance, we were warned about the expansion of the Syrian situation by being alerted to the operation code, it took us some time to realise it was aimed at supporting the Syrian government under the disguise of fighting ISIS. Putin's main reason was to protect his naval base in Tartus but also to spread Russian influence in the Eastern Mediterranean, and he has done that at a low cost. He is now flooding Crete with Russian money, and he has completed a gas pipeline deal with cash starved Greece worth seven billion US\$, organised a deal with Cyprus to service his navy, and is now getting involved with Libya.

'You will appreciate that I am about to give you top secret information and you'll soon understand why. I checked before flying that both of you have in the past signed the Official Secrets Act, and although it was some years ago, it still stands.

'Last week I received a copy of another communication from Russia, and it indicated that there was a new threat called "Operation Open Door." Now that would not have caused concern, but the message also showed that the Duma had covertly earmarked an initial amount of 15 billion dollars with a further 10 billion in reserve. That is 34% of the Russian total current spending on defence.'

Jeremy whistled, 'that's a lot of "bread" but as they are already committed to spending 72 billion for next year, what on earth is a further 25 billion being spent on, and how can they afford it?'

Adrian leaned forward to emphasise his point. 'To answer the second point first, it's thanks to countries like Germany agreeing to purchase Russian gas. So, on one hand they agree to sanctions, and on the other hand pay them billions of US dollars in cash. You're a bit out of date Jeremy, we have information that suggests Russia is going to spend around 108 billion, a 50 billion increase on 2017, but clearly the 25 billion is coming from a separate pot, which is why we think it's political. We know that they tried to interfere with the USA elections, and who knows whether they succeeded, certainly the man they wanted won. Why would they want Trump instead of Clinton? Perhaps because he criticised NATO and the lack of funds from most of the 27 members. You will remember that under the North Atlantic Treaty Organisation which effectively took over from the Brussels Treaty in 1949, each participating country agreed to spend 2% of GDP on defence. This was reaffirmed during the Welsh Pledge meeting of NATO in February 2015. But to give you an idea of who spends what, only four countries meet their commitment: USA, UK, Greece, and Lithuania. It is obviously the big players that Trump is aiming at, such as Germany 1.2%, Italy 1.1%, Turkey 1.6%, and France 1.8%. There are five countries at 1.5%, 6 at 1.2% and several more at 1% or less.'

'So, Trump has a point in criticising European members,' said Jeremy.

'Yes, but the sign that he may pull out of NATO if he does not get what he wants, is worrying many European politicians. He has also indicated that he admires Putin, which rather sends a message, not only to the President of Russia, but to countries nearby that have suffered due to his expansionist policies.'

Ladvia, who had been listening quietly, entered the conversation. 'So where do you think this large sum of money will be spent?'

Adrian turned to her, 'that's the twenty-five-billion-dollar question. We initially thought it might be Greece. Of course, if he took effective control of that country, he would also have access to the NATO base in Crete.'

'That would effectively mean he would control the Suez Canal,' said Jeremy.

'And have huge influence in the whole of the Eastern Mediterranean including the Aegean, which isolates Turkey, and threatens the Balkans including Bulgaria and in the south Israel, Lebanon and Egypt.'

Ladvia frowned, 'but what would he gain from that, apart from it being a major embarrassment to the West. Putin is no fool, and he does not spend money on large projects unless he is going to gain substantially. Also, by taking on Greece, he may be landed with their debt.'

Adrian shook his head, 'I doubt that he would simply welsh on the money owed, mainly to the European Union, thus further destabilising that body.

'Then Greece is certainly a possibility, as you say it would put him in a position to influence a fairly large area that is currently within the strategic interests of the West,' said Jeremy thoughtfully. 'I wouldn't imagine that President Obama's visit to Crete before he handed over to Trump, gave Greece much to shout about as he simply said that America would support them in their quest for a better financial deal on their debt. The IMF have already done that saying Greece's debt should be reduced and has warned that imposing tough austerity programmes on Greece could backfire on its creditors. To quote Obama, he said, "You cannot keep on squeezing countries that are in the midst of depression, at some point, there has to be a growth strategy in order for them to pay off their debts and to eliminate some of their deficits." Well Yuppie do! The Germans who raped and completely destabilised the country after WW2, causing over half a million deaths from starvation alone are holding Greece to account. They haven't repaid their war debts to Greece which would be substantial and in fairness there are many Germans who agree.'

'Yes,' said Adrian, 'you are quite right, and that's why Greece is still number one on our list, as Putin already has recently put navy assets into that area. The problem is that he would not have to spend anywhere near that amount of money to secure Greece as they are particularly vulnerable now. The people of Greece are struggling and only recently the government reduced the amount paid to pensioners from €500.00 a month to €300.00. Prices are rising as VAT increases and all that has achieved is that Greece is effectively paying the interest on its debt, not reducing it. It is not surprising that they are susceptible to some cash plus a lucrative trade deal. Greece doesn't appear to have many supporters in the EU, and I suspect it may consider leaving it in due course anyway.'

'Do you have a number 2?' asked Ladvia

Adrian nodded, 'Putin's sphere of influence is limited, that doesn't mean to say that he won't use whatever influence he has. He was burned with a recent incursion into Lithuania, which was blamed on Belarus, and I really do not see any great advantage for him trying to enter Latvia or Estonia as that would trigger an immediate response from NATO. Finland and Sweden are neutral but certainly the West would support them if invaded. In any case there is no political unrest in either of those countries that could be exploited.'

'Norway? Jeremy asked.

Adrian shook his head, 'again, part of NATO, there are

substantial French, British and US naval assets in the region. He could not use his navy from the Baltic as communication could be cut by Poland Germany and Denmark. Of course, Norway is connected to Russia in the far north, but to invade from there would prove to be a disaster, and there is no way he would have access to the North Sea oil, which is now a reducing asset.

'We must not forget China in all these discussions, we don't know how close they are to Russia, but we do know that they are stepping up their biological weapons research in a place called Wuhan. The easiest way to declare war on the West is not by force, nor by cyber warfare, but they could cripple us by spreading a virus that we have no vaccine for. We do not consider this as a major threat now, as such a virus may act like mustard gas in WW1, if the wind blew the wrong way, the Axis forces suffered more than the Allies. A virus could damage their own population unless of course they had developed a vaccine before spreading it.'

'I agree with that point,' said Jeremy, 'and that would not suit Russia either. With the Chinese however, they do not care how many of their citizens they kill if it furthers their cause. The ravages of Chairman Mao Zedong are a good example of that as was the situation with the MH370.

'Yes,' answered Adrian, 'but at this moment in time the major problem is the number of European countries that rely on Russia for their gas supplies, in addition to Germany. which we've just discussed.' Adrian pulled a document from his briefcase. 'There's some irony here as most European countries are buying energy from Russia which is paid for in US dollars. The fact that the dollar has risen recently is a great bonus to our friend Putin. All the Baltic countries and Finland have one hundred percent dependency. Europe has a thirty percent dependency, the exception being the UK and Norway and further south Spain and Portugal that have none. This is no doubt the reason the major economies such as Germany, France and Italy are showing reluctance in deepening the sanctions against Russia. It may be another reason they are not paying their proper dues on defence. On the other hand, the Americans, under the Obama regime have not been particularly supportive to NATO either. We have all become too complacent. People in the UK worrying about the NHS should consider how they would feel if their daughters or sons were suddenly called up to fight a war with Russia with a force not properly equipped or fit for purpose. This is becoming a real possibility and soon.

'However, I believe Putin will concentrate on an area where there is the greatest weakness on the political front, and that takes us back to Greece. Why otherwise would he take his North Sea fleet into the Mediterranean?' said Adrian finally, 'but we need to know more. It could be why he has secured a base in the Eastern Mediterranean.'

'Moving the Northern Fleet there could be a feint,' said Ladvia quietly. With the sort of money, he has obtained, I would imagine the stakes are much higher than Greece.'

Adrian looked at her in surprise, 'well where else do you suggest?'

Ladvia shrugged, 'as you say we need more inside information, but tell me, what would happen if the Socialist party won the next election in Britain?'

There was silence in the room. Adrian looked shocked, 'I honestly think that's most unlikely, they're a joke and totally disorganised.'

'Sounds rather like President Elect Trump to me.' She smiled sweetly, 'has it not occurred to the establishment in Britain that there is a revolution taking place under their eyes. Looking at the situation as an outsider, it appears that if an election is called, and that is a possibility due to the difficulties emerging from Brexit, the Socialist party could win.'

'On what evidence?' Asked Adrian.

'Common sense' answered Ladvia. 'The government have

done nothing to answer the question of the common man and woman worker. Their tax break helps the rich as well as the poor, they are suggesting that pensioners may not have the triple lock after 2020, they have already changed the interest from RPI to CPI, the latter excluding house prices, which is fine when there are increases in property, but disastrous when property goes down. Now it is suggested that pensioners over 75 will lose their free TV licence, so the Conservatives are aiming at the most vulnerable, who also happen to be their core vote. They have done little to alter the punitive reforms put in by the earlier chancellor. So, the impression given is that the poor will be squeezed even further and the rich will get even richer. There is great talk about money going into infrastructure, lots of money going into the NHS, an organisation clearly not fit for purpose and promises about how everyone will be better off in the future. Well, pensioners do not care a hang about the future because they will be dead. The common worker is fed up listening to promises, they know that their benefits have been sliced, people on disabilities are much worse off, people who needed a two bedroomed house have been evicted, they have great difficulty in getting a doctor's appointment, and if they need an operation they must wait for months. I suspect the people of Great Britain have had enough, and like the end of World War 2, they will vote with their feet and the only real alternative is Socialism. Of course, Brexit is a major factor and that may save the present government'

Ladvia got up and walked to the drinks cupboard. 'I need a drink, how about you two?'

Adrian was a little shaken, not only at Ladvia's vehemence, but at her knowledge and insight into the position in the UK. He also had to remember that he was there to try and persuade her to help draw Validich out in a meeting in Crete.

Taking a gulp of his gin and tonic which Ladvia served to him he smiled. 'I can assure you that the Socialists will not get into power, because if they did it would be a total disaster from a security point of view. The opposition leader has said he wouldn't press the nuclear button if threatened, and the indication is that he would cancel Trident, which would really piss of the Americans.'

'Right,' continued Ladvia, 'now let us get down to business, you've invited me into this discussion because you need my help, not Jeremy's, so what is it you want?' She had a disarming smile.

Adrian, caught off guard, took a deep breath realising that Ladvia was not a woman to take for granted.

'Okay, the asset I am talking about works within the Kremlin and is as I've stated a very high-ranking officer. He will not travel to the UK, so our plan is to ask Oxford University to give a grant for his daughter to go Crete in the Mediterranean to study the history and archaeology of the island. She is doing an archaeology degree incidentally. We will ask her to invite her father and mother to a secure villa we have arranged for her to stay in, owned by a British family that is known to us. Although retired, they are working for the service and as such are discreet. I want you and Jeremy to go with me to meet him there. The villa is large enough for us all.'

Ladvia cocked her head one side. 'Why do you require me there?'

Because you know the asset, as well as his wife and we feel that with someone he knows and trusts, it will make him more comfortable in discussing the business we need to...'

'You mean you think he'll be more likely to open up to a friend rather than a stranger.'

'Yes.'

'What is the name of the asset?'

'General Peter Validich, retired.' Answered Adrian.

Ladvia froze and her hand flew to her mouth as she

gasped, 'oh my God, Peter Validich, so it's his daughter Aleksi that may be going to Crete?'

'Yes, is that a problem for you?'

Ladvia shook her head, 'on the contrary, will Natasha be there too?'

'We will ask Aleksi to invite both to spend some time with her on Crete.'

'You do realise that they both think that I'm dead?'

'Yes, and they will not be told, so it will be a shock to both, but I suggest a pleasant shock.'

Jeremy interjected. 'What about security, don't forget Ladvia had most of the Islamic world plus the Serbs, the Bosnians and the Russians think she's dead and if she is recognised, anyone of them may go to any lengths to ensure her demise.'

Adrian nodded, 'yes we've thought of that, and this is the basic plan, but you can alter any part of it. As soon as it's a go, you and Ladvia will receive a special diplomatic status. I will arrange for the Embassy here to pick you up and take you straight to the British Airways plane, avoiding immigration and customs and you would travel first class to Heathrow. At Heathrow I will pick you up straight from the plane and drive you to the RAF air base in Chelverston, which from memory is not all that far from Northampton. It is really a US air force base now, and we will fly directly to the Chania NATO base in Crete on a US Air Force C130. As soon as we arrive there, a driver in a blacked-out limo will take us to the villa. I will be carrying a weapon throughout, and if you wish to do the same, I will arrange it, I understand Ladvia is a crack shot.'

'Used to be,' Ladvia turned to Jeremy, 'what do you think?'

'Well from what Adrian has told us, you will be kept well

out of public view, and even if you are seen, it is most unlikely anyone will recognise you after all this time but there is that possibility, slight I admit,' said Jeremy, 'the only danger would be on our flight from Santiago to London as there will be others in the first-class cabin.'

'If that's so, it's unlikely that any action would be taken on the flight,' said Adrian, 'in any case you could be armed and no one else will be.'

'They could get at us via the children.'

'Where are they?'

'They go to an English boarding school called Badminton, it's near Bristol. They are due back next week.'

'Ah, so they're both girls.'

Adrian thought for a moment, 'it would be safer for us to withdraw them from the school before you travel, and my wife would happily look after them during the period you are away.'

Ladvia looked at Adrian, 'okay, I'll do it providing the children are safe.'

'Thank you Ladvia it's a deal, I'll get everything organised and be in touch, now how about showing me around the Llama farm?'

It was after dinner when Jeremy had left the house to deal with some items on the farm. Ladvia was standing by the picture window in the drawing room overlooking the Mountain View with a half glass of good Chilean wine in her hand as Adrian joined her.

'It's a magnificent view you have here.'

Ladvia turned and looked at Adrian. 'There's something you're not telling us.

Adrian caught off guard answered with a frown, 'what

makes you say that.'

Ladvia pursed her lips, 'call it a woman's intuition, but you're holding something back.'

'Well, I'm not sure, and I was not going to broach the subject until I had more information.'

'So...' Ladvia cocked her head on one side.

Adrian sighed, 'just before I left, I received some information regarding Operation Gorazde. Someone had put two and two together, which cast some doubt on your untimely death on the basis that it was very convenient, and that British operatives do not shoot people out of hand, particularly women. This report came through an Islamic sect in which we have an asset. These people have launched a full-scale enquiry. At this stage I've no idea of how far it has gone, but I suspect it's in its early stages.'

Ladvia nodded, 'thank you Adrian.' She looked out again at the view as the sun was setting behind the snow-capped mountains throwing a blanket of orange light over the area.

'We will never be able to return, here, will we?'
Adrian did not reply.

After dinner they continued their conversation widening it to world politics. Adrian took a sip of the excellent Blue Mountain coffee which Ladvia insisted be brought direct from Jamaica. He turned to Ladvia, 'You obviously have quite a strong view of the political situation in the UK, what's your view of Brexit?'

It was Jeremy who answered. 'It's mixed to be honest. We know that the British vote was not entirely due to the EU, but clearly that organisation has become a bureaucratic led system that is not arguably democratic.'

'Some people believe it is', answered Adrian.

'Well, it may be better to argue that the democracy is too

far from the proletariat to the extent that it creates a feeling of helplessness that the individual has no direct connection with. It is hugely expensive with little control over the expenditure. A good example is that the staff move between Strasbourg and Brussels, for no good reason. The original idea of a trading partnership was high jacked by the Germans, and to a lesser extent the French who benefit hugely from the system, often to the detriment of the other members. Economically it is a failed organisation and their scramble to bring in new countries before their economies are ready or before they have sorted the problems with the Euro is a disastrous policy. Greece should never have been allowed in at the start, and we all know that Romania and Bulgaria, to mention only two were not ready economically, which is why the financially stronger countries, particularly Britain, were inundated with their citizens looking for a decent wage. The excuse that immigration was overwhelming Britain was nonsense. The UK took in 1 person per 1,000, by far the lowest in Europe. If there was criticism, it should be levelled at the government for not ensuring the influx was spread proportionally throughout the country. It is quite possible that both Italy and France will leave the EU in the future if their politics change, but if not, there is always going to be that possibility in the background.

'The Italian banks are in an extremely poor financial state. Their collapse would seriously damage the EU and the world economy. It is well known that their assets are seriously overvalued. The idea that the EU should set up a new military defence force as an alternative to NATO is laughable if it was not such a serious proposal. It is certainly a good way to say to America, we do not want you anymore.

'As we've already discussed they can't even invest the 2% of GDP they should be doing for their defence, how they imagine they could deal with an aggressive Russia which is planning to increase its spend is an interesting question.

'Certain members of the EU don't want to be reliant on

the USA, but it seems to me they have a short memory. Had it not been for the English-speaking world liberating Europe in 1945, they would have remained under the appalling conditions forced on them by Germany under Hitler. If England had not stood up to Hitler and followed Halifax instead of Churchill, the USA could not have entered the war against Germany for some time, if ever. Yet it is precisely these countries that now are planning to "punish" Britain for leaving their failed community that started as a trading entity not as a political system.

'I remember a little story told to me some years ago which illustrates the point I make.

'In 1966 upon being told that President Charles DE Gaulle had taken France out of NATO and that all U.S. troops must be evacuated off French soil, President Lyndon Johnson mentioned to Secretary of State Dean Rusk that he should ask de Gaulle about the Americans buried in France. Dean implied in his answer that he could not ask de Gaulle in the meeting planned in France, at which point President Johnson then told the Secretary of State: "Ask him about the cemeteries Dean!"

'That made it into a Presidential Order so at end of the talks Dean did ask de Gaulle if his order to remove all U.S. troops from French soil also included the 60,000 soldiers buried in France from World War I and World War II.

'De Gaulle, embarrassed, got up, and left the room without answering.'

Ladvia intervened, 'of course, the winner of any destabilisation in Europe is Putin, and we can be sure he'll take advantage of it.'

The next evening Ladvia flew Adrian back to Santiago and landed in the helicopter area. She turned to shake his hand.

Above the noise of the whirling rotors, he shouted, 'you and Jeremy should consider joining the firm, we need a

Russian expert and Jeremy would be an asset, think about it.'

Ladvia laughed.

'Think about it seriously... I'll be in touch.' With that he disappeared into the airport building.

THE PHOTOGRAPHER

Chapter 6

Abin Abu Kafir an Alawite was a well-known supporter of President Assed in Syria. A wealthy man with business interests in the UK, Ireland, South America, and the Middle East, he had no need to work. He had lived in the UK for over twenty years and had carried out various support roles for a secret Muslim Fund designed to help and support terrorism. He had come to the notice of the UK authorities and although sailing close to breaking the law, he had not been caught doing anything illegal mainly because he worked in cash, leaving no record of what he spent.

He had recently been visited by a shadowy figure from Jordan who asked him to check into reports regarding a certain woman called Ladvia Patricia Silonovic who was supposed to have been shot and killed after the Bosnian war. He was told that the man who had shot her was living near Santiago in Chile with a wife who fitted her description. He handed over a file, which until recently had been closed. The file enclosed a photograph. He was asked to report back within four weeks.

After careful enquiries in the United Kingdom, Abin Abu Kafir arrived in Santiago the day before Jeremy and Ladvia were due to fly to London. Booking into the Matildas Hotel Boutique he spent little time in his suite, only checking his powerful Nikon D7100 camera with stand, along with a

Bower SLY/500PN f8 telephoto lens. They were all compacted in a small carrying bag. He removed the substantial amount of cash he carried about his body and stuffed that into the same bag. There were 20 thousand US dollars, so by the time he had finished he had difficulty zipping the bag closed. He had already established where the Kirkham llama farm was situated, having obtained precise GPS coordinates from Google Earth. He had a light lunch, afterwards calling one of the taxis sitting outside the hotel. He gave the taxi driver the directions and sat back in the rear seat for the drive which he expected to take about an hour and a half. The driver took rather longer because of the Santiago traffic, but after getting on to route 57 north, the driver made good time and after about five miles north of the Gral San Martin junction he turned left and the sign for the llama farm soon appeared on the left-hand side. Abin Abu asked the driver to slow down, and he searched for some cover in sight of the house within the estate, which he could see from the road. Finding a convenient clump of bushes on the right-hand side opposite a security fence which circled the estate, he asked the driver to drop him there and to pick him up just before sundown that evening. As he got out of the car, the driver asked for payment. Abin Abu said he would pay after the return journey, but that was not satisfactory to the taxi driver who had experienced passengers disappearing in such circumstances before. Abin Abu was of course concerned that the driver might not return for him, so on opening his bag he promised the driver a double fare after he was collected. There was a slight breeze coming down from the mountains in the east, and that caught the packed US dollars as he unzipped the bag blowing a couple of the wads out onto the ground. Abin Abu quickly collected them and paid the driver, but the remaining stash of notes was clearly visible, and the driver's eyes bulged at the sight. He took the payment and drove off promising to return on time.

Abin Abu waited until the taxi was out of sight and took the bag behind the bushes and carefully unpacked the camera with its stand and fitted the telescopic lens. He then used a knife to cut some of the foliage and settled down to sight the camera on the front door of the house about a quarter of a mile away. He realised that he may have to return to the spot for several days before getting the picture he required. After several hours he started to suffer from cramp and it was while he was stretching his legs that he noticed a 4x4 being driven up to the door, the driver's side being on the same side as him. A man got out and he saw some luggage brought out and stacked in the rear of the vehicle. Abin Abu adjusted his lens and could see the man perfectly, so he took several pictures. While he was doing so a young woman arrived at the door carrying something which she placed in the back and then an older woman appeared and walked around the back of the 4x4 climbing into the driving seat. Abin Abu took several more pictures. The car was driven off with the man now in the passenger seat leaving the young woman waving from the front door. He then noticed the vehicle speeding towards a small runway where a helicopter was being pulled out of a small hanger by a young man on a quad bike. The car stopped near the helicopter, the bags were transferred to the aircraft, the woman climbed into the left-hand seat and the man the right hand. The rotors started to turn, and it took off heading south in the direction of Santiago. The young man moved the car into the hanger and locked the door. All this had been faithfully recorded by Abin Abu, taking some 120 photographs. He could hardly believe his luck to have achieved his mission on the first day and he silently thanked Allah who he felt was helping him with his exertions. He packed the equipment away apart from the camera, extracting only 100 US dollars which he put in his pocket and awaited the return of the taxi. While waiting he went through the photographs he had taken, the camera being digital, allowed him to do so via the 3.2-inch monitor at the back of the equipment. As soon as he returned to the hotel, he would download the pictures onto his laptop and email them to his Jordanian contact. He realised that the old picture of Ladvia he had was the same person who was flying the helicopter.

Diego Diaz, the taxi driver had much to think about on the drive back with the empty cab. He realised that the Arab he had taken to a spot north of Santiago was carrying a great deal of money. He thought about his wife currently in a local hospital where his son was in urgent need of a lifesaving operation that could not be carried out because he did not have the funds to pay for it. It was likely his son would die within the next two weeks. Diego decided instead of driving to the hospital, he drove to his bank drawing out his meagre savings of 338,000 Pesos, an amount equal to around US $560. He then drove down-town and made an illegal purchase.

THE SCOTTISH PREROGATIVE
Incorporating
THE WUHAN AFFAIR

THE JOURNEY

Chapter 7

It was two weeks since Adrian had visited them, and all the arrangements had been made during that time. It was only three days ago that they received their special diplomatic passes along with first class tickets for London on British Airways. The person delivering the items to the Kirkhams' was Oliver Swanson, who oversaw the political department at the British Embassy in Santiago and who was known to Jeremy. The senior embassy staff knew that Jeremy had been connected to SIS. They did not however know of Ladvia's background and because she spoke English without an accent, everyone assumed she was British, as her passport showed.

Ladvia and Jeremy left the helicopter at the airport and not knowing when they would return, they asked the company who originally sold them the aircraft to deliver it back to the estate. They stayed the night at the Holiday Inn and after an early dinner they went up to their room as their flight in the morning took off at 07:00 hours.

The flight connection was at Guarulhos International Airport, and they arrived in good time to catch their direct flight to London. The nineteen-hour connecting flight was about twenty minutes late arriving in London, the passengers were told the delay was due to a headwind over the Atlantic Ocean. Before any passengers disembarked,

Adrian went on board and told Jeremy and Ladvia that everything was going according to plan. Their luggage had been kept in the steward's area, and the car to take them all to Chelverston Air base was waiting alongside the aircraft, so they did not have to go through immigration and then the wait to retrieve their luggage, before going through customs.

As it was early, the morning traffic was light with most of it going into London as they were going out. They arrived at the base in time for breakfast. Take off was scheduled for 10:00 hours, which would mean them arriving in Crete after dark as they plane had to stopover in Gibraltar to drop off some equipment.

Adrian had confirmed in a recent telephone call that Peter Validich and his wife had agreed to holiday in Crete with their daughter and through a careful coded letter the daughter had indicated that her Lecturer would be there too.

The C130 is not the most comfortable of planes and although special seats were available for the party, it was noisy and not very warm. The flying time took over 7 hours, the stop-over in Gibraltar was over 3 hours before carrying on to Crete.

On arrival a limousine with darkened glass windows, originally used for the recent visit from Barrack Obama, was waiting on the tarmac, and the party were glad to disembark and climb straight into the limo. The drive from the NATO base took them through the town of Souda the main port attached to Chania, the capital of the western region. From there onto the National Road which stretched right across the northern part of Crete. They turned off after about thirty minutes into a small town called Kalyves and from there to Almyrida a favourite place for tourists because of the fine beach. The next smaller town was Plaka and the villa they were to stay was situated at the top of a very steep hill about

200 metres above the town. They were warmly welcomed by the owners James and Kate Alexander, and Kate showed them to their rooms which overlooked the whole of Souda Bay. Although it was dark, the lights across the bay were burning bright. The rather brighter lights from the NATO base could also be seen from the villa.

James took Adrian to his room and told him that Aleksi had already arrived and that her parents were arriving on Aeroflot at Heraklion Airport the next day. She had hired a car and was going to meet them off the plane and because she had had a long flight she had already gone to bed. Kate saw Jeremy and Ladvia into their suite.

They had a very pleasant evening, and an excellent dinner was prepared by Kate who it turned out was an extraordinarily good cook. They agreed that the next day's discussion would not start, until Aleksi had left to meet her parents. James and Adrian had a brief discussion on the situation in Crete, but everyone was in bed well before midnight.

The next morning Aleksi left before the Kirkham's had risen. She said she had a two-hour drive to Heraklion to pick up her parents and wanted to get to the airport in good time. After breakfast those staying behind discussed tactics for the forthcoming meeting with the Validich's. James and Kate decided that they would not take part, as James felt that their presence would be unnecessary. Jeremy said that he was quite happy not to join the discussions, but Adrian disagreed.

'No Jeremy, I want you both in on the conversation. I mentioned to Ladvia before I left Santiago that I was keen for you guys to join the firm as I have a particular role, I want you both to get involved in, but I'll discuss that with you once we've spoken to Validich.'

As he finished speaking, his secure mobile phone rang. He had left a message with his secretary that he should not be disturbed, so he answered testily, 'yes?'

He listened as his secretary put him through to Geoffrey Williamson. As he continued to listen, he looked grave. 'Are you saying they're being accused of murder?'

'Yes.'

'Geoffrey, ask Oliver Swanson to call me at once.'

'Er, it's a little early in Chile they're about ten hours behind where you are at this moment.'

'I don't care a damn Geoffrey; I need this sorted and I won't be available later today.'

'Okay boss, I'll get on to it.' He put his phone down.

Jeremy had overheard the conversation and recognised the name of Oliver Swanson.

'A problem?' He asked.

'Could be but let me speak to Oliver first.'

THE SCOTTISH PREROGATIVE

Incorporating

THE WUHAN AFFAIR

THE MURDER

Chapter 8

Driving back to pick up his passenger, Deigo Diaz found his fare in the same place where he had left him. He was standing by the side of the road, still carrying the bag. Diego quickly climbed out of the taxi and opened the rear door. Abin Abu started to climb in and as he did so there was the sound of a pistol shot. Abin Abu cried out and slid to the ground writhing with pain. Diego fired another shot which did not stop the screaming. Now thoroughly frightened, Diego emptied his gun into the figure sprawled on the floor. Abin Abu was dead. Fearing that a car would come along the road, Diego tried to drag the bloodied corpse behind the bush, but he saw a truck approaching some distance away. He dropped the body and reached for the bag. It seemed heavy, so he opened it and saw the camera and the lens on top of the cash. He fleetingly thought of taking the camera, but then decided that it could implicate him if the authorities found it, so he took all the equipment out throwing it on the verge and zipped up the bag. He quickly climbed into the car, did a U turn, and headed back towards Santiago. He found his hands were shaking uncontrollability and so he took a turn off the main road and stopped. Getting out he opened the rear door to get at the bag where he had thrown it and was horrified to see the rear seat and carpet was heavily bloodstained. He had nothing to clean it with, so he just checked the bag and was pleased that the money was still there. He quickly assessed that there was about US$20,000 a huge sum for an average taxi driver in Chile representing about six and a half years wages. Deigo calmed down and thought how he was going to clean up his car. He then had a sudden thought, fingerprints, in his haste he had not wiped the camera and he knew his prints were on the police records. He decided to return to the scene of the crime.

He headed back up route 57 but as he neared the scene, he saw several cars stopped by the roadside. It included the truck that he had seen behind him in the distance. He made a second mistake, braking hard he carried out another U turn, but this time the truck driver recognised the taxi and was close enough to get the registration number. The Carabiñeros de Chile (Chilean police) had just arrived, but both officers were out of the car and by the time the truck driver could get their attention Diego had disappeared.

An ambulance was called and while waiting, one of the officers searched the body as the other carefully picked up the camera equipment placing it into a large plastic bag. The contents from his clothing were placed in another plastic container. Once the corpse was removed the police returned to the station just off Avenida Vicun, opposite the Parque San Eugeno and handed in the contents of the man's pockets and the camera in the plastic bags to the Criminal Investigation branch. They dusted the contents for fingerprints and because it was a foreign national the murder was treated as a priority. That same evening the pictures in the camera were scanned and printed out. The officer looking at the pictures recognised Jeremy. The next morning when Ladvia and Jeremy had just arrived at Chelverston a senior police officer tried to contact Jeremy at the estate and was told that he had left for London the day before. After checking the airlines, he found that the Kirkham's had left on a British Airways flight on a special diplomatic pass. The officer then contacted the

British Embassy and was eventually put through to Oliver Swanson.

'Good Morning Senor Swanson, I'm calling you because we are trying to contact Senor Kirkham who I know has connections with your Embassy, I understand he and his wife left the country on a diplomatic pass. However, this is a murder enquiry.'

Oliver Swanson frowned, 'You're surely not suspecting Mr Kirkham?'

'Well Senor, we found the body of an Arab gentleman by the name of Abin Abu Fakir just outside the main gate to the Kirham's property and we found a high-powered camera which has several pictures of the Kirkham's, so obviously this man was spying on them.'

'That doesn't mean to say that this man's death was anything to do with either Mr or Mrs Kirkham,' said Oliver Swanson.

'What we do not understand is why someone killed this man, he was taking illegal pictures, it is true, but why?'

'I really don't know,' replied Oliver Swanson, but his brain was racing for an answer. 'Was there any form of transport nearby?'

'No, we have checked, a lorry driver spotted a taxi that was near the scene, and we are having the registration number checked.'

'So, he was either driven there by someone or he used a taxi.'

'It's possible Senor, however in view of his connection I thought I would call you first. There are prints on the camera so we will run it through our data base and let you know the result. We may need to ask you for the fingerprints of Senor Kirkham.'

Oliver told the policeman that they would of course cooperate and rang off. He then picked up a secure phone and contacted Adrian Bradley with the news.

Diego Diaz drove to his house and found a note from his wife that she had left to go to the hospital. He put US$8,000 in a large envelope and went around to her mother's house nearby telling her that she should use the money to help her grandson, but on no account tell anyone where it came from. He gave her another US$4,000 to help his wife live until he could sort his life out and that he would contact her in due course. With that he left in his taxi heading south. He was never caught nor was he ever seen again.

It was two days later that the fingerprint division produced the owner of the prints and the taxi driver named. Oliver Swanson was phoned at once, and he asked for the pictures to be sent to the Embassy. As soon as he received them, he sent them to Adrian Bradley who by that time was back in London.

THE SCOTTISH PREROGATIVE

Incorporating

THE WUHAN AFFAIR

THE ENLIGHTENMENT

Chapter 9

Aleksi arrived from Heraklion Airport just before lunch and introduced her father and mother to James and Kate who then showed them to their room. After unpacking, they walked through to the large drawing room and were offered lunch, but neither were particularly hungry having had a large breakfast before leaving Moscow. They did however accept a cup of tea.

Adrian, Jeremy and Ladvia had been out walking, arriving just as the Validich's had sat down. Aleksi saw Adrian come through the front door and jumped up to introduce him to Peter and Natasha. Jeremy followed but Ladvia saw some flowers in the garden and went to pick them. Adrian introduced Jeremy. Peter Validich put his hand out and at once withdrew it. He scowled, 'Aren't you the man who was reported to have shot and killed Ladvia Silonovic?' Peter had seen a report in the London newspapers at the time about her death.

Jeremy looked grim, 'yes, sadly, I was the man that killed Ladvia.' At that moment Ladvia appeared at the door, but hidden to Peter Validich, as she was behind Jeremy. Natasha gave a cry and as Peter turned, Natasha rushed past him and embraced Ladvia. Both dissolved into tears. Peter still could not see Ladvia as Natasha enveloped her. Natasha broke off and turned to Peter and he saw Ladvia for the first time. 'My God, it can't be...' It was many years since tears had been brought to Peter's eyes, he said afterwards, but it was a shock, a delightful shock, and he turned to Jeremy. This time he shook his hand. Jeremy smiled, 'I was going to introduce my wife to you, but Natasha beat me to it.'

'Your wife?' Peter asked.

Jeremy nodded, 'her name is Patricia Kirkham. Ladvia Silonovic had to be killed off, as too many people wanted her dead.'

'Of course, I should have guessed,' he said wiping his tears away. Ladvia looked at Peter he was looking older but still had a reasonable figure for his 6-foot frame. A few more lines perhaps and his hair now completely grey was thinning but he was still a handsome man. Natasha however looked much older and had put on quite a bit of weight. She remembered someone saying to her years ago that Russian women tended to age more quickly than those in the West.

Ladvia was delighted to meet Aleksi. Ladvia put her hand at waist level indicating that Aleksi had been that high when they last met. Aleksi laughed and said she would always remember Ladvia, as when she visited, she always brought plenty of sweets.

The rest of the afternoon was a delight for Ladvia, and she and the Validich's caught up on tall he news, after dinner the question of a meeting the next morning came up. They agreed that Aleksi, Natasha, Kate and James would drive down to the old town in Chania leaving the others to have their discussion.

The next morning after breakfast, James went to fetch his car from the garage situated below the villa, and as he took a little longer than normal, Kate led Natasha and Aleksi out to the garden area just as James was driving through the gates into the gravel compound.

As the women were climbing into the car, James said he had left his wallet inside and getting out of the car he went through the front door and saw Adrian, Ladvia, Jeremy and Peter sitting in the comfortable chairs drinking coffee. 'I've just told the girls that I've come back for my wallet,' he explained, 'as I didn't want to worry them.'

'As I was walking down the hill at the side of the house to get the car, something made me look back and I saw the sun glinting on something from the villa set back from ours by about 200 metres. I know that the owner, a Norwegian, is not in the country, although he occasionally lets it for short periods in the summer. However, this is not the holiday season. I looked up and immediately looked away so as not to show I had seen anything unusual. I then carried on down, opened the garage and drove the car out and up to the car parking space in front of our villa. The girls are in in the car. Now the only window in this villa open to the south is in my office. All others open to the North, which is normal for houses in these temperate climates.' He picked up some powerful binoculars on the sideboard and entered his office which was next to the drawing room and standing well back from the window he trained them on the villa above. He saw two men, one holding the binoculars he had previously been looking through. Of course, that man could have been simply looking at the view, but when James saw two other men walking around the house his sixth sense told him that his villa could be under surveillance.

He walked back into the drawing room and asked Peter if his car was followed from Heraklion Airport. Peter shook his head, 'I wasn't aware of anyone... but wait a minute I do remember a black Mercedes 4 x 4 that was well behind us, but when we stopped for petrol, it carried on past. We were chatting for most of the journey, so I did not notice it again. But I did see another black 4 x 4 just before we turned in to your drive, but again it went straight on.'

'Okay, I have feeling about this Peter. There is no sign of a car in their driveway, but it may be behind the house. They would not have been able to get in the villa without the permission of the owner, and as even you didn't know exactly where you would be staying, they would have had to check where you ended up and then go to the next town to the agent who handles the lets for most of the houses around here. Assuming they have someone here who knows the agent concerned, and there are plenty of Russians who live in this area, they would have been able to rent the house. Now I reckon that would have taken some time to arrange, so they have just arrived and would not have seen Adrian, Ladvia and Jeremy returning from their walk earlier this morning. I will call Vien Hodal, the owner of the house from Chania and find out who these people are, in the meantime, I'll go through security with you.'

Just as he finished talking, Kate appeared looking a little irritable. 'James, what are you doing, our guests are...'

'Go back to car with a smile on your face,' said James, 'there is a problem I will tell you about later. Don't at this stage worry Aleksi or Natasha.'

Kate stopped and nodded, 'okay, I read you, but try not to be too long.' She turned and went back to the car smiling.

'Right,' said James. 'The house behind is slightly higher than us and therefore they have an excellent view of most of the front of this villa including the front door. At the west wing of the house there is a water pumping station which is where the private entrance to the west wing is. There are no windows on the south side of the villa except for my office. And before I go, I will close the shutters, it will just look as though I am closing for security purposes. There is a security gate between the water pumping station and the west wing. The private door is the other side of this gate, so it is secure, and no one can walk around the house without a key to that gate.

'In the back of the villa is our swimming pool and a wall about 6 metres high down to a cul-de-sac created to allow delivery vehicles to get to the house in front of us. Because we are situated on a very steep hill, the houses in front are well below us, and anyone even standing on the roofs would not be able to see the interior of where we are now. So, to sum up, the front of the villa as far as the west wing, the front garden and parking area and the very steep tarmac road down the side of the villa where we have access to the garage are all in full view of the house behind. Assuming the guys in the house are on a surveillance mission, they have a perfect view of the area, but they don't know if there is anyone else in the villa apart from Peter who they would expect to see at some stage. Indeed, when I walk out to the car you can come with me Peter and look as though you have been invited but have decided against the trip. In the meantime, I am going to close all the window shutters, so you will have to talk in artificial light. If you want to make telephone calls only Peter should do so, the same for answering the phone. Do not open the door to anyone. This place is like Fort Knox, so there's no chance of anyone breaking in without a bulldozer.' James laughed, and quickly secured all the shutters on the south side of the house which sported 16 French windows. Once done he opened the front door and walked out with Peter following him. As he was climbing into the driver's seat, Peter made a gesture of laying his head on his hands, suggesting he was going for a sleep. Out of the corner of his eye James had noticed the man with the binoculars studying them.

As soon as they reached Chania about half an hour later, James took out his mobile and called the owner of the house in Norway. 'Hi Vien, forgive me for calling you, but I noticed some men inside your house... and as this is not the holiday season, I wondered if...'

'Ah, thank you James for phoning, yes, it is okay there are six Russians apparently going to snorkel in Souda Bay, they have taken the villa for a month.'

When the shoppers had left, Adrian introduced himself and Peter was impressed that the head of Britain's security service had travelled out to meet him. 'I decided that the number of people who knew what I was doing should be very few, indeed very few in my organisation know that I'm here. Obviously, the fact that you've indicated that there may be a mole in a reasonably senior position is of concern and I would like to discuss that with you after you tell us what "Operation Open Door" refers to.' Peter Validich nodded. The four of them sat in comfortable chairs in the drawing room which overlooked Souda Bay, without the stunning view when the shutters were open.

Peter pulled out a folder from his briefcase. 'I'm going to give you a rough precis of Putin's master plan, although you would not need to be a rocket scientist to understand what he's up to.' He spoke in perfect English. 'Why am I doing this?' He looked at Ladvia, 'you know that I'm a patriot and love my country.' Ladvia nodded. 'Putin was exactly the right man for Russia after the humiliation the country suffered after the collapse of the Soviet Union and that drunken fool Yeltsin.

'Russia is a great country, and the Russian people are much the same as any other in the world in an advanced economic community. The average Russian wants security, the chance to earn enough to look after his family and the opportunity to better his lot. The sacrifice made during World War 2 was horrendous and it created a feeling of total insecurity among the population. The rulers of Russia at the time did not trust the West and the result was the cold war that eventually ruined the economy of Russia and created a situation where the police state ruled. There was no law, no freedom of expression, no free press.

'The idea of it accepting a democratic system was received with some relief by most and for a time it worked. Unfortunately, there were still those in the background that considered democracy weak, and the tender shoots of the new system were hi-jacked by a conglomerate of rich and powerful people. Putin: originally chosen as a reluctant leader by people who thought they could manipulate him to their will. Just as the right wing in Germany thought they could manipulate Hitler. He is by far a cleverer man than the Chancellor of Germany was and had the patience to ensure his position as head of government was secure. Anyone who came close to opposing him, whether old friends, or those in disagreement with his policies, were either murdered or jailed, indeed he has been known to simply sack senior officials who were becoming too popular.

'The West continued to humiliate Russia after the collapse of the Soviet Union, but for a time I hoped that we would be able to join hands with respect and create a friendly and jointly beneficial agreement between us. Indeed, there was a time when there was talk of Russia joining NATO and even the European Union.

'There is no doubt that Putin has benefited from the humiliation felt by the Russian people and has used that to strengthen his hold on government. The decline started when George W. Bush made certain promises and then was seen in Georgia with the new prime minister when they declared independence. Then Putin found the Americans

77

were involving themselves in the Chechen situation and allying with the terrorists there. He also felt rebuffed by Tony Blair who he thought of as a friend when the British Courts refused to extradite certain enemies of Putin's. Once Obama became President of the United States, Putin realised that this was an honest man, but one who would shrink at even the thought of outright war. Obama backed down on the idea of putting defensive missile sites into Poland and other countries close by, which was supposed to be for the defence of an attack from Iran. Hardly believable. The realisation came when Obama created a Red Line which he said he wouldn't cross regarding chemical weapons in Syria and this was welcomed by the Western world, but he then backed down giving Putin a green light to take a much more aggressive stance there. The British parliament turning down the suggested strikes proposed by the military, gave Putin the chance to interfere without risk.

'Putin feels that democracy is weak, uncontrolled capitalism creates greed, and shrinking from using extreme force is politically feeble. He also realised that Russia was weak. Its economy was in tatters and its military tested and found to be technologically wanting. Corruption was rife and the Russian people disenchanted with their lot.

'He looked at what was strong in Russia. The first thing he realised was the tremendous reserves of energy in both oil and gas. The landmass also contains virtually every known mineral known to man. Russia has the largest nuclear stockpile and a large army. The wages paid to Russians is one of the lowest in the advanced economies which meant that he could export his gas and oil at lower prices. In only a few years, he ensured that his power was absolute, while amassing a huge personal fortune, he is the wealthiest man on the planet. He has also made Russia the greatest gas exporter and the second greatest oil exporter in the world.

He has laid claim to over 463,000 square miles of Arctic territory based on the Lomonosov Ridge which goes as far as the North Pole. This is an area rich in oil and gas deposits. To ensure Russia's claim he has built 40-armed ice breaking ships. The USA has 2. You will hear him shortly boasting that Russia has developed a cruise missile that can avoid any detection by the west and that they now have underwater drones that can seek and destroy submarines. This is for home consumption only, as we know the west have developed similar technology. But this information was to boost his standing in the recent election, which he won by devious means. Anyone standing against him was either murdered or jailed. Putin needs to persuade the Russian people that they are strong and not at the mercy of the United States or the Western World. Russia is now selling gas to most of the European nations and in some cases, such as the Baltic States and Finland they are dependent on Russian energy. Belarus, Czech Republic, Slovakia and Bulgaria 80-100%, Ukraine, Austria and Greece 60-80%, Poland and Slovenia 40-60%, Germany, Italy, Luxembourg and Hungary 20-40% and Romania, France, Croatia, and the Netherlands more than 20%. Only the UK, Sweden, Switzerland, Spain, Portugal, Norway, Ireland, Denmark, and Belgium do not rely on Russia for their gas, although frankly you would have to be an engineering genius to determine where all the gas goes. You would have thought that he had achieved all that was necessary for the country and that it would continue to prosper, becoming one of the richest trading nations based on the raw materials held under the vast landmass. He could have utilised the new riches for the betterment of his people still on an average monthly wage equivalent to US$ 533 per month. But no, he now wants to destroy Europe, divide NATO to marginalize the United States and the West, achieve regional hegemony and become a global power.

'He is doing this by his six-point plan:

1.   Weaponisation of Energy
2.   Military intervention without risk
3.   Hybrid propaganda
4.   Influencing any organisation with generous cash payments that can destabilise areas that he wants to have some control over, particularly Europe, but also the Middle East and the United States.
5.   Cyber-attacks and using social media to perpetrate fake news into the target countries.
6.   Build up a huge military structure comparable to the USA. Russia already has more nuclear weapons in its arsenal, and he is updating them as we speak.

'He has recognised the weakness of the European Union, NATO, and the unwillingness of the democracies to stand up for their beliefs.

'Now he is embarking on a policy of aggression, which I believe will lead Russia to ruin. Democracies are always slow to deal with despots and invariably suffer as a result. On the other hand, once they have woken up to the dangers they face, they will react. The West has a hugely powerful military, their technology, their industrial might, along with their ability to respond. All it needs is the political will to do so, and at the end of the day, it is when the people of the democracies come to their senses and replace weak leaders with strong ones.

'Let us now look at what Putin has so far achieved of his plan.'

Ladvia jumped up and went to the refrigerator bringing back some glasses of chilled water. Peter took a sip and turned to her. I had hoped this would be something a little stronger.' He smiled.

She got up again and brought a bottle of vodka from the drinks cupboard. 'It's not good for you at this time of day, Peter,' she chided.

'You've obviously been in the West far too long,' he joked.

He drank the water and then poured himself a liberal amount of vodka in the same glass, before offering it round. Everyone else refused.

'Now, where was I? Ah yes, what Putin has achieved.

'He has used the gas he sells to good effect, and don't forget he only sells for US dollars. He has at times cut supplies to Ukraine, which affected Bulgaria, Greece, Macedonia, Romania, Croatia, and Turkey. The excuse was non-payment by Ukraine, but it sent a message to Europe that Russia could close most of the European Countries at will, effectively using the supply of energy as a potent weapon. There is no doubt that this prevented Europe from deepening the sanctions requested by the USA and Great Britain. One also must ask oneself, if Putin walked into say Latvia, would NATO stop him? It is doubtful that the European nations would do so as their energy supply could disappear, causing chaos. They would huff and puff, take the matter to the United Nations who would also huff and puff, but nothing would be achieved, particularly as there are 25% of Russian citizens within the whole country, and 50% in the capital city Riga. Despite NATO's stepped-up activities, there are still less American troops in NATO than there are policemen in New York City.'

'Do you have an alternative?' asked Jeremy.

'It is a fact that most of the larger European countries including the UK and Ireland have substantial gas reserves under the ground. The way to obtain this resource is by fracking. The USA already has become more than self-reliant by using this method. I appreciate that countries with a higher population per square kilometre have political problems, but you must know that Russia is highly active in supporting those individuals and institutions that are against fracking.'

Adrian nodded, 'yes, we are aware of Putin's interference and the fact that he is pumping cash into not only those bodies against fracking, but Russia is also very active in other areas, such as those against nuclear power, military or otherwise.' Adrian took a sip of water. 'He is also putting funds into certain political parties in Europe that he deems will either weaken the state or be more friendly to Russia.'

'Can't you identify these funds?' asked Ladvia.

'In a lot of cases we can,' answered Adrian, 'but they are not generally illegal. Often the Kremlin pays a wealthy supporter or an investment company or in some cases directly to the political party concerned, often as a loan via a Russian bank. If it appears that someone, a company, or individual is supporting something that either destabilises or is not necessarily in our country's interest, we can take steps to stop the flow of finance, however it is sometimes good policy to watch how the money is used and gather intelligence by doing so. In some cases, the recipient may not be aware where these funds originate from and who is supporting his or her cause, in such a case we have ways of letting them know where the money is coming from. I have to say though, that here are a number of recipients who ignore our information, and they are then placed on a security list.'

'It is quite true,' said Peter, 'The UK are much better at identifying such people and organisations than most of the other European countries, and the reason for this is that most of the funds are cleared through London. This point however is noted in clause 4 of my list of six.

'While we are on the subject of funding, Russia spends a considerable amount on what we call hybrid propaganda, this is aimed at Russian speaking communities within what Putin would term Russia's sphere of influence and that really includes any country that is adjacent to the Russian land mass, plus a few others. So, as I have already said Latvia and Estonia have a Russian population of 25% and Lithuania about 6%. These are Russians who were living in these countries when they became independent after the fall of the Soviet Union. They did not take the citizenship of the countries they were resident in.

'Russia has the most international borders with 16 sovereign states, including two with maritime boundaries (US, Japan), as well as with the occupied Georgian territories of South Ossetia and Abkhazia. With a land border running 20,241 kilometres, the second longest border. Only China has a larger border.

'Where there are Russians living within sovereign states, we target them specifically with propaganda, sometimes inventing stories designed to unsettle the Russian communities, and it is fair to say, with some success. This was particularly successful in Eastern Ukraine and the Crimean Peninsula.

'At the moment Russia is on a similar ideological sphere as China, but eventually we all know that China must be a major threat as they build their economy to outstrip even the USA. We are aware of their interest in biological warfare, which is a method of crucifying your enemies without having to declare war. Of course, by releasing such a terrifying weapon it could create many deaths within their own country. Only China and North Korea could get away with killing its own population for what they consider to be a coup of all coups, to create economic superiority. If you consider that Putin uses his people to retain power, the Chinese use their military as a complete system of control, they do not have to rely on elections, and it has been shown that they care little for the Chinese people. Remember Tiananmen Square where the military killed an estimated 10,000 people who were protesting. Remember Hong Kong.

'Russia also has biological weapons but is restricted in the use of them. Instead, we make exceptionally good use of social media, again inventing stories and, in some cases, creating difficulties for politicians we do not like. Some of the stories are true, thanks to Mr Snowden who now lives in Russia, but some sophistication is used in slightly twisting a story to make it more damaging. A lot of this went on against Hillary Clinton when she was a candidate for the US presidency.

'Cyber warfare is another area Russia is adept at, creating problems, hacking various companies or institutions that hold sensitive information, thus in some cases weakening various organisations and, or stealing critical secrets from government papers including the military. It is now well known that Russia hacked into the e-mails of both the Democratic and Republican parties in the USA. Because we preferred Trump to Clinton, we arranged for details of Hilary's e-mails to be leaked through WikiLeaks. Trump won, although I frankly believe that Putin may have made an extraordinary error in supporting him, we shall see.

'It may surprise some in the West that Russia is now a much greater threat than it was during the cold war. We sell our energy for US$ dollars so we have benefited hugely by the increase in the value of that currency, which is ironic, as the gain far surpasses the sanctions the West placed on them.

Nevertheless, our whole economy relies on that one area, and as countries shocked by Putin's methods of energy control diversify, Russia could suffer with little to sell apart from arms. This means that there is a window of opportunity where Russia can gain its ascendancy. Putin has a limited time too; he is now 66 years of age and thus he needs to achieve his aims within the next few years.

'It is worth noting that our GDP has lowered over the last few years, where most of the west's has increased.

'Although Russia has a large military force and that is doubling in size, it has been built up because of low wages and plentiful mineral resources within the land mass, so comparing military expenditure against GDP is not necessarily an accurate picture. We know that Russia is moving its military expenditure up from 6.84% to about 10% of our GDP, i.e., 87 billion to 101 billion, against the UK 2% representing 53 billion and the USA 3.3% representing 596 billion, all in US dollars. NATO, Including the USA spends about 871 billion on defence, a figure far below what it should be if every country met its commitment, and it has been decreasing over the last few years.

'The GDP figure for the USA is 18.56 trillion, UK 2.65 trillion and Russia 1.268 trillion, China 14.1 trillion.

'Russia still has a low debt figure, and still has 386 billion US$ in foreign reserves, considerably more than either the United States at 116 billion or the UK at 163 billion. The gold reserves are USA 8,133 tons, Russia 1542 tons and the UK 310 tons. The external debt ratio for the democratic nations is huge compared with Russia, nevertheless it is obvious that only two countries far surpass Russia in terms of military expenditure and that is China and the USA. In a situation of outright war, Russia would not stand a chance of winning a war of attrition if the West pooled its economic and military resources. It is therefore a matter of political will and taking the view that the West will shrink from any confrontation.

'So, to sum up, Russia is far weaker than you are led to believe, but we are using our reserves which 2 years ago stood at over 700 billion and utilising our low cost of labour and materials to build up our military strength which as we've seen, Putin is quite capable of using. He has no compunction in killing women and children as well as non-belligerent civilians and would not consider human life a necessary factor when achieving his aims, whether they be his own countrymen or those belonging to the West. He is ruthless, but an excellent poker player. At some stage, the West will have to call his hand, and the longer he can delay the more powerful he becomes as he will draw more and more countries to serve his ambition. You only need to look at the Syrian situation to understand how he glibly votes for a ceasefire and then completely ignores the United Nations decisions. What do the West do? They criticise him in the United Nations thinking it will harm him, but of course in Russia he gains even more support by being strong.

'His strength is his military. They are well trained and equipped. He has S-100 missile sites in Abkhazia and South Ossetia which gives him de facto control over Georgian airspace. In Kaliningrad on the Baltic, he has 35,000 troops, 2 mechanized brigades and hundreds of armoured vehicles. More importantly he has SK720 Iskander missile sites there which effectively cover an area of over 400 square miles, (this figure is incorrect as their area is nearer to 800 miles, thus breaking the treaty created to contain the distance covered) threatening the airspace of the Baltic States, Poland, and a large part of Germany. Of course, there is nothing in the NATO treaty that deals with overt threats, only actual invasions. With his army of 845,000 active, plus reserves of 2 million and Paramilitary of 519,000 plus 15,398 tanks he could invade any European country with ease and secure its borders before NATO could even think of reacting. Of course, the nuclear deterrent is a factor, but is there really a European politician that would use it? My contention is only if their own country suffered invasion and even then, it would depend on the circumstances.

'The Russian navy is being upgraded as is the equipment used by the army – the new T-14 Armata battle tank is more than equal to anything the West can put in the field, but of course you are aware of all these figures, so I'm not divulging any secrets to you.

'The new investment in military satellites is high and it is well known that the West is susceptible to their continued use of programmable logic computers which control virtually everything from hospitals, water supplies, dams, electric generators, to name but a few. Because these items are not state run, most in the control of local councils, or communities, many do not have encryption.

'It is also well known that your internet cables run underneath the sea, ripe for either cutting or listening in via special submarines. Your exit points on land are often unguarded and open to the public.

'There are a number of us in high command who are extremely concerned that Putin's sabre rattling could flare into a world war. Indeed, it may be inevitable even now, but politicians in the West need to start preparing the populace for the worst. In the UK, your voters are worried about the state of your NHS, but what would you think if I told you that within a period of between 2 to five years your sons and daughters could be called up to fight for their country, what would you feel if you were suffering the same sort of attrition being brought on the heads of those poor individuals who live in Aleppo. I and many others are saying wake up Europe, it's not too late, but you'll have to bring an end to Putin's plans before it is.'

Adrian thanked Peter for setting out his warning. 'We are of course aware of most of what you've been saying, but it is one thing to be aware and another to get people within a cosy democratic environment to recognise the real dangers we face. As you know it is public knowledge that we have recently built 2 new aircraft carriers and are building new frigates, but the changes we are currently facing, with a new President in the USA, Brexit at home, and the poor Greek, Italian and Spanish financial situation we are in a disaster mode. The elections in France didn't change the political map as feared but we are still unsure about Germany, where they are struggling to rule with a coalition government. All this dissension is obviously a great help to someone like Putin as he feeds on uncertainty. All we can do now is to keep our intelligence at the fore front of this battle, and ready ourselves as best we can for the worst.

'There is one matter which I would like to know about, however. You have mentioned that there is a new situation called "Operation Open Door," we have assumed that this could be referring to the Eastern Mediterranean, the Baltic States or perhaps Norway.' Adrian looked at Peter with raised eyebrows.

Peter smiled. 'There you go, Putin is a master of creating surprises. "Operation Open Door," does not apply to any of those areas, it is a daring plan that will completely take the whole of Europe by surprise and compromise most but will only be enacted if certain political situations are created. The first one has already happened and that is the election of Donald Trump as President.'

Jeremy frowned, 'I recognise that Trump said he admired Putin because he was a strong man, but I don't believe for a moment that he will not strengthen the US military, and indeed he has already put some fairly strong military leaders into his cabinet.'

Peter nodded, 'I agree with you, but he has also indicated that if the Europeans don't put at least the 2% into their military budgets, he may not consider them as part of the NATO alliance. There are 23 countries out of 27 that fit into that category. All the indications are that Trump is an isolationist, which again suits Putin.

'What if I suggested to you the following? That the current Prime Minister of the UK may have to call an election to enable them to move the UK into a form of Brexit which was agreed after the referendum. Let us assume that the opposition remains with Marxist thinking, with substantial funds and fake news fed in from Russia. Assume the leader of that party is a pacifist and would not press the nuclear button and would further run down your military by say cancelling your purchases from the USA, for Trident. This could create a situation where the USA may well withdraw its military support. The Scots, again with substantial funding supplied by Russia, secedes from the United Kingdom as did Ireland in 1922 and allows Russia to station troops in the new country to protect it from any intervention from England, what would Putin have achieved?'

Adrian drew in a quick breath, but before he could speak, Peter continued. 'Putin would have complete access to the North Sea and the oil fields therein, he would have control of your nuclear submarine base at Faslane on Loch Gare, your nuclear stockpile opposite at Coulport all just above Glasgow and have access to the Firth of Clyde thus controlling the Irish Sea. He would have control of the Rosyth shipyard above Edinburgh on the Firth of Forth where your aircraft carriers are stationed and the Clyde where your new type 26 Frigates are being built, and yet he would not have had to use any force, as he would be in Scotland by the invitation of the new government. He might even be able to take over Scapa Flow for his navy thus controlling the area between the Orkney Islands and Iceland. Then let us fantasise a little further, say he then threatens England, either you surrender your sovereignty, or we will nuke London. Then what happens, you have a leader that would not retaliate. So does the UK surrender and join Putin's idea of a completely unified Europe under Russia's control?'

Adrian pursed his lips. 'That's making a lot of assumptions Peter, it is extremely unlikely that the First Minister of Scotland would secede to let Russia in, it is also unlikely that the present Prime Minister would lose an election.'

'Putin's plan has already started, first the election of the American President who he feels will isolate the United States from the rest of the world.' Peter leaned forward in his chair.

'There is little doubt that it was a British firm that supplied something like fifty million pieces of personal data to the Trump Campaign, which helped Putin's scheme, add to that a plethora of what appeared to be individual comments on social media, a large percentage traced back to Russia which may have influenced both the Trump campaign and Brexit. Fake news also played a part.

'The plan is quite simple, isolate your enemies and then strike in the confusion. Sun Tzu the ancient military philosopher said one thousand five hundred years ago, "victorious warriors win first and then go to war." He also said, "supreme excellence consists of breaking the enemy's resistance without fighting." So, the idea is to encourage the UK to break away from Europe, which will upset the Scots and possibly create a situation where there would be more of the population that would accept a breakaway from the United Kingdom. His pièce de résistance would be to offer the Scots a monetary deal, possibly of oil and gas for zero, thus allowing Scotland to reap in all its exported energy, which would be roughly equal to the amount it currently receives in subsidy from the United Kingdom. This would make Scotland one of the richest states in Europe, assuming it left the United Kingdom.

'For the moment let us leave the last two assumptions and concentrate on a sudden and unexpected secession. You will have heard of Angus Stuart who is a senior member of the SNP?'

Adrian frowned and nodded.

'What you may not know is that he is in Moscow now discussing political matters. It is not his first visit. That may not be all he is discussing. You will certainly be aware that Angus hates the English, to the extent that he refuses to use the language in public, he speaks only Gaelic. My understanding is that his lineage goes back to the Jacobeans who tried to usurp the English throne in the 1700's.' Said Peter.

'It's true that I didn't know he was negotiating a deal with Russia, but even then, I can't see the First Minister agreeing.' Argued Adrian.

'Unless the First Minister was to be eliminated,' said Peter. 'It is quite easy nowadays to arrange a spectacular car accident by obtaining control of a vehicle via a nearby computer. That done, Angus would seize control, with Russian help of course. The Russians would already be in the country probably in a greater force than most would realise.'

'Hmm, is that what you're telling us would happen?'

'All I can say at this juncture is "Operation Open Door" pertains to the seizure of Scotland, without using obvious force. It will be over within 24 hours and is highly unlikely that English troops would be sent to fight Scottish troops, but again it depends how it is accomplished and who is involved.'

'Wow,' said Jeremy sitting back in his chair, 'that would give Putin the pincer movement of pincer movements and effectively block the USA or NATO from intervening even if they wanted to, Scotland then being a sovereign country. Do you have a suggestion as to how we stop him?'

Peter took a large swig of vodka, 'Act now, before it's too late, remember Hitler when he started out, by walking into the Rhineland, if he had been stopped, that would have been the end of the matter and would have given the Allies plenty of time to re arm properly.'

Adrian was silent for a minute. 'I'm most grateful for the information you've given to us Peter and remember, if you ever need to leave Russia, you can count on us. Just one more thing, you have mentioned we have a mole in our organisation, do you happen to know who it is?'

'No, but I do know that he or she quite highly placed'

'Do you know what party he/she belongs to?'

'No, but I'm reliably informed that the person is not necessarily a politician and is definitely in it for the money. Follow the money and you may find him... or her. There is another possibility. There are situations where relatives living in Russia have been compromised by the FSB and as a result open the possibility of blackmail to close relatives in Britain. The FSB are past masters at this sort of skulduggery. There is something else you should be aware of.'

Adrian raised his eyebrows, 'Go on...'

'I am also reliably informed that there is a new purge on named defectors, particularly those still working for the West. Litvinenko was one, Sergei Skripal another, but there will be others. The elimination of Litvinenko was just before he was due to appear to give evidence in a Spanish court about nefarious dealings between the Mafia and the Russian hierarchy which would have compromised Putin.

'Sergei was very active in the UK, despite indications that he had retired, and the use of Novichok was quite deliberate to spread the word to others that if you cross Putin, you will be eliminated. If he knew I was here talking to you, my life would not be worth a rouble.

'As you know, Novichok, is particularly deadly, and it cannot be detected by NATO sensors. Moreover, it is designed to infiltrate protective clothing, but your people at Portland Down will be familiar with this fact.'

THE SCOTTISH PREROGATIVE

Incorporating

THE WUHAN AFFAIR

SHEREPOV RETURNS

Chapter 10

Andropov Sherepov, head of the FSB, the equivalent of MI5, was sitting at his desk in Lubyanka Square in Moscow when his phone rang. It was the special phone connected to the Kremlin.

'Sherepov?'

A female voice answered. 'General Sherepov, the President wishes to see you within the next half hour, please make yourself available at his office, you know where that is?'

'Yes of course, I will be there.'

Sherepov put the phone down and pondered what was in store for him. It was a year ago since he received promotion from a Colonel in charge of Moscow security to head the FSB. He had been diligent in his task, but a plan which he had created and was agreed by the President had not achieved the required result.

He knew he could be relieved of his position. Putin did not treat failures with equanimity and as he stood up to leave, he looked around his office. It really showed the man he was. There were no pictures on the walls, only statistical charts. No pictures on his desk of a family because he did not have one. Sherepov, as everyone knew, was married to his job, a job which he had done to the best of his ability. He picked up his briefcase and asked his secretary to call for a government limousine. In a past encounter he had been wounded in his leg, and his worry and concern made it appear even more painful. Arriving at the Kremlin, he realised that he could be shot, which is what the Western press had expected, or at the very least incarcerated in Lubyanka prison.

He was shown into the President's office and offered a chair opposite the President's desk. Much to his surprise the chair behind the desk was empty.

It was some five minutes later when the President came in with an aide. Sherepov assumed that he was there to escort him out to a lifetime of misery.

The President signed some papers on his desk, handed them to the aide, and as the aide left, he sat back in his chair.

'Well, Sherepov, our previous plan to take over Greece didn't go quite as we planned, did it?'

Sherepov took a deep breath, 'no sir.' He was not a man to make excuses.

'The man you employed to act as our middleman turned himself over to the Americans, but they have chosen not to publicise the matter, as to do so, would compromise their security service. However, we did make some gains, despite the problem in Greece, we still achieved an energy deal with them which puts them under our influence and because of the upheaval in the Middle East we were able to take over control of the Syrian situation from the British and Americans. The American President, aware of our resolve, backed down over the chemical weapons fiasco, which he said was a red line for him. The truth is Sherepov, we aim high and gain some, even if we do not achieve everything we plan to. We failed with our input in the Scottish referendum, but we arguably helped to split Europe with the Brexit vote.

What I like about you is your professionalism and your loyalty to me.' He stopped and stared at Sherepov. 'You are married to the Russian State but more so to me, the President, and you steer clear of politics which so many military and others cannot stay clear of once in a high position, and as long as that continues, I will support you.

'Now, I am removing you from the position of the Head of the FSB.'

Sherepov felt a tightening in his stomach. Here it comes he thought.

'I am replacing you and transferring you to the position as head of the SVR, this to include an overall control of the GRU. This will give you ample opportunity to use your skills in a more productive manner.'

Sherepov was trembling, although it did not show. He was in fact being promoted to the head of the Russian foreign Intelligence Service a similar organisation to MI6 and the Russian military spy network, previously a separate entity.

'Now there are some matters which you may be unaware of as we have devised a forward plan it's called "Operation Open Door".'

Sherepov had heard whispers and rumours about a daring plan but had not being privy to the details and had deliberately stayed clear of delving further. He showed surprise. 'It has not crossed my desk Mr President.'

Putin was pleased that the secret plan developed by his close associates in the industrial sector had not reached the ears of the head of FSB. He then went on to explain the plan which he claimed was his idea alone. 'Of course, it does rely on certain matters coming to fruition. Our efforts to ensure President elect Trump won the US elections was the first step and with that we were successful. It was not too difficult as many voters disliked his opponent, and us being able to hack into the Democratic Campaign's e-mails, was a great help. We were able to throw some doubt onto the personal e-mails of Hillary Clinton, to the extent that the FBI was forced to say that the investigation would be reopened. Of course, once they realised that the new information was invented, they quickly stepped back from their original stance, but by then the damage was done.' He laughed, 'it was all so easy, and the Americans think they own the digital industry, but we have made great strides in the last couple of years, particularly with the help of Mr Snowden and Wikileaks.

'You will also handle the hacking department as well as the hybrid propaganda. This gives you complete power over all our external spying operations and the successful completion of "Operation Open Door". You realise that we should not be waiting for events to happen, we must make them happen to our benefit.'

'I fully understand Mr President, and I will spend the next few weeks assimilating my new department and...'

Putin held up his hand. 'There are two matters which I want you to deal with personally.'

Sherepov raised his eyebrows.

'I have seen an opportunity to have a further plan to destabilise the United Kingdom. Tomorrow we are expecting a man called Angus Stuart to visit Moscow. I want you to meet him. He is here for talks on us continuing to support the building of a new factory in Scotland near the border with England. The factory, which is almost ready for production, will produce new earth moving machines for export to the European Union, but it will also have another purpose that will ensure the English cannot interfere with our plans. Stuart hates the English and will be our contact going forward. He is now leading the Scottish industrial expansion scheme and is well thought of by the First Minister. She will not be aware of any plan we agree on except the building of the factory, built by picked Russian workers with Latvian passports. The company involved is Swedish. Originally there was an industrial corporation in Sweden called Bolinder Munktell. This was defunct and the assets are now part of Volvo Construction Equipment. Our Swedish friends set up a new corporation called Munk Ny (Monk New). We have covertly financed the operation and it comes under the oversight of the Russian Economic Development, shortly to transfer to the SVR. The directors are all Swedish but will report directly to a person who you will appoint. I have a suggestion of names that will be suitable. A Greek businessman who owes us. The company although structured to build earth moving equipment, will be much more. If the true ownership is traced, it will point to North Korea. As you know we are using this criminal State to further our grip on hacking and false news. Angus Stuart will not be aware of the true purpose of the corporation other than it will employ about 400 people in an area of high unemployment near the Scottish and English border. The company have already built an airport on the site to facilitate the direct importation of parts. I have arranged for a top-secret report to be sent to you and I will go into more detail once you have read it.'

'Are the directors aware of any secondary interest for the corporation?' asked Sherepov.

'No, nor is our Greek businessman, but he is the only one who is aware of the true ownership, and he will report directly to you. He will be well paid for the job.'

'Secondly, I am aware of certain members of some of our highly placed liberal military plan to halt our expansion plans in Europe and concentrate on peaceful solutions with our neighbours. We tried that, and they simply took advantage of what they saw as a weakness. We will not make the same mistake again. The reason I am putting the GRU under your control, is that I do not wholly trust the military, as they made it plain that they were against our infiltration of the Crimean situation.'

'Do we have names...'

'No one has been caught being disloyal to the State, but you should keep your ear to the ground Sherepov. Any high-ranking person going overseas should be watched carefully to see if they are meeting people from the other side. There is one that we know who has very recently gone to Crete with his wife for a holiday, his name is General Peter Validich.'

'Peter, I'd be surprised, he is very well thought of by military and politicians alike.'

'Yes of course, but he is more liberal minded than most. Of course, there are a few them, but all senior military officers going overseas should be checked, as should senior civil servants and politicians. You will find that I have already given that instruction through your predecessor.'

Sherepov felt that there was something behind Putin's remarks but decided not to take the matter further, until he had moved offices and assessed the situation.

When he returned to his office, he instructed his assistant, who was to move with him to dig out the file on Validich and report back.

His next few days were taken up with moving from central Moscow to the SVR headquarters situated in the Yasenevo District south west of Moscow.

A week had gone by before he questioned his assistant about Peter Validich.

THE SCOTTISH PREROGATIVE

Incorporating

THE WUHAN AFFAIR

THE SURVEILLANCE

Chapter 11

A key inserted in the door interrupted the talk as the shoppers returned. Peter confirmed to James that no telephone calls had been made or received. As Kate made some tea, James sat down. 'There is no doubt that the Russians in the house above are not here to scuba dive,' he said. 'They are obviously in Crete to carry out surveillance on Peter. That is not a problem, it only becomes one if Adrian, Jeremy and Ladvia are seen.

'I have given some thought as to how we deal with the situation. I telephoned the NATO base via my secure mobile and spoke to Major Carter, who is incidentally one of us. This is our joint suggestion. It is imperative that the three of you get out of here, tout de suite. I have therefore planned how you can do so safely, but if you disagree, I can change the plan. Next door is a villa that is currently unoccupied, as indeed are all the villas below us. This is not unusual at this time of year. While our front is on the north side, the next-villa faces south, we can reach it by negotiating the fence between us. You can then walk down the steps to the cul-de-sac below. All this can be achieved without being seen from above.'

'What if the ungodly have someone posted in one of the villas the other side of the cul-de-sac, bearing in mind any vehicle collecting us would be visible to them once it reaches the road going downhill?' Jeremy asked.

'All the villas are well and truly locked,' said James, 'and unless they've been broken into, there will be no one there. To be sure however, I will check each villa before you leave. I can do that without being seen,' he added. 'And before you ask,' James smiled, 'there is no way that they could have attached any listening devices to this villa that would be of any use to them. The front of the house is alarmed, the rear of the villa is unassailable because of the steep hill. It is at least 30 feet up from the cul-de-sac, and on the side of the house where the road runs down the steep hill, there are two bedrooms and my office all constructed from stressed concrete to be safe in the event of a medium earthquake. What I have arranged for you is a van owned by a local contractor, who is known to us. He looks after most of the houses in this area. He will drive up the hill and turn into the cul-de-sac at 20.00 hours precisely. There is turning space at the end, and he will turn around and drive very slowly past the gate to the house next door. The sliding door of the van on your side will be unlocked and all you need to do is to open it and climb in. He will then drive down the hill at some speed and meet the limo you came in on the outskirts of Plaka. You will transfer into that. The limo will drive towards Georgioupolis, it being in the opposite direction to the NATO base and once it reaches the National Road, it will turn right and take you to the base. The van will carry on to Omalos near the Samaria Gorge to provide a decoy. When you reach the NATO base, you will fly back to Chelverston in the C130 that brought you here, leaving Peter and family in Plaka to enjoy their holiday.

The plan worked without a hitch, and James was amused when looking out of his small office, he saw panic from the Russian's when they saw the van turn into the cul-de-sac and almost immediately drive out and go down the steep hill. It took four of them several minutes to get to the 4 x 4 and drive out in pursuit. They caught up with the van just before the entrance to the town of Almyrida, and followed it all the way to Omalos, the town near the famous Samaria Gorge where the driver parked outside a taverna leaving it unlocked. The disappointment at the Russians finding the van empty did not improve their day.

The limo with darkened windows drove straight to the C130 on the tarmac and the occupants climbed on board. Within ten minutes the plane was in the air.

Adrian turned to Jeremy, 'when we arrive, my plan is as follows, I have arranged for a car with chauffeur to collect you and drive you to one of our safe houses in South London where you will stay the night, and tomorrow you will be collected at 10.a.m and brought to my office. I have a proposal to put to you, which I would like you to consider.'

The journey as before was uneventful, but as they did not have to go via Gibraltar, it was much shorter.

The safe house was in fact in Richmond, where Ladvia had stayed for a brief period many years before, and she was pleased to see that it had been upgraded since that time.

That evening, in the Crete villa, when most had retired, James was left talking to Peter Validich. After discussing the recent events, James brought the subject around to Peter's future. 'I remember the old days of the KGB when normal Russian citizens were restricted from travelling overseas and those that did were heavily escorted or at the very least carefully watched.' James took a sip from his gin and tonic. 'I thought those days were behind us, so the fact that you are under surveillance from the new regime, suggests that you may be under suspicion. You should consider at the very least getting your family out of Russia while you can. If the unthinkable happens, you should consider joining them in either the UK or the USA.'

Peter pursed his lips and laughed, 'that does not necessarily secure my safety as both Alexander Litvinenko, and Alexander Perepilichy would be able to attest if they were still alive, but there are others that I'm aware of that died of "natural causes". All my children are grown up now, and most live overseas as does Aleksi. I have one son at university in Moscow and of course my wife who lives with me there, but the powers that be would not be foolish enough to kill me as this would send the wrong message to the military, something our leaders rely heavily on.'

James grimaced, 'Unless of course they could pin something on you. I should tell you that I had Nemtsov and his girlfriend stay with us only last year, and he told me the same thing, "Putin would not dare to have me killed as I have too large a political following." He was shot and killed in Moscow shortly afterwards.'

Peter nodded, 'yes, he was careless and perhaps a little naive, but a politician who is against Putin, is different from a senior member of the military.'

James nodded, 'Well, I have been authorised by Adrian to offer you and your family a permanent residence in the UK, should you need it, simply use the word "residence" in your correspondence and we will make speedy arrangements.

'The best time to do this would be when Aleksi graduates, which I understand is within the next three months. There would be no better excuse for you to travel to the UK except for her graduation celebrations.'

The subject was left there, and they moved on to other matters.

THE VILLA

VIEW FROM BALCONY

NATO BASE

SOUTHERN SIDE SHOWING THE CUL DE SAC

FRONT SHOWING STUDY WINDOW ON RIGHT & WATER STATION BEHIND CAR

THE MAP

1. THE VILLA FRONT 2. THE RUSSIANS 3. THE CUL DE SAC
4. THE STEEP HILL   5. THE WATER TANK 6. THE ROUTE OUT

THE SCOTTISH PREROGATIVE

Incorporating

THE WUHAN AFFAIR

THE NEW RECRUITS

Chapter 12

A government driver collected Jeremy and Ladvia from the safe house and took them to MI6 headquarters at Vauxhall Cross. A secretary escorted them up to Adrian's office where coffee was served along with some delicious shortcake biscuits. After enquiring about the comfort of the safe house, Adrian got down to business. 'The meeting with Peter Validich was absolutely crucial,' he said. 'It is thanks to you Ladvia that he opened up to a much greater extent than I could have hoped for.'

'Yes, that was a surprise for me too,' she said, 'he knows he is under threat, and wants to get his side of the story out. I am worried however, as to his safety going forward.'

'Yes, so am I,' answered Adrian, 'but confidentially I have given James Alexander the authority to offer him and his family secure residence in the UK should he wish to take it.'

Ladvia, shook her head. 'No, Peter would never accept that, even if his life was in danger, he is a Russian patriot to the core. He is in a similar position to those who opposed Hitler in the 1930's, regrettably they didn't succeed, and neither will Peter Validich. Putin has captured the reins of power and will not give them up. He is infinitely cleverer than Hitler, and he is the biggest danger to the democracies, as he knows how to fight a war without declaring it. Of course, he has the "weapon" of social media to help him, which is considerably more potent than Herr Joseph Goebbels.'

Adrian nodded, 'yes, you may be right Ladvia, and I will be taking this point up at our COBRA meeting tomorrow. Now I want to talk about you. I have had confirmation that there was surveillance on your home in Chile. The man involved was from Jordan, and we happen to know that he is someone used by the Muslim Fund. His name was Abin Abu Kakir. This suggests that they suspect that you are still alive. This man was killed by the taxi driver that took him to an area near your house and our Embassy there managed to persuade the authorities to release a copy of the film that Abin Abu had taken. It showed you getting into the helicopter, and there is no doubt that anyone looking at that film would recognise you from the files that were kept when you were in the Bosnian security service.'

'So, you have the film...'

'Yes, but we cannot be sure that the photographs were not passed on to the Muslim Fund as well, certainly we have to assume they were. The police in Chile are not necessarily completely loyal to Great Britain. While the Bosnian's were embarrassed by you working essentially for MI6, they were the benefactors of the deal that was secured over Gorazde, so they would not be on your tail, neither indeed would the Serbs as the political situation has changed hugely since those days. The Russian's wanted you for the murder of the commandant of the air base near the border with Belarus, but thanks to Peter Validich, this was reversed when the truth of the matter came out. This then leaves the situation with the Muslim Fund, from which you took about $1.3 million of their money, and it has never been returned.'

'That's true,' interjected Jeremy, 'but as we had Ladvia "killed" it was not possible for her to return the money, otherwise they would have realised she was still alive.'

'I quite understand that' answered Adrian, 'has the money been used?'

Ladvia shook her head, 'no, it was my late father's money that we used to buy the estate in Chile, the Muslim Fund money has remained untouched in an account in the Cayman Islands, in fact I have a copy of the bank statement in my folder.'

'I had a feeling that maybe the case,' Adrian smiled. 'With your permission, I would like to get the fatwa removed, it is important to obtain that so I can discuss an idea I have, which would help the us deal with this Russian threat.'

'That's fine with me,' answered Ladvia, 'but what do you have in mind?'

'From our conversation with Validich we know that there is a highly placed politician within the Scottish SNP who appears to be cosying up to the Russians. He hates the English, due to his father being killed during the Iraq war. He was a senior officer in a Scottish Regiment out there. He met his end, along with others, because of a stupid error made by his commanding officer. I will not go into detail, except to say that the officer was retired early in disgrace, but the War office suppressed the details. However, Angus Stuart, which is his name, blamed Tony Blair for the debacle and since then he will not even speak the English Language in public, he speaks only Gaelic. We know that he is a heavy drinker and a womaniser. We also know that he is negotiating some sort of deal with the Russians, but we do not yet know what sort of deal he is trying to organise. My concern now, is that this could well tie in with "Operation Open Door."

'So, how can Ladvia and I help?' asked Jeremy.

'We have been aware of this man for some time and have kept a careful watch on his movements since the days of the Scottish referendum. What was not publicly known at the time, was that had the British government lost, we would have created two sovereign territories within Scotland, one in the area Argyll and Bute and the other in part of South Fife. This to protect our submarine base where we currently store our atomic weapons and a part of south Fife where we have the Rosyth shipyards. Angus somehow got wind of this and threatened to publicise it if the Scottish referendum was won by the Scots.'

Jeremy looked surprised, 'So, are you saying that these areas would have been British sovereign territories, like Gibraltar and Cyprus?

'Exactly.'

'What about the Govan shipyard on the Clyde?'

'You mean BAE Systems; we were prepared to leave that and use it as a bargaining chip. However, his threat cost us some considerable time, as we needed to know who had blown our secret plans and what alternatives were available if it became politically impossible to create sovereign territories. The problem we had was to find an area that had the port facilities but a low population count. This meant that Portsmouth and Plymouth were out, and eventually we fixed on Barrow-in-Furness in Cumbria.'

'Yes, I can see why,' said Jeremy, 'Cumbria already has Sellafield, perfect for storing atomic bombs and nearby Barrow could soon be converted into a submarine base.'

'Yes, but we never did learn who tipped him off, we suspect it may have been the Russians, quite possibly from the "insider" within our government, but now we have an idea of what the Russians may be up to, we need more detailed information of "Operation Open Door" We have assets within the Scottish government, so we do get a certain amount of information and we know that Stuart is looking for a Russian linguist, as of course he doesn't speak the language. The last person he employed was a Scottish girl called Maggie McDonald who had a first in Russian from Edinburgh University. However, the story is that Stuart sexually harassed the poor girl who told her husband and he put in a formal complaint. She was then sacked on some trumped-up charge. So far, he has not been able to replace her, so we would like Ladvia to apply for the post. He has a trip planned to visit Moscow again next week, so he is desperate to find someone competent. Reading your record, I have no doubt that you would be quite capable of dealing with any sexual desire this man may have,' Adrian smiled.

Ladvia nodded, 'he sounds to me to be a rather nasty misogynist, but I'll do what I can. But what do you advise I should do about the Muslim Fund?'

'Leave the Muslim Fund to me, obviously I would not expose you to this job if that were not settled, so give me a couple of days.' Adrian turned to Jeremy. 'I want you to set up a department within MI6 to deal with "Operation Open Door", you know the ropes, Jeremy. You will have your own budget to work with and only my number two and I will be aware of the situation so it will remain secret. Just after the Scottish referendum, we took a leaf from the CIA and invested in a company in Scotland. You will remember that they created a company called Saint Lucia Airways in the 90's which did an excellent job of running a local airline among the Caribbean Islands.'

Jeremy nodded, 'Yes, by having a national airline they were able to obtain a slot in Brussels where they used a C130 to take arms down to Angola. Unfortunately, the plane landed in an unsafe area, and the crew were all killed. A friend of mine was one of the pilots.' Jeremy grimaced.

'Well in this case we bought a catering firm based in Scotland that has substantial contracts with the Scottish government. As we have access to all the government offices, we pick up a fair amount of information. The company have about twenty vans on the road, six of them dealing specifically with sensitive areas run by our own operatives. The managing director is going onto a technical IT company, owned by us, which is nearer to his discipline, and he will be based in one of the Baltic States, an area that is extremely sensitive now. In the first instance you will take over his position, but like him, your job will be to obtain and sift information, not to run the company, your number two, who is also one of ours, will do that. By both you and Ladvia working in unison, I hope we will expose any Russian plan. The company offices are in Edinburgh with depots in Dundee and Glasgow, so you can choose where you live within that triangle. However, this is just a precursor to a new department we are setting up, again pinching an idea from the Americans.'

'Oh,' Jeremy raised his eyebrows.

'The Central Intelligence Agency has created a department with the acronym SAD. This stands for the Special Activities Department but might just as easily stand for Search and Destroy as their main purpose is to do just that under a covert umbrella.

'We don't like the acronym "SAD" for obvious reasons,' smiled Adrian, 'so we've chosen the new department to be called the Special War organisation for Research and Defence, "SWORD", interestingly, this was used by our forces during WW2 during the D-Day invasions. I will discuss the detailed duties with you in due course, but effectively it will include the newly expanded listening post near Scarborough, Yorkshire and a priority access to a section of the SAS.'

Jeremy nodded, 'so it will encompass real military infiltration as well as the use of technology?'

'Yes.'

'Okay, Ladvia and I will discuss your idea on the basis that the Muslim Fund matter is resolved and that we are only involved for the period concerning "Operation Open Door" and then we obviously need to discuss your other plans going forward.'

Ladvia handed a folder over to Adrian. 'This statement contains the total expenditure for Operation Gorazde, and you'll note that there is U$ 1.023,000 left in the account.'

Adrian took the folder and called in Geoffrey Williamson to whom he handed the file. 'Geoffrey, as we discussed, please fax the contents of this file over to Al-Salhi once I have spoken to him.' When Geoffrey had left the office, Adrian turned to Jeremy and Ladvia.

'Now my wife is reluctantly waiting for you to pick up your two charming children who have been our guests. We have very much enjoyed having them stay with us, and I suspect they have been thoroughly spoiled. As you may know, my wife has a genetic problem and we have not been able to have our own.   I will give you a call on your mobile as soon as I have some news.'

THE 2nd MEETING OF COBRA

Chapter 13

The next day Adrian put through a call to a Mohammed Al-Salhi, a Saudi citizen who he knew was a senior member of the Muslim Fund, situated in Jordan. The Al-Salhi was not available, so he told his secretary to arrange for a convenient time to speak to him if he called back while he was out.

He then took the lift to the basement where his driver was waiting for him to go to the COBRA meeting. He had already been advised that the Prime Minister would not be able to attend due to a visit to China, so the deputy, Malcom Phipps, attended instead. Sir George Pemberton was voted as chairman for the meeting. Sir Ian Crowley of MI5, Admiral Sir John Scott-Jones joint head of the military and Sir Harry Booth the commissioner of police and the foreign Secretary, Charlie Grimes who was newly appointed, were present. Again, the people attending were kept to the bare minimum for security purposes.

Sir George opened the meeting ensuring that the last meeting minutes were agreed. Each handed their copies back, as the meeting had decided that only Sir George would hold them.

He then handed the meeting over to Adrian Bradley.

'Well gentlemen, I have some important news to impart to you. I now have information as to the origin and intent of "Operation Open Door". We were all wrong at our guesses at the last meeting, the target is Scotland.'

There were gasps around the table. 'But how...' Admiral Scott-Jones started, but Adrian waved his hand. 'we discussed at the last meeting that the President of Russia was a clever man, well I have worked out a scenario where he could it pull it off, it does assume quite a lot of "what if's" but with the amount of funding allocated to the result, it is a serious possibility. Let me elucidate: We are aware of a senior member of the SNP, who is cosying up to the Russians. We do not yet know what he is doing but suspect it may be some sort of trade deal. We are currently trying to get one of our people on the inside. The SNP has already shown it is against Brexit but consider a situation where we do not get the sort of trade deal with the EU as promised, or a no deal scenario. It would not take much persuasion for those who are still keen on separation to create trouble, assisted by fake news, cyber interference and hard cash supplied to those individuals and companies who believe Scotland would be better on their own. Do not forget that it is less than a century since the Republic of Ireland seceded from the Union. Secondly, assume that we have an election, due to the Brexit situation and a different party win. There is little doubt that they would further reduce our ability to defend our country by cutting the military budget, already at the very minimum. They may cancel Trident and have already indicated that they would not press the nuclear button. Even if the present government remains after a forthcoming election, it may be that enough damage will have been caused by forcing Scotland out of the EU, thus giving the ruling body up there the excuse required. If a referendum is denied, they could take matters into their own hands.

'Thirdly, Russia promises to support Scotland's budget to a level that would make them substantially better off financially.'

Giles nodded, 'Yes, I was briefed by Sir George on the last meeting. Russia have reserves of US dollars to the tune of around $350 billion, so $25 billion would be well within their grasp to support a seceded Scotland.'

'Precisely,' answered Adrian. He continued, 'fourthly, If America decides to isolate themselves further from Europe and the way they are talking about a trade war, indicates that is a possibility, one cannot be sure this policy would not spread to NATO. If the UK, under a different government cancel Trident thus essentially reducing our 2% of GDP defence expenditure, it could well be that our cousins across the sea would no longer support us. In any case, NATO offers protection to an invaded member country, which would not be the case with a secession. Fifth, with Russia effectively controlling Scotland, they would have access to our submarine base at Loch Gare, our nuclear weapon storage area at Coulport, Govan shipyard on the Clyde and the Rosyth shipyard. They would effectively control the North Sea and Irish Sea and be able to block off the Baltic, thus prejudicing all the countries in that area, including Finland, Sweden, Norway, Denmark and all the Baltic States: Estonia, Latvia, and Lithuania, and threatening Poland Germany and France. A pincer movement without precedent, and all without firing a shot.'

'You are surely making a lot off assumptions Adrian,' said Sir George, 'even if Scotland were to secede, we could put a stop to them doing so militarily. Ireland was quite a different case.'

'Yes, in theory we could stop them, but what with? We know that Russia has a powerful army, and their fleet, although powerful, is not yet at a technological state to defeat ours, but gentlemen, what if we were threatened by a nuclear strike, then what is our policy?

'In my scenario we have lost the support of the USA, Russia supply most of the gas to the countries in the European Union, and he has used his energy reserves as a weapon before, we would be alone, without support and an army not fit for purpose.'

Admiral Scott-Jones agreed. 'I have to say that Adrian's scenario's may be suspect, but if such a situation came about, we could probably stop them landing an army on our shores, but would we have the political will to use our nuclear power and if Trident were cancelled, we would not even have that option. Secondly, we would not under any circumstances send our forces against the Scots. If, as in the case of Hitler taking over Austria with the compliance of most of the populace, we would have to accept it as a fait accompli. No, gentlemen, this is a serious threat, and we must work to prevent it from becoming a fact. We must also recognise that our naval warships have been reduced to a fraction of what we had only a few years ago.'

Adrian nodded in agreement, 'there is one other matter that we should consider,' he said. Everyone looked up expectantly. 'The President of Russia holds supreme power, there is nothing to stop him from within the country he controls with an iron fist. Anyone showing the slightest objection to his policies is either jailed or assassinated. He was born in October 1952; now 66 years old, it could be that he wants to carry off a major coup to prove his legacy, what better than to take effective control of Europe. He may even be planning to become Head of State for life rather like Xijinping.'

'We did not take the Kaiser seriously, we did not take Hitler seriously, until it was almost too late, now it appears we could be sleepwalking to disaster.' Scott-Jones interjected.

Ian Crowley agreed. 'Adrian is right, we have assumed that the Muslim militants were our only enemy, and our efforts have gone into preventing them from taking over the world, but in real terms, although serious, they are but a distraction from the real threat, which the British public are not really aware of. For a change of government to take place, as Adrian suggests, would certainly be a disaster because of the concentration of social issues to the detriment of our security. Every week at PMQ's the previous Prime Minister was assaulted with sometimes tragic incidences of personal social injustice. The response is "we are putting more funds into... whatever." It gives the impression that the present government does not care about the individual. More and more funds pour into what is believed to be the present crisis. Security, always the strong suit of the current party is submerged in a morass of social injustice. I wonder sometimes if the electorate would prefer to give up their freedoms so jealously guarded by their fathers and grandfathers, for a completely funded NHS. Do we really believe that Russian control would keep our freedoms? Of course, they would not, we need to spell out the dangers we face before it's too late.'

'Brexit has also been a huge distraction,' said Sir Harry Booth, 'and the fact that the negotiations appear to be in disarray doesn't help either because there is so much uncertainty both politically and financially.'

Adrian agreed. 'Gentlemen we need to start preparing for the worst. The fact that the Russians can attack our digital systems from satellites is concerning, we need to ensure that all important public systems are safe.'

'What do you mean by safe,' asked Sir George Pemberton.

'Every piece of major equipment has a PLC (programmable logic controller), which controls it. Some machinery has several. For instance, hospitals, electricity generators, dams, all factory heavy machinery, trains, ships, motor cars built after 1983. All these items have computer chips, which are susceptible to hacking. There was a time when they were isolated and we had teams going around maintaining them, then some bright spark suggested if we put them on central computers within the World Wide Web, they could all be controlled by very few people, thus saving thousands of pounds in maintenance costs. Unfortunately, a lot of these items are not encrypted, and even those that are, need only a four-digit pin to get into the control of the machinery they serve. Another open problem we have is undersea cables that we rely on to process substantial amounts of data, financial and otherwise, underneath our oceans. Apart from the possibility of enemy submarines cutting these cables, they also have the capability of reading the messages sent through them, assuming they can decrypt the data. As most of the encryption is sent via RSA (named after its inventors, Ron Rivest, Adi Shamir, and Len Adleman), which is a public key cryptography algorithm, we know this has been compromised, so we are open to theft of important and sometimes secret data. If you are interested, there are certain sites around the UK where the undersea cables surface and there is usually a small building which holds the link. Would you believe that most are not even behind a locked door? Most members of the public do not know where these buildings are, but you can be sure that our enemies do. The asset I spoke to in Crete was aware of all these facts. Frankly, I do not see it is even necessary for a change in government for Russia to carry their plan through.'

Sir George looked worried, 'so what are we doing to secure these items?'

'Some work has been done,' answered Adrian, 'but we lack the funding to complete it, because it would take billions to do so, and even if we encrypt everything, what method of encryption would we use? With super computers moving into the quantum range, we may find that nothing is safe using our current methods, which is why we should be looking at completely new methods of data encryption.'

'Do you have any suggestions, Adrian?' Asked Harry Booth.

Adrian smiled, 'Yes, carry the secret data in a diplomatic bag. Seriously though, we need a new system, a wireless laser bounced off satellites may supply an answer, assuming of course we can keep the satellites in orbit. GCHQ and NASA are also looking at a method of using Photons which would be a much more secure way of encrypting data. The beauty of using a system based on photon technology is that anyone breaking into a communication, would be immediately make the sender aware of a break in, and the message would be destroyed. The problem at the moment is, that an enemy can create havoc without having to declare war, as signals can be bounced around the world making it extremely difficult to trace where they originated.'

'But if the enemy can do this, presumably so can we,' said Sir George.

Adrian smiled again, 'yes, we can and do, but the smarter the equipment, the easier it is to hack. Why do you think that we have had several of our young men with Asperger's being able to hack into top secret US military systems? Russia has its huge landmass, so undersea cables are not so crucial to their military. Also, their technology rode on the back of ours, so while they are not so advanced, their systems are harder to infiltrate. Their system of government makes it easier for them to control items within the public sphere.'

'Do we have an answer to this problem?' Asked the Deputy Prime Minister, who had remained quiet throughout the discussion.

'Yes, Deputy Prime Minister, persuade your chancellor to create a special fund for us to identify the key areas of security that could be compromised in both the military and civilian sectors, and we will start the ball rolling. I have just taken on the man for the short-term project we were talking about earlier and he would be perfect to head up an investigation team.'

The Deputy Prime Minister nodded and then apologised saying he had further appointments, but that he would raise the matter with the Chancellor when he met him later in the week. He would also speak to the P.M.

When he had gone, Sir George turned to Adrian. 'Do you really feel that the threat is as bad as you indicated?'

Adrian looked grim, 'your party will almost certainly lose the next election unless there is a change of focus, and dare I say it, regrettably a different Prime Minister. The opposition is trying to persuade the electorate that the social problems are more important than the real dangers we are facing. In eighteen months. We could be facing a humiliating defeat from foreign sources and far more interference in our affairs than we could ever have experienced by being a member of the EU. The main problem as I see it is the younger generation are lapping up promises from politicians, but most haven't read their history books.'

Giles Fortescue agreed. 'Adrian is right, we must beef up our defence, there is one particular incident you should read up on, and that is Operation PB Success and Operation Sherwood.'

Sir George looked surprised and puzzled, 'never heard of either, tell me more.'

'Well, it's not surprising you are not aware of it as it was carried out under Eisenhower's presidency in the early 1950's. The Americans at that time, fearful of any politician with a communist background, deposed the democratically elected Guatemalan President Jacobo Árbenz, and instead installed the military dictatorship of Carlos Castillo Armas, the first in a series of U.S. backed authoritarian rulers in Guatemala. Giles smiled, 'The key here is how it was done Well before the technology we have at our fingertips today. The two main ingredients were money and fake news. There was no social media then of course, so the Americans set up a clandestine radio organisation, the pretence being that it was utilised by Guatemalan rebels, but it was The CIA. That ran it. It was extraordinarily effective. I mention this because although the situation is quite different now, we are in fact much more susceptible to fake news and media manipulation than we were in 1953. Add cyber warfare and the use of satellites interfering with our digital systems, and you can see that we are wide open to this type of intervention, particularly so, when the perpetrator can easily deny their involvement. And one other matter we seem to have forgotten from our history. The French tried for over 200 years to invade England and they eventually did so by utilising what they termed our back door.'

'Scotland,' answered Scott Jones.

'Yes, we may have forgotten our history, but you can be sure Putin hasn't.' Giles, known for his knowledge of history, sat back in his chair.

Sir George looked worried, 'so what is our defence?'

121

'I am putting a paper to the next COBRA meeting for approval. I intend to set up a new quasi military department to actively deal with this type of interference, not only digitally, but by covert interference on the ground by highly trained officers,' said Adrian.

OFF THE HOOK?

Chapter 14

Adrian left the meeting feeling a sense of unease. He was aware of the pressures on politicians, and the sense of a divided country. It did not auger well for the future.

Arriving back at his office, his secretary told him they had received a call from Mohammed Al-Salhi, and he would call back later.

Mohammad worked in a tiny office on the second floor of a building in Zeryab Street only a stone's throw away from the great Sport City Park. His desk almost filled his room and many of his visitors were surprised that a man with such power should do his worldwide business from such an unpretentious building. His male secretary entered. 'There is a brother to see you, he tells me that you are expecting him.' Mohammad raised his eyebrows. 'His name is Jaber Bin Hayyan,' he passed the man's card across the desk.

'Show him in, I have been waiting for him to contact me.'

A small, wizened man came into the office and the secretary brought in some thick treacly coffee. He sat down opposite Mohammed on one of the rickety chairs supplied.

'Well, Jaber, what have you got for me?'

'You are aware that the man we sent to Chile was murdered?'

'Yes, your office phoned me last week, do we know who was responsible?'

'We initially thought that the murder was carried out by the target, but the police have confirmed that they believe it was the taxi driver that drove him to the surveillance area, but while he was waiting to be picked up, he contacted us from the surveillance point and confirmed that the target was the person we were looking for.'

'Did we get any pictures?'

'No, the camera was left at the scene, and the police recovered them. My contact there has confirmed that copies were sent the British Embassy.'

'Ah, I wonder why they should be involved, Ladvia Silonovic was a Bosnian, who we later learned was working for the Serbs. Unless of course she was a triple agent working for the British, I wonder.'

Jaber answered, 'we learned that she was married to a Jeremy Kirkham as a Patricia Johnson, which we believe was one of her aliases. We also know that Kirkham was attached to the British secret service. We believe she is now in the United Kingdom, so it should not be difficult to track her down and complete the fatwa.'

'Ah, that may explain a telephone call I received here earlier, thank you Jaber, I will let you know if we require your services any further.'

'Do you want us to pursue...?'

'I will be in contact, thank you for your diligent work my friend,' he repeated.

Realising the meeting was closed, Jaber quickly drank his coffee and rose from the chair bowing slightly with his hands clasped together and left.

It was about two hours later that Mohammed received a call from London. Adrian switched on his recording machine before making the call. 'Good afternoon Mr Al-Salhi, my name is Adrian Bradley and...'

'Yes, I know who you are Mr Bradley. It is not every day that this humble servant receives a call from the head of the British secret service, what can I do for you?'

Adrian realised that his secretary had indicated who was calling him earlier in the day.

'We have a joint interest in a woman called Ladvia Silonovic. We are advised that there is a fatwa out for her,' said Adrian, 'may we know the reason for this?'

'Surely. The woman you mention stole 1.3 million United States dollars from us and then disappeared. It was rumoured that she was dead, but then we began to wonder where the money had gone. We also found it strange that she was apparently shot and killed by the British secret service, not something you are known for, so we reopened our files, and found that a person living in Chile married the man who was supposed to be Ladvia's killer.'

'Yes, you are correct,' answered Adrian, 'it was necessary for her to be removed as there were several countries at the time who wanted her dead. However, what she achieved was what you paid for; her actions saved Gorazde from falling into the hands of the Serbs. She obviously could not repay the Muslim Fund as to do so would have exposed her position. Now, my question to you is this, if you received those funds back, less the expenses connected to the

125

operation which I understand was around US$ 250,000, would you release the fatwa?'

'Well, I would have to clear that with my brothers and we would have to have a detailed expenditure account of what the funds were spent on, but providing we receive back a million plus, we may consider the matter closed.'

'In that case, I will organise that, if you can give me assurances, your word will be sufficient. If, however, the fatwa is not removed after the money has been repaid, then we would fall out and that could be detrimental to your organisation, particularly as your transactions are cleared through the City of London.'

'My word is my bond. I will contact you later this week with an answer, and if positive we will supply you with bank details.'

The phone clicked at the other end.

THE SCOTTISH PREROGATIVE

Incorporating

THE WUHAN AFFAIR

A RUSSIAN MESSAGE

Chapter 15

Sherepov's assistant, a Captain, responded to Sherepov's request on General Peter Validich and brought in a folder holding a report from the surveillance team that had returned from Crete.

Sherepov raised his eyebrows before looking at the contents. 'It doesn't look good sir; you will see from the report that General Validich may not be totally loyal to the State.'

'In that case Grigori, I will read it over my coffee, later this morning, and depending on what it contains I will consider my decision from there.' His assistant walked out and closed the door.

When his coffee was brought later that morning, Sherepov opened the file.

Report on General Validich's visit to Crete, dated from the first day of Validich's arrival there with his wife. Major Andrei Balishev signed the report.

The unit sent to carry out surveillance on General Validich consisted of six operators including myself. We did not know where he was going to stay in Crete, so on being advised by the airline of his arrival time, we followed him and his wife from Heraklion Airport to a villa north of Plaka in

Chania province. We dropped two of our operators off in the village nearby who pretended to be walkers while the rest of the party contacted a house agent recommended to us by a local Russian patriot. It was quite easy to rent a house just above the property which gave an excellent view of the villa where the Validich's were situated. Fortunately, because of the time of year, there were many villas empty.

We set up a watch on the front of the villa where Validich was staying but had difficulty in watching the rear because of the villa being on a steep hill, there appeared to be no exit from the property on that side, and certainly we could not see into it from outside. The villas below, although empty, had no windows on the cul-de-sac running between the target and indeed the target villa only had one small window facing us. The steep hill running to the right of the target property was the only entrance and exit road, so we were satisfied that anyone coming or leaving the target would be seen and photographed.

On the second day we observed the owner of the target villa taking his car from a garage underneath the property and driving it into the compound where the wife of the owner, Mrs Validich, and a girl who we have since learned was Aleski Validich, the daughter, came out of the villa and were driven away by the owner. Although General Validich appeared, he did not go with them. We assumed therefore that the General was the only person left in the target villa.

Later in the evening, we were surprised to see a van driving up the hill and turning into the cul-de-sac below the villa and at once driving out again. We realised that it may have been possible for anyone in the target villa to climb the fence to an adjoining property as their entrance led directly to the cul-de-sac. We immediately sent four of our operatives in the 4 x 4 to chase after the vehicle. It took about 3 minutes to do so, but by the time our vehicle started, sight of the van had disappeared. We caught it up just outside Almyrida and followed it for several miles. It eventually stopped outside a taverna, and when the driver went inside. We checked the unlocked the vehicle and found it empty.

At this time, we did not alert the driver of the van that he was under suspicion, but later carried out a careful investigation of who he was and what he did for a living. In some cases, we had to bribe certain officials for personal information. He is a genuine contractor who looks after the maintenance of villas in the area, having about sixty on his books. We found that he was Albanian and well respected as the work he carried out was first class. We understood that his main motivation was to earn enough money to send his son to university. On further enquiries we found out that his son was at Moscow University. Once we knew that, we realised that we could apply pressure on him, which we did, making it plain that unless he told us who he was carrying that evening, we would find some pretext to arrest his son.

He broke down under questioning and pleaded with us not to interrupt his son's education and we are satisfied that he told us the truth.

James and Kate Alexander are genuine owners of the luxury guest house who only take one family at a time. If they are connected to any organisation, this is certainly not known to the Albanian. In fact, as both are in their seventies, it is unlikely that they are connected to any secret organisation. He told us that he received a telephone call in the late afternoon to pick up three people in the cul-de-sac at the bottom of the steps from the adjoining villa. He assumed that they had been staying there as he knew that the Alexander's looked after the villa while their Norwegian owners were away. The reason given for the van to collect the people instead of using a taxi service was that they could not obtain a taxi immediately, and the people concerned had suddenly realised that the tickets for their flights were for the same evening, not the next day and they were desperate to get to the airport. In fact, on their way out of Plaka, they asked to be dropped at a small road where they said they had arranged a car to meet them there. They then paid him €200 to deliver a parcel to a taverna in Omalos, which he did, but the recipient had no knowledge of the parcel and when opened it held a pewter beer mug. After having a coffee, he called James Alexander and was told that it was a mistake, and that he should keep the mug. He showed it to us, and it had inscriptions of the Kings and Queens of England from 1066.

We received descriptions of the people he carried, there were two men and one woman, and all in the age bracket 45-50. The woman was particularly attractive, and the men obviously well educated, but appeared much the same as any normal English holidaymakers.

We continued our surveillance on the target villa and noted that the Validich family remained there for a further two weeks, the General returned to Russia and the mother and daughter to the United Kingdom.

However, our surveillance team at Chania Airport did not report two men and a woman together leaving and again through bribery we were able to obtain passenger lists for planes leaving that evening, although if they were travelling under assumed names, it would not show up on our data system.

Our assessment.

It seems clear to us that the possibility of the 3 strangers meeting General Validich is strong, but the meeting was very well arranged. I believe that they may have been surprised by our presence, and it would not have been difficult for James Alexander to find out that we had taken the villa behind his.

We did notice that he used his binoculars trained on us from within his office, which had the only window on that side of the house.

Because we did not initially know where the Validich's were staying, we had no time to set up listening devices, but in any case, that would have been difficult due to how the target villa was structured.

We believe that the 3 people picked up in the van were hiding their departure from the target villa and that they switched to another vehicle as soon as they were out of sight. The Albanian contractor was simply doing Alexander a favour and knew nothing of the plot of which he was an inadvertent accessory.

The fact that he was told to take a parcel to a taverna in Omalos, was obviously a blind, as the perpetrators would know that we would follow the van to its destination. This may suggest that James Alexander is not what he appears to be. It is not unusual for SIS to remain in contact with retired agents.

I realise that this report is inconclusive in that we cannot be sure that Validich met with anyone, but my suspicion is that he did so.

Recommendations:

1. Investigate James Alexander's background.
2. Ask the surveillance teams we have at London airports if any high-powered people returned from Crete that evening.
3. Our technical services trace all foreign military planes, did a flight take off from the NATO base in Crete that evening or in the early morning the next day and if so, what was its destination.

Sherepov placed the report back in its folder. He turned around in his chair and looked out of the window behind him looking at nothing. *'What would I have done in similar circumstances,'* he mused, *'and what does Validich know that would be so important as to arrange a meeting with a foreign power out of the country?'* He pressed the bell on his desk, and his assistant appeared almost immediately. 'Gregori, you are aware of 'Operation Open Door?'

'Yes sir, I am aware of the name, but not the content, I believe it to be highly restricted.'

'Hmm, bring me a list of people who are aware of its content.'

A few minutes later, Gregori brought in a file market TOP SECRET. Sherepov opened it and noticed only 10 names including his own. General Validich's name was not listed.

Sherepov was a careful man and he decided to put the question of Validich on one side while he dealt with other matters. It was two days later that Gregori came into his office with further information.

'You will know sir, that we monitor all outgoing and incoming foreign mail including e-mails to and from military personnel and politicians. Our special investigative section has trawled through Validich's mail over the last 12 months and the vast majority are to his daughter who is a student at Oxford University in the United Kingdom. They have found an anomaly and while not being conclusive, it highly suspicious.'

'In what way?' asked Sherepov.

'They picked one out in particular where within the text were the words OPERATION OPEN DOOR. The letter was innocuous family correspondence until one linked those words with the date of the letter. It's not a system that is often used as it is very restrictive to the information that could be passed over. Having realised the method however, other bits of important information have been passed over in similar letters. I should say here that there is no information leaked regarding military equipment or strategy, only areas that concern the state expansionist policies, which as you know, is something Validich and many other high-ranking Generals believe is counterproductive to the safety of the Russian state.'

Sherepov pursed his lips, 'the problem is Gregori, once you have senior military officials covertly contacting a foreign power, it lays them open to blackmail and is highly dangerous.'

'I agree sir, do you want me to have Validich arrested?'

'Hmm, not yet, I understand from his file that he has four children. I am aware that his eldest is in the United Kingdom, and his wife has recently joined her there. Find out where his other children are, as if they are in Russia, we have a better hold on the General. In the meantime, I am going to discuss the matter with the President. It is time we dealt with traitors including those who no longer live in Russia.' Sherepov waited until his assistant had left the room and then he picked up the direct line to President Putin. The phone was answered by a female voice, who told him that the President was busy, and he should phone back after one hour.

Sherepov did so and explained the situation he had discussed with Gregori including the report from the surveillance team in Crete.

'Sherepov, you must deal with this matter at once. Because Validich works within the Kremlin, he may have picked up more than he should, find out if you can, exactly what he knows, and then deal with the problem. "Operation Open Door" is essential to our future policy of disassociating the United States from Europe and for our State to hold the reins of power in the European region. We also need to send a message to other like-minded military and political personnel that those who meddle with the decisions of the executive, will be punished.' The phone clicked as the President cut the call.

It was later in the day that Gregori told Sherepov that Validich's children were all in the UK having travelled there to witness the graduation of their eldest sister.

'In that case Gregori, please contact General Validich to come to my office tomorrow at 10.00 hours, say to him that I have some important information to disclose to him. Also, ask the special operations executive to see me as I have some specific instructions for his department.'

Later that day the special operations delivered a sealed bottle of Whisky to Sherepov's office along with a small bottle of tablets.

General Validich arrived on time and was greeted warmly by Sherepov. 'It is good to see you again General; I hope all is well with you?' without waiting for a reply, Sherepov continued. 'I understand that your eldest daughter is about to graduate from Oxford, you must be proud of her, are you intending to travel...'

Validich smiled, *so that's what this is about, he thought to himself.* 'No, Russian Generals do not generally travel overseas unless it's on state business, but of course you know that General Sherepov. You will be aware that my wife and I recently went to Crete for our holiday and met our daughter there, but you will see that I reported this before travelling, and it was approved.'

Sherepov nodded, 'Of course, but that is not why I asked you to see me. You may have heard the phrase "Operation Open Door"?' Sherepov raised his eyebrows.

Validich answered cautiously, 'there is a rumour regarding the operation, but there is no detail...'

'Yes, which is why I have decided to fill you in with the plan.'

'I'm surprised comrade because I was not aware that it affected my department.'

'Oh, but it will comrade, the air force will be involved.' Sherepov then went on to explain in detail the plan and Peter Validich was amazed at the simplicity and audacity of it.

'You don't think that this will trigger a nuclear war?'

Sherepov shook his head, 'no, if such a situation proves to be the case, it would be cancelled. However, "Operation Open Door" will only launch if certain circumstances are met but of course, we will do everything possible to ensure that the end game falls into our orbit.'

General Validich asked a few questions, which Sherepov answered and just as he was about to leave, Sherepov stopped him. 'I have been given a bottle of Glenlivet 12-year-old single malt whisky by Mr Angus Stuart, who I mentioned during our conversation,' he smiled as he drew the bottle from a cupboard nearby. He placed 2 glasses on his desk and opened the bottle which Validich saw was sealed. 'I know you are fond of scotch so, to celebrate your daughter's graduation I thought it fitting that I should share it with you. He poured the liquid into the two glasses, took his glass, and downed the drink in one go. Peter Validich did the same.

Peter looked at the empty glass approvingly, 'my goodness that was a superb malt.'

'Another?' Sherepov asked.

Validich smiled, 'thank you but no, I have some detailed work to do, and need to ensure I am Compos Mentos for the rest of the day. Thank you for the information, it is appreciated.' With that he opened the office door and walked down the long corridor towards the building entrance. As he reached the entrance to the building, he suddenly felt unwell and as he tried to turn the doorknob, he missed it and fell heavily to the floor.

Some fifteen minutes later there was a knock on Sherepov's door and Gregori entered. 'I have some bad news for you comrade General, your visitor, General Validich collapsed before leaving the building. Despite our medical team trying to resuscitate him he died. It appears to have been a heart attack.'

Sherepov showed astonishment. 'I am deeply sorry to hear it; he was a good man and he seemed fine when he left my office.'

Gregori nodded, 'heart attacks like strokes can happen without warning and...'

Sherepov held up his hand, 'It is important that he did not die in this building, you understand. People may draw wrong conclusions from his death.'

'Yes sir, I understand, should I contact his wife?'

'First, his body should be taken and cremated immediately, his wife should be contacted tomorrow saying that because of the sensitive political situation it was decided to give him a military funeral with full honours, which means that she will continue to receive his pension. I am sure she'll understand.'

When Gregori had left to carry out his instructions, Sherepov picked up the internal phone to the head of the special operations department. 'I have to congratulate you. I took the antidote, and everything went according to plan. One of these days, you must tell me how it works.' He put the phone down and picked up the phone to the President. 'The Validich situation has been dealt with comrade President I am about to write up a positive eulogy which will hit the newspapers tomorrow.'

There was no answer, just the click of the phone being replaced.

THE SCOTTISH PREROGATIVE
Incorporating
THE WUHAN AFFAIR

THE INTERPRETER

Chapter 16

It was several days later when the telephone rang on Adrian Bradley's desk. His secretary told him that a Mr Mohammad Al Salhi was on the line.

'Good Morning Mr Al-Salhi, do you have news for me?' Adrian asked.

'I do, and it is good news, my brothers have agreed that if the amount you suggested in your last communication is paid, the fatwa will be removed, and that will be an end to the matter.'

'Very well,' answered Adrian, 'to avoid any complications you will receive the funds directly from the British Government, if you give me your bank details, I will ensure the payment reaches you within the next two days.'

'May Allah go with you.' The phone call ended.

Adrian picked up the external direct line phone and punched in a number. 'Jeremy, it's Adrian. Are you two free, if so, I would like you to join me for lunch tomorrow so we can chat. Ask Ladvia to bring her bank details as I have struck a deal with the Muslim Fund, which incidentally means you can return your children to their school. For your interest, I have arranged through a security company who look after some wealthy Nigerian girls there, to keep a watching brief, but I'm satisfied that it should not be necessary to do more than that.'

'Okay Adrian, we'll probably drop them back this afternoon and we'll hire a car...'

'That's not necessary, I'll send a driver down, and take you to the girls' school and bring you back, picking you both up again in the morning.'

Jeremy thanked him and rang off.

The next morning the government driver picked up Ladvia and Jeremy as arranged and took them to Mi6 HQ. After normal greetings, Adrian asked for the bank details of the Cayman Island account and arranged for Ladvia to pay a special government account with the funds for the Muslim Fund. 'The reason I'm doing it this way is so they are not aware of the bank you use in Cayman, so we will settle the bill as soon as the funds are received.'

Ladvia nodded, and gave Adrian the necessary bank account password, and this was handed to Adrian's secretary who already had the bank information of the Muslim Fund.

'Now, I suggest we have some lunch, I'm a member of Boodles so we'll go there and talk.'

Half an hour later they were sitting in a quiet corner of the club and Adrian ordered champagne to celebrate the lifting of the fatwa.

'I am afraid I have some sombre news to impart. Peter Validich died yesterday of a suspected heart attack. Our sources say that it was most unlikely that he died of natural causes, particularly so, as he had just had a meeting with General Sherepov, the head of their foreign security services.'

'Oh my God,' said Ladvia, 'I must call Natasha straight away.' She started to get up from her seat, but Adrian waved her back. 'Please, not yet as the announcement of his death is not public knowledge yet, so she will be unaware of his demise. They have already cremated the body, so there is little point in her returning. The story is that he received full military honours, which means that Natasha will continue to receive his pension, but it would be unwise for her or the children who are over here now, to return. A general's pension in Russia is substantial, but the Rouble is worthless in the West, so we will look after the family financially, and I have alerted the department that deals with these things to contact her as soon as the news is out. I have to say it is unusual for them to kill their own within Russia, but I suspect they wanted to send a strong message to others in the military.'

Ladvia sat down, wiping a tear from her eye. 'The bastards,' she said. Adrian nodded. 'This is what happens when there is no law and the leadership have total authority. It should remind us what we could face in the future, which is why I need your help more than ever.'

'Okay,' said Ladvia, 'you have it. In the meantime, please let me know as soon as the news breaks so I can meet up with Natasha. Now, what is your suggestion?'

'I want you to apply for the job of interpreter which Angus Stuart's department is advertising. We have ensured the position has not been filled as the woman heading the personnel department in the Scottish government is one of ours. She is therefore waiting for you to call her, and I will give you the number once we get back to the office. We need to act quickly, as you have to get an emergency visa for you to travel with Stuart on his trip next week.'

'Does Ladvia use her passport?' Jeremy asked.

'Yes, there should be no problem there, as it is in the name of Patricia Kirkham, but your background will change somewhat. You are Welsh, born and educated in Cardiff and received your degree in the Russian language from Oxford University. You stayed on and received your PhD five years ago, and then retired to look after your children. So, this will be the first job you have applied for. You can be sure that all the relevant details of your time at Oxford will be searchable public knowledge. We are issuing you with a new passport in your name including your degree, but obviously without any foreign stamps in it. We have already written your application form, and we will give you a copy before you travel to Edinburgh. My suggestion is that you both travel up there tomorrow or the day after at the latest, and once you have seen Margaret McDonald at the Edinburgh office, which is in St. Andrew's House Regent Road, Edinburgh, EH1 3DG, you should look for a suitable apartment as near as possible to that address. Whether you decide to also have a country address where you can spend your time outside the city, is entirely up to you. Now Jeremy, your offices are also in Edinburgh and Mark Johnson is waiting for you to call him, so that he can hand over the reins and introduce you to the General Manager. You will discuss what "Open Door" is and stress to him that he should give complete priority for the collection of any connected data from his team. The financial budget for the business is more than adequate, and I will get finance to discuss that with you this afternoon. You will pay Ladvia from those funds, although of course she will also receive a salary from the Scottish government. You will both appreciate that this is quite a big change in the way we normally do things, but there is nothing more important than finding exactly what the Russians are up to, their timing and their strategy. There is something else you should be aware of. Stuart has been active in supporting Scottish interests and over the last year he managed to secure a deal with a Swedish company to manufacture earth moving equipment in the south of Scotland, quite near the border. We started to take an interest when an application was put in for an airbase, so that CKD (completely knocked down) parts could be flown in directly from Sweden. This made sense as the original parts are made there to be assembled in Scotland, and that is quite normal. We have many CKD plants in various areas around the world.'

'So why the interest?' asked Ladvia.

'We carried out a check on the directors of the Swedish company, and they did not appear to be either experienced or competent enough to run a large company. They are however "clean" but the finance for the company is difficult to trace and our financial people in the City have tracked it to Greece. However, there is a lot of Russian money in that area, and we cannot be sure of its origin. If it is Russia, then we are much more concerned. That does not mean it is in any way illegal, as there are many pseudo-Russian investments in the UK, not necessarily connected to the Kremlin. It is only when we start putting together what we now know from Validich and the fact that Stuart is negotiating something with Russia, that we need to investigate whether there is a connection. Of course, Stuart may well be a willing supporter of Scottish interests without realising what he is getting himself involved in. We need some answers.' Adrian smiled, 'and I hope you will be able to "Open a Door" for us.'

The next day Ladvia spent with Natasha and her children, all completely shattered at the news they had received. Natasha wanted to fly immediately to Russia, but the woman assigned to their case from SIS advised against it and eventually she agreed to stay in the UK and with help from SIS find a suitable accommodation for the family until matters were clearer. Jeremy bought a new Jaguar F- Type car and travelled up to Edinburgh promising to meet Ladvia from Edinburgh airport the next day. Ladvia arranged to meet Margaret McDonald and rang Jeremy to tell him that flights were full so she had hired a Jet Ranger Helicopter which she would fly up herself and she gave him an ETA.

The next few days were busy, finding new accommodation took almost no time at all, as they were able to take over Mark Johnson's apartment in Eglington Crescent. Leaving Jeremy with Mark, Ladvia went to see Margaret McDonald who had by that time received a C.V. as set out by Adrian.

'It's good to meet you Patricia, I know that you have a different background from that shown on your CV, but I am not aware of what you really did before, nor do I need to know.' She smiled. 'You have the job of course, and I suggest you start tomorrow, it's rather urgent as the man you are working for is going to Moscow shortly and will want you to accompany him. Your job title is Assistant to the Deputy First Minister, and you therefore fall into a senior pay grade. Now privately, let me tell you a little about the man you will be working for. You will already know he is a strong Nationalist and does not like the English, so as you are Welsh it will be helpful. He is a prick and quite how he managed to manoeuvre himself into his present position is not something I understand. He is a misogynist bully, and uses violence on his partner, his wife of fifteen years. They have two children. He drinks heavily and is the type that gets nastier the more he drinks. He is also a womaniser and his last assistant, although sacked for being late for an appointment, was let go because she put in a formal complaint about his behaviour towards her. The matter was covered up, and she received a hefty payment by agreeing to remain silent. I would not of course normally give this sort of information to an applicant, but then you are a rather special case.'

Margaret gave Ladvia the details of where the office was situated and that she should report to Stuart's secretary Maureen Nolan. She wished her good luck and told her to be careful.

Ladvia reported to the office at 9 am the next morning and met Maureen who took her to a private office from where Ladvia would be working. 'Mr Stuart will see you at 10 am this morning so he can brief you on the trip to Moscow next week. I assume you are up to speed on your Russian?'

'Da,' answered Ladvia,

Ladvia spent some time organising her new office, and looked at several files in the filing cabinet, selecting a few to look at after she had seen Stuart. At 10 am Maureen came through and asked Ladvia to go with her to meet her new boss. She introduced her as Patricia Kirkham and left the office. Angus Stuart was a heavyset man sporting a small beard and moustache. He was in shirt sleeves, and his large belly protruded over the top of his trousers. He had a tie that was askew, *not a very impressive image* thought Ladvia to herself. He spoke in a broad Scottish accent. He did not shake Ladvia's hand, simply pointed to a chair in front of his large desk. After sitting down, himself, he then spent some time looking at a file that was open on his desk.

He looked up, 'Mrs Kirkham I have read your references and they are excellent. Just to put you in the picture, you are to accompany me to Moscow on Thursday next to meet with officials there. The discussions we are to have concern trade links but because of present sanctions against Russia, we are discussing other ways of dealing with that problem and they have some suggestions for our consideration. This will be the third visit I have made, but this time we will be meeting a very senior official.'

Ladvia smiled, 'do you have a name of the person we are meeting?'

'Yes, it is a General Sherepov, who is now leading the negotiations, he is the head of overseas development.'

Ladvia knew precisely who General Sherepov was, but she said nothing.

'Now, as far as the Russians are concerned you are simply my assistant, I do not wish them to know that you speak Russian. Your job is simply to listen to their conversations and let me know what was said after the meeting. I will provide you with a hidden recording device.,.'

Ladvia shook her head, 'that is not necessary, in any case the Russians will have the ability to detect such devices.'

'Mrs Kirkham, you will do as you are told, you will wear a listening device. We are not dealing with espionage here and I want to retain a copy of all the conversations so we can review what was said.' Ladvia nodded, 'of course if that is what you want, then I will do as you say, but I must warn you that once the wire is detected, the information we pick up in Russian will be useless. These people are not stupid.' It was clear that Stuart had not thought that point through and the idea of Ladvia wearing a wire was not brought up again.

'Very well, now the logistics. Maureen will organise tickets for the flights. We must fly down to London and pick up another plane there to fly to Moscow as there are no flights currently from Edinburgh. You will be flying economy and I will be in first class, so we will not see each other until we reach Moscow. You will not need to show your passport there, as you are already cleared, and your name will be recognised.

'I will be driven to the hotel by a member of the negotiating team, you will catch a taxi from the airport. The hotel we are staying at is the Ritz-Carlton at Tverskaya Street 3, Moscow. It is near the Kremlin. The room number is 313. Our meeting is at the Kremlin at 10 am Moscow time which is 3 hours ahead of ours. The current rate of exchange is 1.27 pounds sterling to 100 roubles.'

'Is there anyone else accompanying us?'

'No, it's not necessary, because we are simply discussing options not signing any documents.'

'And when do we return?' Ladvia asked. 'The next day, after our meeting, we will be leaving early. In the meantime, you can go through the files of earlier visits created by your predecessor, but they are not informative due to her inefficiency. Thank you, you can go now.'

Ladvia got up and walked back to her office. She had just sat down when Maureen entered without knocking. 'Is everything all right?' she queried. Ladvia shrugged, 'It seems fairly clear to me,' she answered, but received the impression that Maureen was expecting more. 'Oh good, I will need your passport, to put the details on the list. You will not need it for Moscow, but you will require it going through London when returning.' Ladvia smiled, well at least I won't require it from Edinburgh to London.' She noticed a very strange look from Maureen as she handed her the passport and she filed Maureen's look into her memory.

Ladvia went through the previous account of his visits to Moscow, but only the last one had been written up, so clearly on the first two Stuart had been alone. The last notes were quite vague and there was little Ladvia could do to retrieve the information, then she remembered that the girl involved had been sacked on her return, so perhaps she did not have time to qualify her report.

She met up with Jeremy in the evening and he told her that he had booked them into the Murrayfield Hotel and House, where they would stay until Mark left the flat, which was to be at the weekend. Mark had offered for them to use the flat and that he was leaving the furniture so the Kirkham's could move in without having to go out and buy new.

Driving to the hotel Jeremy asked how she had got on. Ladvia grimaced, 'Stuart is full of own importance, not a nice individual and his immediate staff are not particularly friendly, but that's unimportant. The files on what he is talking to people in Moscow about are virtually bare, so I suspect he has removed them, perhaps I should talk to his previous interpreter who may shed some light on the problem. The main interest is that he is meeting General Sherepov who Stuart says is head of overseas development. I know that he used to be head of the FSB and I would be surprised if he has suffered demotion. In Russia, they do not demote people, they either jail them or have them killed. When Ladvia made enquiries as to the location of her predecessor, she found that she had taken herself off to New Zealand, and no one appeared to know where she was.

Jeremy and Ladvia moved in to the flat and at the same time carried out a search for a residence outside of Edinburgh. They found one that Ladvia said was ideal, a country house between Blairgowrie and Perth. It was a converted farmhouse with surrounding land that was not overlooked.

On Monday evening, Ladvia took a call on her secure mobile, it was from Adrian Bradley, after asking if she and Jeremy had settled in, he asked her if she had followed the story of the poisoning of Sergei Skripal?'

"Yes, I have. and am not surprised. Validich told us that there would be other factors including interference in the affairs of sovereign countries, well this is just a start, and you may find that there are others that have not hit the headlines in the past or have been deliberately suppressed. Putin has scored on this latest incident in that the Russian people are happy that a spy has been assassinated, just speak to the average Russian in the street. It is all good for ensuring an election landslide and particularly so when his rivals have been disenfranchised. He is also sending a message to others who defect, that they will never be safe.

'So, you are saying that he wanted this to be publicised?'

'Of course, it sends a message to the British people that they may not be safe either. He knows that it is going to be difficult to prove, and that the British will 'huff and puff' to use one of your expressions, but he is quite safe in his position, and he simply strengthens his hold on power.'

'From an interest point of view, what do you feel should be the British government's response?'

Ladvia laughed. 'Stop accepting political money from Russian emigres. You do not know where it comes from or how it was accumulated.

'Secondly, ensure much better security for defectors. Most continue to work for the British or American security services, so they should be better protected. If you do not ensure that defectors will be safe, you will find it much more difficult to entice the right people. There are antidotes for nerve gas, Atropine being one of them, and it may be good practice to ensure that all those susceptible to being targeted by a foreign power are supplied with some. At the very least they should have emergency numbers they can call if they believe they have been targeted.

'Thirdly, stop buying Russian Gas, I was appalled to read last week that Britain had decided to do so. All you are doing, like most of your European allies, is giving Putin a lever which he can use against you, and supplying him with useful Petro US dollars, which helps him build his forces.

'Fourthly, increase your defence expenditure and persuade your allies in Europe to do the same. We are starting to look at a 1930's situation all over again. Putin is consolidating his power, and as he does so, he will become more belligerent and eventually he will act more aggressively. Most will be surprised, but then it will be too late.

'Fifth, start to warn the public of the fate they could face.'

'Yes, I agree with all those points, Ladvia, but what's your take on our response after this latest debacle?'

'It depends on how grave you determine the act was and if you can prove it was instigated by Russia. It is a declaration of war, without it being declared. Send the Russian Ambassador and his team home, withdraw our Ambassador from Moscow, and cut all ties with Russia while Putin is in power. That would damage his image in the world and even make the average Russian think. In any murder, one looks at motive. Who else would have a motive to kill a Russian defector along with his daughter? Having said that, it appears to me that the poison was ingested slowly, which means that it was either something sent to his home or something a trusted friend gave to the daughter. Chocolates or more likely a favourite Russian food such as Veal Orlov or Beluga Caviar, both of which could pass through the postal system or airport security without any concern. Of course, if agents were involved, then it would be easy for them to discover Sergei Skripol's address. I know that they have used nerve gas in other parts of the world, and their current

148

favourite is novichok, designed to escape the notice of NATO sensors at airports. Simply by smearing this onto an object touched by the victim, would be enough to kill. Novichok was also designed to percolate normal safety clothes, so those dealing with it, should be made aware of the dangers.'

'Hmm, your points are well taken Ladvia, thank you for that. Jeremy tells me you are going to Moscow toward the end of next week, take care. The Skripol's are still alive and our scientists at Porton Down think there is a chance they could pull through.'

'Well, that is good news, and if so, that will suggest that those responsible for the murderous act did not do a particularly good job. I wouldn't like to be in their shoes when they return to Russia.'

'We think there were two of them from the GRU, and we suspect they were met by a Russian Major General when they first entered the country, all have recently returned to Russia.

'Oh, and we believe General Sherepov has recently been promoted to head the Russian SVR, which now includes the GRU, who we know was behind the Sergei Skripol poisoning. It may be that this change took place because of the botched job carried out by them.'

'That's certainly a possibility,' answered Ladvia, 'but if Sherepov is involved in the affair we are looking into, then we better take it very seriously indeed.'

THE SCOTTISH PREROGATIVE

Incorporating

THE WUHAN AFFAIR

CHINA EXPOSED

Chapter 17

Adrian had just arrived in his office when Geoffrey Williamson buzzed him on the intercom. 'I have the report on China you asked for.'

'Thank you, Geoffrey, bring it in and on the way and ask my secretary to order some coffee for us.'

The coffee came in shortly afterwards, as Geoffrey spread a map out on the coffee table.

'Here is China,' his stubby nicotine finger jabbed the centre of a map; 'China is a very large country encompassing almost nine thousand six hundred square kilometres, about the same as the USA, but where the USA has a population of 310 million, China's is 1.340 billion making it the most populated country on earth, yet the density is only 140 persons per square kilometre. To give a comparison the next largest population in a single country is India with 1.185 billion but a density of 360 people per square kilometre. The United States is only 32 the United Kingdom,' he looked at Adrian, 'is 253. China is surrounded by potential enemies and has had border disputes with most of them, which they have managed to solve by using the "carrot" method. Occasionally they have used or threatened to use the "stick", but what is left is becoming extremely disabling for the region.' I have put the main report in a separate folder for you to read at your leisure.' He placed it on the table marked Appendix.

'I also have an interesting article taken from the Wall Street Journal.'

Adrian sat down in his chair, 'okay read on...'

Geoffrey put on his glasses. 'The Communist Party has made strenuous efforts to keep signs of its enduring power out of sight of the Chinese public and the rest of the world. Richard McGregor writes on the secrets of the world's largest political machine and its role in Beijing's growing influence.

'On the desks of the heads of China's 50-odd biggest state companies, amid the clutter of computers, family photos and other fixtures of the modern CEO's office life, sits a red phone. The executives and their staff who jump to attention when it rings, know it as "the red machine", perhaps because to call it a mere phone does not do it justice. "When the "red machine" rings, a senior executive of a state bank told me, "you had better make sure you answer it."

'The red machine is like no ordinary phone. Each one has just a four-digit number. It connects only to similar phones with four-digit numbers within the same encrypted system. They are much coveted, nonetheless. For the chairmen and chairwomen of the top state companies, who have every modern communications device at their fingertips, the red machine is a sign they have arrived, not just at the top of the company, but in the senior ranks of the Party and the government. The phones are the ultimate status symbol, as they are only given out under the orders of the Party and government to people in jobs with the rank of vice minister and above.

'The phones are encrypted, not just to secure party and government communications from foreign intelligence agencies. They also provide protection against snooping by anyone in China outside the Party governing system. Possession of the red machine means you have qualified for membership of the tight-knit club that runs the country, a small group of about 300 people, mainly men, with responsibility for about one-fifth of humanity.

'The modern world is replete with examples of elite networks that wield behind-the-scenes power beyond their mere numerical strength.

'None can hold a candle to the Chinese Communist Party, which takes ruling-class networking to an entirely new level. The red machine gives the party apparatus a hotline into multiple arms of the state, including the government-owned companies that China promotes around the world these days as independent commercial entities. As a political machine alone, the Party is a phenomenon of awesome and unique dimensions. By mid-2009, its membership stood at 76 million, equal to about one in 12 adult Chinese.

'China's post-Maoist governing model, launched by Deng Xiaoping in the late 1970's, has endured many attempts to explain it. Is it a benevolent, Singapore-style autocracy? A capitalist development state, as many described Japan. Neo-Confucianism mixed with market economics, a slow-motion version of post-Soviet Russia in which the elite grabbed productive public assets for private gain, Robber-baron socialism, or is it something different altogether, an entirely new model, a "Beijing Consensus", according to the fashionable phrase, built around practical, problem-solving policies and technological innovation?

'Few describe the model as communist anymore, often not even the ruling Chinese Communist Party itself.

'How communism came to be airbrushed out of the rise of the world's greatest communist state is no mystery on one level. The multiple, head-spinning contradictions about modern China can divert anyone. What was once a revolutionary party is now firmly the establishment, the communists rode to power on a popular revulsion against corruption, but it appears they have succumbed to the same cancer themselves. Top leaders adhere to Marxism in their public statements, even as they depend on a ruthless private sector to create jobs. The Party preaches equality, while presiding over incomes as unequal as anywhere in Asia.

'The gap between the fiction of the Party's rhetoric ("China is a socialist country") and the reality of everyday life grows larger every year. However, the Party must defend the fiction because it represents the political status quo.

'The Party's defence of power is also, by extension, a defence of the existing system. In the words of Dai Bingguo, China's most senior foreign policy official, China's "number one core interest is to maintain its fundamental system and state security." State sovereignty, territorial integrity and economic development, the priorities of any state, all are subordinate to the need to keep the Party in power.

'The Party has made strenuous efforts to keep the sinews of its enduring power off the front stage of public life in China and out of sight of the rest of the world. A decade into the 21st century, the Beijing headquarters of the big Party departments, whose power far outstrips that of mere ministries, still have no signs outside indicating the business inside and no listed phone numbers. For many in the West, it has been convenient to keep the Party backstage too and pretend that China has an evolving governmental system with strengths and weaknesses, quirks, and foibles, like any other country. China's flourishing commercial life embracing globalisation is enough for many to dismiss the idea that communism still has traction, as if a Starbucks on every corner is a marker of political progress

'Peek under the hood of the Chinese model, however, and China looks much more communist than it does on the open road. Vladimir Lenin, who designed the prototype

153

used to run communist countries around the world, would recognise the model immediately. The Chinese Communist Party's enduring grip on power is based on a simple formula straight out of the Leninist play book. For all the reforms of the past three decades, the Party has made sure it keeps a lock-hold on the state and three pillars of its survival strategy: control of personnel, propaganda, and the People's Liberation Army.

'Since installing itself as the sole legitimate governing authority of a unified China in 1949, the Party and its leaders have placed its members in key positions in every arm, and at each level, of the state. All the Chinese media come under the control of the propaganda department, even if its denizens have had to gallop to keep up in the Internet age. In addition, if anyone decides to challenge the system, the Party has kept ample power in reserve, making sure it maintains a tight grip on the military and the security services, the ultimate guarantors of its rule. The police forces at every level of government, from large cities to small villages, have within them a "domestic security department," the role of which is to protect the Party's rule and weed out dissenting political voices before they can gain a broad audience.

'China long ago dispensed with old-style communist central planning for a sleeker hybrid market economy, the Party's greatest innovation. However, measure China against a definitional checklist written by Robert Service, the veteran historian of Soviet Russia, and Beijing retains a surprising number of the qualities that characterised communist regimes of the 20th century.

'Like communism in its heyday elsewhere, the Party in China has eradicated or emasculated political rivals; eliminated the autonomy of the courts and press; restricted religion and civil society; denigrated rival versions of nationhood; centralized political power; established extensive networks of security police; and dispatched dissidents to labour camps. A good example of this was the

British businessman Neil Hayward who was poisoned after he threatened to expose a plan by a Chinese leader's wife to move money abroad.

'The Party in China has teetered on the verge of self-destruction numerous times, in the wake of Mao Zedong's brutal campaigns over three decades from the 1950's, and then again in 1989, after the army's suppression of demonstrations in Beijing and elsewhere. The Party itself suffered an existential crisis after the collapse of the Soviet Union and its satellite states in 1992, an event that resonates to this day, in the corridors of power in Beijing. After each catastrophe, the Party has picked itself off the ground, reconstituted its armour and reinforced its flanks. Somehow, it has outlasted, outsmarted, outperformed, or simply outlawed its critics.

'Few events symbolised the advance of China and the retreat of the West during the financial crisis more than the touchdown in Beijing of Secretary of State Hillary Clinton in February 2009. Previous U.S. administrations, under Bill Clinton and George W. Bush, had arrived in office with an aggressive, competitive posture towards China. Before she landed, Ms. Clinton publicly downplayed the importance of human rights. At a press conference before leaving, she beamingly implored the Chinese government to keep buying U.S. debt, like a travelling saleswoman hawking a bill of goods.

'Deng Xiaoping's crafty stratagem, laid down two decades earlier, about how China should advance stealthily into the world, "hide your brightness; bide your time"—had been honoured in the breach long before Ms. Clinton's arrival. China's high-profile tours through Africa, South America, and Australia in search of resources, the billion-dollar listings of its state companies (including Petro China and the Industrial & Commercial Bank of China) on overseas stock markets. Its rising profile in the United Nations and its sheer economic firepower had made China the new focus of global business and finance since the turn

155

of the century. China's star was shining more brightly than ever before, even as its diplomats protested, they were battling to be heard on behalf of a poor, developing economy.

'The implosion of the Western financial system, along with an evaporation of confidence in the U.S., Europe and Japan, overnight pushed China's global standing several notches higher. In the space of a few months in early 2009, the Chinese state committed $50 billion in extra funding for the International Monetary Fund and $38 billion with Hong Kong for an Asian monetary fund. It extended a $25 billion loan to cash-strapped Russian oil companies; set aside $30 billion for Australian resource companies; offered tens of billions more to various countries or companies in South America, central and South-east Asia, to lock up commodities and lay down its marker for future purchases. In September, China readied lines of credit of up to $60 to $70 billion, for resource and infrastructure deals in Nigeria, Ghana, and Kenya.

'Beijing's ambition and influence were being lit up in ways that would have been unthinkable a few years previously. The Chinese central bank called for an alternative to the U.S. dollar as a global reserve currency in early 2009 and reiterated its policy as the year went on. France obediently recommitted to Chinese sovereignty over Tibet to placate Beijing's anger over the issue, after Beijing had cancelled an E.U. summit in protest at Paris's welcome for the Dalai Lama. On its navy's 60th anniversary, China invited the world to view its new fleet of nuclear-powered submarines off the port of Qingdao.

'The giant Chinese market had become more important than ever. Just ahead of the Shanghai auto show in April 2009, monthly passenger car sales in China were the highest of any market in the world, surpassing the U.S. A month later, Wang Qishan and a team of Chinese ministers met Catherine Ashton, then the E.U. trade commissioner, and about 15 of Europe's most senior business executives in

Brussels to hear their complaints about Chinese market access. Sure, Wang conceded after listening to their problems over a working lunch, there are "irregularities" in the market. "I know you have complaints," he replied. "But the charm of the Chinese market is irresistible." In other words, according to astonished executives in the meeting, whatever your complaints, the market is so big, you are going to come anyway. Even worse, many of the executives realised that Mr. Wang was right.

'The rise of China is a genuine mega-trend, a phenomenon with the ability to remake the world economy, sector by sector. That it is presided over by a communist party makes it even more jarring for a Western world, which, only a few years previously, was feasting on notions of the end of history and the triumph of liberal democracy.

'In just a single generation, the party elite has been transformed from a mirthless band of Mao-suited, ideological thugs to a wealthy, business-friendly ruling class. Today's Party is all about joining the highways of globalisation, which in turn translates into greater economic efficiencies, higher rates of return and greater political security.

'In the absence of democratic elections and open debate, it's impossible to judge popular support for the Party. However, it is indisputable that support for the Party has grown with reform since Mao's death. The Chinese Communist Party and its leaders have never wanted to be the West when they grow up. For the foreseeable future, it looks like their wishes will all come true.'

Geoffrey looked grim. 'A lot of what is written in that article is already known of course, but it's only when you put things together that you realise with some real concern what the outcome could be.'

'Yes. I agree,' said Adrian, 'and I sometimes get the feeling that we are sleep walking towards disaster. I remember my father once saying to me, "let China sleep, for when she wakes, the world will find it is facing its biggest challenge".'

Geoffrey nodded, 'yes, that's true, but we also know for a fact that China is actively trying to steal our technology. We know that they are speeding up spending on their armed forces; we know they are coercing neighbours to fall in line with their policies. We also know that they are becoming belligerent in their maritime policies in an area of huge strategic interest to the USA and the Western democracies. We know that they are using their economic might to gain interests in strategic areas of the world that are vital to the free world. We are committed to defending Taiwan, Japan, and the Philippines and this is going to become more difficult as China's power increases in the region. It seems to me that the problem is becoming urgent and that we should act sooner rather than later, while we have the power to do so.'

Adrian nodded. 'It's no different from the 1930's and early 1940's when both US and British business worked overtime to sell to German and Japanese industry which was instrumental in helping them to re arm. Churchill was one of the few who started to send out warnings, warnings that few wanted to hear. The first thing is to recognise the problem, and then develop a strategy to deal with it. The biggest danger to us now, is their increased expenditure toward biological weapons, now that their method of using computer hacking is challenged. Their facility in Wuhan is known to be working on an advanced type of virus. Their main target is the USA because of the sanctions placed on them by the President Trump. China tried to hit back by aiming at the US States that supported Trump, but that failed. My fear now, is that they cannot afford to be seen to be losing face and in desperation, they may try something much more sinister. Biological weapons can be a powerful method providing the country concerned does not care about its own population because the spread can be enacted without fear of reprisal.'

THE SCOTTISH PREROGATIVE

Incorporating

THE WUHAN AFFAIR

MOSCOW

Chapter 18

Ladvia arrived at Edinburgh Airport in good time, but due to delays, she missed her Moscow connection in London and had to get a later flight. The result was that Stuart arrived in Moscow on time but without his assistant. It was later in the day when she reached Vnukovo International Airport. It took over two hours for her to clear, even though she was only travelling with hand baggage. Catching a taxi to take her the 38 kilometres to the hotel, took a further hour because of the traffic, so she arrived at the hotel Ritz-Carlton at 21.00 hours. When she arrived at the hotel reception, she was told that Mr Stuart had arrived some hours before and was in the room. Ladvia assumed that it was a suite with two bedrooms, so she caught the lift to the third floor and found the door to the room open.

Stuart was not in a good mood and demanded to know why she was late. Ladvia told him of the problems at Edinburgh airport, and said she was surprised that he managed to arrive on time. Stuart said he had gone to London the day before.

She put her bag down and asked Stuart where her bedroom was. He looked surprised, indicating the double bed in the room. 'We're not made of money you know; you're sleeping here.'

'And may I ask where you are sleeping?' Ladvia asked.

Stuart walked unsteadily towards her, and for the first time she smelt alcohol on his breath. 'We are in the same bed; you surely don't think I just brought you all the way to Moscow to listen to Russian speakers?'

Ladvia remained calm, 'Mr Stuart, you have misunderstood the situation, I have no intention of sleeping with you, or of sharing a room, so...'

Stuart snarled, 'well where are you going to go, the hotel is full, so get used to it. I employ you, and you'll do as you are told,' he sneered, as he moved closer to where she was standing.

'Now, Mr Stuart, I must warn you, that if you make a further step toward me, you will find I am not the type of woman you appear to have mistaken me for. You should remember that this bedroom will almost certainly be bugged, and any thoughts you may have of forcing yourself on me will be faithfully recorded by the Russians and used to blackmail you down the line.'

'Yeah, that is a great story, now get yourself undressed, or I'll do it for you... He moved toward her and grabbed her coat, roughly removing it. He then tried to turn her round to get at the zip of her dress, moving quite quickly for a man of his size. As he did so he tried to force her onto the double bed. Ladvia was unbalanced and knew that once he was on top of her, she would have difficulty in removing him. She sidestepped slightly and suddenly her right arm moved with lightning speed towards the soft tissue to the left side of his throat where the carotid artery is located. He at once fell heavily to the floor, gasping for breath. As he started to recover, he managed to get onto one knee, 'why you fucking bitch, I'll show you...' Ladvia used her foot to strike again but this time just below the left ear and caught the vagus nerve with a whack. Stuart fell to the floor unconscious. She was worried that she had killed him but found a pulse and reckoned that he would be out for some time.

Ladvia realised that she would not be able to attend any meetings with Stuart, and so she decided to move out of the room and exit from Russia as soon as possible. She put on her gloves and picked up her coat using it to cover his briefcase she walked into the bathroom, took out a heavy file marked Russia negotiations, and with her smart phone, she photographed what appeared to be sensitive documents. Once she had done so, she sent them to her private computer in Scotland and a copy to Jeremy's phone. With that she placed the file back in the case and again hiding it under her coat she put it back in the exact place in the bedroom. She knew that while her actions would have been seen by a surveillance crew, who would almost certainly have been monitoring what was going on through a camera in the bedroom, they would not have been able to see her take the files into the bathroom. Ladvia knew their report would be telephoned to the headquarters of the SVB sometime during the day, so she picked up her case and left the room. Once outside the hotel, she telephoned the airline she had travelled on and changed her ticket for the first flight to London the next morning, so that anyone checking would assume she would be on that flight. Then she took the battery out of her phone, ensuring she could no longer be tracked. Ladvia ignored the local taxis and walked quickly down Tverskaya Street, where she picked up a passing cab. She smiled as she saw a sign for the Ministry of Communications only two streets up on Nikitskiy Perevlok, which was certainly where the monitoring team were situated. While she had a second-class air ticket to take her back to the UK,

Ladvia was cautious. Instead, she told her taxi to take her to the Kurkskaia Railway Station. Once there she booked on the next train to Saint Petersburg, she paid the equivalent of £50.00 in cash so that there was no record of a card payment. She only had to wait a couple of hours before boarding the train. The journey took 3 hours thirty minutes. When she arrived in Saint Petersburg, she found her luck was in, the Saint Peter Line ferry that travelled twice a week to Helsinki, was due to sail later that day and she was able to get a cabin for that night so she could sleep during the 13-hour trip. She had some time before boarding so she took a cab to the Winter Palace looking around the Hermitage Museum, at one stage having to leave a disappointed male who had asked her out to dinner that night.

Once in Helsinki. Ladvia phoned Jeremy, told him what had happened and asked him to relay the situation to Adrian. She received a phone call later to say a ministry car would meet her at Heathrow Airport.

THE SCOTTISH PREROGATIVE

Incorporating

THE WUHAN AFFAIR

BACK IN RUSSIA

Chapter 19

Members of the SVR had burst into the hotel bedroom about 30 minutes after Ladvia had left and found Stuart sitting on the bed nursing his injuries

General Sherepov was sitting in his office when he received news of the situation in the hotel between Stuart and Ladvia. He was not happy and called for Angus Stuart to be brought to him. When he arrived, he looked decidedly worse for wear as he had not even had time to wipe the blood from his forehead.

Soon afterwards a local alert was put out for Ladvia, but by that time she was on the train to Saint Petersburg. The airline ticket office reported that Ladvia was booked an early flight to London. It was only the next morning that a general alert was issued, but by then she had arrived in Helsinki.

General Sherepov started to ask Angus Stuart questions. 'How long have you employed the woman, Patricia Kirkham?'

'She was taken on as my new assistant, as the last girl I had left my employment to go to New Zealand.' Stuart, took his handkerchief out of his pocket to wipe some blood from his forehead, caused by his fall.

'How careful was the scrutiny when employing this woman, obviously she is very accomplished in martial arts.'

'I didn't realise...'

There was a knock at the door.

'Come,' shouted Sherepov.

A Captain entered the room holding a large file. 'It is probably more serious than we thought sir,' he handed Sherepov the file.

Sherepov opened it, and gasped in surprise, 'are you sure?'

'Yes sir, the resemblance was slight, so we checked the DNA we found in the hotel bedroom, it is definitely Ladvia Silonovic.

Sherepov stared at the two photographs in front of him. 'My God, you are right Captain, this is profoundly serious indeed.' He looked at Angus Stuart. 'You have just managed to employ one of the most dangerous spies we have known. It was thought this woman was killed many years ago, but that is clearly not the case. We understand that she has changed her flight to London for early tomorrow, so we will pick her up before she boards.

'My main concern is the files you have in your briefcase, my aide has looked through them and they are very damaging to our well laid out plan, if Ladvia saw them, we may have some major problems.'

Stuart sniffed, 'she would not have had time to read them, and as they are not missing...'

Sherepov interrupted, looking at Stuart contemptuously, 'My dear Angus, this woman is an expert, I know, we trained her. We must assume that she has copied the sensitive files which included notes from your earlier meetings with us. This could compromise what we are doing to help you free Scotland from the English. I am going to assign you a male assistant, he speaks perfect English, and he will travel back with you when you go, he already has diplomatic immunity in Britain, so there will be no problem in getting him into the country. Now, I have a phone call to make, so if you would like to get yourself some coffee from the canteen, I will only be a few minutes.'

Angus Stuart, got up, and a secretary went with him to the restaurant in the building.

The Captain who had accompanied Stuart from the hotel was told to stay. 'Sit down Captain.' Ordered Sherepov, the Captain did so. 'Before we start, I am going to make a phone call to a friend in the Middle East.' He dialled a number, not wishing it to go through the switchboard. 'I would like to speak to Mohammed Al-Salhi, this is General Sherepov, I am phoning him on a secure line from Moscow.' The line was connected after a brief time frame.

'Ah General, how nice to hear from you, what can a humble man like me do to help one of the greatest men in Russia?'

'I have some interesting information for you Al-Salhi, it concerns a person who I understand you have been looking for.' There was silence at the end of the line. 'Her name was Ladvia Silonovic, presumed dead, but has now suddenly appeared as Mrs Patricia Kirkham, she is living in Scotland and is an employee of the Scottish government.'

'Do you know where...?'

'Yes, I will get a member of my staff to e-mail you, I assume the Fatwa is still active?'

'You can rely on me to take the necessary action General; I am in your debt.'

Sherepov put the phone down. 'A necessary precaution in case our fly escapes our net, and as she is known to be very resourceful, it would not surprise me, now let us look at the damage that has been caused.'

The Captain pulled out the files. 'Most indicate the financial loans offered to Scotland should it become independent. Because Angus Stuart is not fully aware of the deal we are intending to force on Scotland when they secede from the Union. It does not say what will happen to the First Minister if she does not agree.'

'Good, good, go on...'

'There is however, rather more regarding the financing of the factory that has been set up in the south of Scotland and the names of the directors, although they are Swedish, could lead the British to trace a Moscow support.'

'Go on...'

'The files show the underground size of the factory, which could make the local authorities suspicious, as it is known that the earthmoving equipment constructed in the factory is at ground level. It shows that the airstrip built is longer than that agreed by the local authority. It also shows that no local workers are employed after 6 pm and flights from Sweden are sometimes known to come in after HM customs have left the premises. There is a piece about the security arrangements being particularly tight with armed guards, and that a double security fence was constructed after a breach was found. It indicates that workers were flown in from Latvia to build the factory including the area below ground but were flown out again leaving only a security contingent. Questions could be raised as to what production is going on in the basement area. They also state that 250 Latvian workers were subsequently flown in to start the production but of course it is only local people who have been employed in the production area. The "workers" are Spetsnaz and members of an armoured brigade capable of manning tanks and they have all been living under the factory, being involved in putting together all the military equipment, so any investigation in that area would compromise the operation.

'Finally, there are some figures showing the number of diggers produced which would not agree with the amount of parts imported.'

'Hmm, the piece about the Latvian workers brought in for the production area could cause a problem, particularly as they were Russian with false Latvian passports. These men were obviously flown in unbeknown to the immigration department.' Sherepov took a drink of water from a glass on his desk.

The Captain nodded, 'yes sir, there is sufficient information to create awkward questions, but we could of course claim that all the second wave of "workers" were sent back once the locals were employed. No one would be able to disprove that. However, we must hope that the files were not seen or copied.'

Sherepov grimaced 'Never underestimate your enemy Captain. The British may be complacent, but they are not fools and if our fly is not on that flight early tomorrow morning, whatever the case, we must assume that she saw the files, and almost certainly copied them, It does not take a genius to send the data by phone, so you should contact our communications people to establish what information was sent from her mobile, if any. Of course, she may have a secure connection. It is possible that she may be lying low, as she is known to have contacts in Russia, on the other hand she may have found a way of exiting the country. I suspect that she has been in touch with her base, which means we will have to move more quickly. Now perhaps you could get Mr Stuart out of the canteen and bring him back here.'

THE SCOTTISH PREROGATIVE

Incorporating

THE WUHAN AFFAIR

THE DECISION

Chapter 20

It was weeks later that The Minister was called to a meeting of top ministers in the State Council of the People's Republic of China. The Deputy President was presiding. Two further people had been invited, the Ministry of State for China and the senior member of the PLA, the People's Liberation Army that consists of five branches: Ground Force, Navy, Air Force, Rocket Force, and the Strategic Support Force.

The Deputy Premier addressed the group. 'Gentlemen, I have convened this special meeting to discuss one thing and one thing only. I will invite the minister in charge of our Biological Facilities, and the major plant in Wuhan to present his report, Minister?'

The Minister whose name was Bo Chen, described his recent visit to the Facility in Wuhan and the details of the virus that had been manufactured.

There was a moments silence in the room when he had finished.

The deputy Chairman spoke, 'and what do you suggest we do with this information?'

'My colleague, the head of the Ministry of State and I have discussed this matter thoroughly, and we have produced a plan. I will therefore hand over to Mr Chang Hou.'

Chang Hou had a copy of the original folder in front of him. 'I have had discussions with the Ministry of Finance and we both agree that our biggest economic threat is the USA and to a lesser extent, Western Europe. Long-term, India, the latter from both an economic point of view and militarily.

'We should use our vaccine which we have produced to inoculate all senior members of the Republic, the higher ranks of our armed forces and other strategic people such as our overseas ambassadors. A list will be drawn up by the Minister of Health.

'We should accelerate the production of the vaccine.

'Then we should order that the virus be dropped in an area like the fish market in Wuhan. Once it takes control, we can then shut the facility down and send all the people home. If the information we have is correct, the virus will spread rapidly causing panic around the world. We assess that it will quickly reach the United States and have a major effect on the economy there, ensuring that Donald Trump loses the next election.

'We are aware of the damage his sanctions have caused the people of China, and this is a perfect way of creating panic in the Western World, which can only be to our benefit.'

The Minister for the National Security of China intervened. 'But surely, this would have a huge effect on our population, if none of our leaders suffer from the virus. Will that not look suspicious?'

'Initially it would,' agreed Chang Hou, 'but China is in a good place to deal with such an outbreak. We will simply shut down various areas to stop the virus spreading and then after a reasonable period, we will use our vaccine to ensure the safety of our people. We cannot do so until we see the result of the infection, as it may then indicate that we had deliberately spread it. In the first instance we will ignore the contagion, taking at least six weeks before declaring with horror to the World Health Authority that we believe the virus came from the fish market due to improper hygiene. As far as our leaders are concerned, they can lie, just as we can continue to lie about the number of deaths that the virus will cause. One of the beauties of our system of government is we control everything, including the media and the press.

'We estimate around 10,000 deaths at most, and these will be older people and people with health problems, so the State will benefit financially by the saving of pensions and health care of the elderly. We will build new hospitals to show what we can do to deal with the virus and thus bring admiration from the world indicating how well we look after our people.

'Finally, when our situation is regularised, we will sell our vaccine at a huge profit. Of course, we will do this through our interests in the Pharmaceutical industry in Europe, one that is not apparently connected to China.'

'Well gentlemen,' The Deputy Premier, spoke. 'Thank you all for your input. To sum up, it appears that we can catch the Western world at its weakest. The UK will almost certainly leave the European Union next year, which will leave the EU with a gap in its future budget, The USA have their elections, India has a problem with the Muslims within the state, and according to our treasury, debt is piling up in the Western world, Russia is now stuck in a war in the Middle

East, Turkey is beset by Immigrants as is Greece. Early next year, 2020 would be a good time to strike. The beauty of this idea is that China would appear to be the most damaged party. Indeed, instead of selling our vaccine covertly, we could offer to sell it direct, and claim that we are saving the world, not destroying it.

'I am now going to put this to a vote, and the people who have spoken will handle the implementation. Just one other idea, once the virus is 'floated' we may consider ensuring that it is spread into certain Western countries that have a weak economy. Italy perhaps?'

The vote taken was unanimous and each member rushed to inform their departments.

'Oh, and one other matter before you disperse,' said Chang Hou, 'I believe we have manufactured thousands of testing kits for the virus and the western world will look to us to supply them. Please make sure that one in ten are faulty, so they will believe we have tried to help them, but after they have paid their money, they will come to realise that they cannot rely on them. This will spread further panic within their medical systems.'

As often happens, those at the top, often forget those at the bottom that must implement such decisions. One of these was a young Chinese woman trusted to take notes during the meeting. Events would change her views dramatically, especially when her doctor brother died of the virus...

It was two days later that the Minister phoned the Laboratory manager. 'We have been given the go ahead, you are to instruct a responsible man to take the virus to the wet market and break a Covid-19 vial in the area.

The Manager was about to ask for written confirmation, but the phone clicked. He tried to call back, but the Minister was unavailable.

THE SCOTTISH PREROGATIVE

Incorporating

THE WUHAN AFFAIR

THE INVESTIGATION

Chapter 21

Adrian had just put the phone down after telling Jeremy the timing of the flight from Finland with Ladvia on board and that he should travel down from Edinburgh to meet her at Heathrow Airport and contact the ministry driver as soon as Ladvia arrived. Both should travel to the MI6 Headquarters.

It was about ten minutes after talking to Jeremy that Adrian's secretary buzzed him on the internal intercom. 'I have a Mohammed Al-Salhi on the line, he wants to speak to you urgently.'

Adrian frowned, was this to break their agreement, he wondered? 'Put the call through but switch on the recorder,' he waited a few seconds.

'Ah, Mr Bradley, I am sorry to disturb you, but you should know that I had a call from General Sherepov yesterday, I am sorry to tell you, but your Ladvia Silonovic has been "blown". I have no idea what she has been up to, nor do I need to know, but the call was made on the basis that the fatwa was still in place. I did not disabuse the General, but I suspect that as soon as the Russians realise that we are not interested in her any longer, they will take extreme measures. I thought you should know, one good turn, deserves another, isn't that what you say?'

'Indeed, it is my friend, and we are most grateful for the information, thank you.' The phone clicked at the other end. Adrian replaced his on the receiver. He pressed a number on the intercom. 'Geoffrey, come in please, we have a problem.'

Geoffrey Williamson entered the office and Adrian proffered a seat opposite his desk. Geoffrey raised his eyebrows as Adrian told him of the call he had just taken.

'That puts the fly in the ointment,' he said. 'I assume you'll have to pull her out, and as Jeremy is her husband, he too will be compromised.'

'Damn,' exclaimed Adrian, 'I was hoping to engage them both in the SWORD project, particularly as the new Prime Minister is keen for us to sort out the Iranian affair.'

Geoffrey nodded, 'Well there is no connection between the two, why not consider giving them leave while the "Open Door" matter is resolved and then bring them back when the dust has settled?'

'Hmm, that does seem a sensible idea, leave may be the answer, I'll give it some thought. We need to re think, It is true, that the situation may now appear to require more of a military intervention. I was going to speak to the Chief of Staff about SWORD anyway, perhaps this would be a good opportunity to test out specialist forces to help us solve "Open Door".'

'Good thinking,' said Geoffrey, 'would you like me to arrange a meet...?'

'No, I'll give him a call and offer him a lunch at the club, thank you Geoffrey.' He picked the phone up as Geoffrey exited the office. Adrian noticed that a red light on his intercom switchboard was still on. He tried to turn it off by juggling the switches, to no avail. After arranging a lunch with the Chief of Staff he buzzed his secretary. 'Mary, there seems to be a problem with my intercom, would you call the relevant department to come and fix it?' Adrian knew that it was normal practice for there to be regular bug sweeps for all offices, so he was not concerned.

Later that morning Jeremy and Ladvia arrived, and once settled in the office with coffee and biscuits, Adrian listened to the report that Ladvia had sent through to Jeremy.

'It seems to me,' said Adrian, 'that there is enough in your report to insist on an investigation of the plant up there.'

'Hmm, probably, but that would alert the ungodly,' answered Jeremy, 'I would recommend you carry out a secret incursion by those who are skilled to do so.'

'The SAS?' Adrian raised his eyebrows.

'Yes, they are past masters at this sort of surveillance and would ascertain what they are up to, if anything, and if it was found to be illegal, then you could react with the heavies. On the other hand, if everything is in order, then no feathers would be ruffled. It is after all an important area of employment, where previously, there was virtually none.'

Ladvia intervened. 'I know from some of the reports I saw in the office in Edinburgh that there are fairly regular inspections of the factory by Scottish officials, and the reports are clean. Of course, it could be that Stuart has somehow falsified them, but Jeremy is right, politically, if you send English inspectors up there, it could cause bad blood, which would no doubt, please Stuart immensely.'

'Okay, I am having lunch tomorrow with Scott-Jones, the Chief of Staff, and will discuss the matter with him. Now, we have an immediate problem.' Adrian looked at Ladvia. 'I am afraid that you have been "blown".'

Ladvia looked surprised, and then frowned. 'But how, the fact that I stopped Stuart in his sexual tracks, would not have given the Russians any indication of my identity, in fact, I never met anyone while I was there.'

Adrian nodded, 'I agree, it does seem strange, but I had a call from our Muslim friend, who told me that he had received a call from General Sherepov indicating that you were employed in Scotland by the government there. He received the impression that they were hoping the Muslim Fund would do their dirty work for them.'

'Hmm, of course, once someone had alerted the SVB that I was still alive, they would have carried out DNA tests in the bedroom, which would have confirmed who I was. But that still does not answer how they found out originally. I am assuming that the Muslim Fund could not have been involved, as they would have had no idea I was in Russia, or indeed working for the Scottish government.'

'I'll get my people on it straight away and see if we can produce an answer.' Adrian said.

Jeremy looked thoughtful, 'I must agree that with Ladvia exposed, my position as her husband would also make it impossible for me to continue in the UK.'

'Damn it, you're right,' answered Adrian, 'but I may have another suggestion that may suit us. A position has just become vacant in Washington DC. The present incumbent has resigned after he made a derogatory remark to a journalist about the President. I have had a word with our Embassy in Washington and providing you agree, I have arranged for Jeremy to take over the position of the political secretary there. The job would be similar to that which you filled for us when you worked as a liaison between the services, except in this case you would be liaising between the various security services in the US, as well as other friendly intelligence services, such as Mossed in the Israeli Embassy there. Ladvia will act as your number two. Your first job would be to enquire how the Americans control SAD and what sort of brief they have. You would be secure there and the children could go to school in the area.

'I am under pressure from the Prime Minister regarding the Iranian situation and what we can do regarding the British subjects held at the Elvin Prison in Tehran. There are US subjects there as well, and at least one Israeli.'

Jeremy nodded, 'yes, our usefulness in the UK is over, we know how intrusive the Russians can be, take the case of Sergei and Yulia Skripal,' he said. 'the children are the weak link in our case, so we need to rethink.'

'Okay,' said Adrian, 'why not take two weeks leave, and go and consider the US job, and let me know as soon as possible. I don't think you can consider going back to Chile to live, and I will consider what sort of protection you may need whilst on leave. It is possible that the Russians will try something within the next couple of weeks.'

They continued to talk for a further hour before Jeremy and Ladvia left Adrian's office. When they were alone in Jeremy's hotel suite at the Barclay Hotel in Knightsbridge, they discussed the matter further. 'How do you think the Russians got onto you?' asked Jeremy.

'There is only one way, and that is through the mole indicated by Validich, but that means the person is much closer to Adrian than we were led to believe. It also means that any idea originally discussed with Adrian, is surely

178

compromised.' Ladvia grimaced. 'However, the position in the States could be interesting. I have the feeling that you continuing as a llama farmer is no longer challenging enough.'

Jeremy laughed, 'nor you, I have no doubt we can sell our interests there, in fact you will remember we had an offer only three months ago, so we could place it on the market and see what happens.

'Okay, let us enjoy our leave, we'll take the children out of school, and I fancy Devon at this time of year. There is an excellent place to stay, it is called Gidleigh Park Hotel, near a small town called Chagford.'

THE SPY UNVEILED

Chapter 22

Adrian was about to leave his office to meet the Chief of Staff for lunch, and as he was passing through his secretary's office, she told him that the "communications man" would be calling during the lunch hour. 'Okay Mary, let him into my office, but for the moment, do not indicate to anyone, and I do mean anyone, that we have someone looking at the system.'

Mary affirmed that she would not do so.

John Scott-Jones was in mufti, so as not to draw too much attention to himself, he had seated himself at the table 5 minutes before Adrian arrived. Adrian noticed John looking at his watch and he apologised for being late. John laughed, 'typical of a bloody civil servant, time means nothing to them. Whereas we in the military are sticklers for time keeping.' Adrian just smiled as he sat down.

'Well as my department is paying for the lunch, you can grant me 5 minutes.'

'I should bloody well hope so,' laughed John, 'with your massive budget, I could build another bloody navy.'

They ordered drinks and John ensured that he ate well, Adrian however was more circumspect, asking only for a plain dish of salmon in a lemon sauce.

John took a sip of the excellent wine, 'well, how can I help?'

'I have had an idea for some time that MI6 need a body like the US SAD team, where we could utilise them covertly to ensure certain projects were carried out without using the military. Mossad have been doing this for some time, of course...'

'You are surely not suggesting that we have a murder squad like the GRU?'

'No of course not, but a highly trained body used to infiltrate a foreign country and carry out surveillance and if necessary real force. If anyone was caught, we could deny responsibility. We have a situation now that may concern a foreign power but the situation in Scotland is more urgent and one which you are already aware of.'

John nodded, 'okay, tell me more.'

Adrian told John of the situation regarding Jeremy and Ladvia. 'I cannot use them for this project any longer, but it perhaps it now demands a rather different approach. The problem with MI6 is that too many people are aware of what goes on, and from time to time we find that a trusted colleague has blown the whistle, as it appears in the case of Ladvia. However, with a body under the name of SWORD, "Special War organisation for Research and Defence," it would come under my budget and report to me directly, nevertheless the top team would still be registered soldiers, so ranks and promotions would be for the War Office.'

John nodded, 'It could work, as a matter of a fact, I may just have a team that would suit you. They are well experienced in the type of work you are alluding to. They are all SAS and commanded by an exceptional officer. They have recently been involved in the Ukraine, Belarus, Lithuania,

Nigeria, and Greece. There are five members on the top team but are well capable of leading a much larger body of men, as indeed, they did on the island of Crete. My problem, is that I cannot currently utilise their skills, as to do so could expose the military to severe political criticism.'

'Is it possible I could get a meeting with their commander?' asked Adrian.

'Hmm, I need to run this across the bow of the new Prime Minister, perhaps both of us could get a meeting with him. I have the feeling that he might be quite enthusiastic, as he has some concern about the Iranian affair. To solve problems without directly involving the military, would be right up his street. No political comebacks.'

Adrian agreed, and John said he would set up a meeting with the PM within the next available time frame. Adrian said it would not be necessary at this juncture for him to be present at such a meeting. They finished their lunch and Adrian walked back to his office, only a few hundred yards away.

As he entered, Mary told him that Jeremy had left a message on his machine saying where he and Ladvia were staying. 'Oh, and one more thing, the man from the communications department is awaiting your return, he is in the canteen, shall I call him for you?'

Adrian said yes and entered his office deep in thought about his recent meeting with John Scott-Jones.

There was a knock on the door, Mary entered with a tall intelligent looking man behind her. 'This is Mr Charles Duncan; he is the gentleman who looked at your intercom.'

Mary closed the door as she went out, and Adrian shook the man's hand and showed him to a seat in front of his desk.

'Well, Mr Duncan, did you...?'

'Yes,' Duncan interjected, 'but the fault I found will not make you happy, I'm afraid.'

Adrian frowned, 'go on...'

'Well sir, your intercom is connected to the switchboard, so it acts as a telephone with an outside line as well as being connected internally. You also have five other phones within that system that are direct lines.'

Adrian nodded.

Duncan continued, 'you will understand my department screens for bugs, listening devices and the most recent was completed by me today. However, on examining your intercom, I noticed that one section has been modified so that any call coming through this phone, whether it be internal or external could be picked up by another on the same system.'

Adrian leaned forward, 'are you saying that it is possible for someone to have listened in to all my calls, both inward and outward?'

'Precisely sir, but only those channelled through the intercom and there is only one station that could do that.'

'And that is?'

Duncan gave Adrian the number of the connection and noticed his skin paling. 'Good God, this is serious.' He sat back in his chair, completely shocked. Duncan was talking again. 'I am sorry to tell you that this was a deliberate modification by someone who must have had access to your office, and it is quite clever, because it would never show up on any of our scans.'

'So, let me get this completely straight, anyone phoning me on this line, means that a certain unauthorised person could listen in to my conversation with the other party?'

'Yes sir.'

'What if someone called when I was not in the office, would it go through automatically to my secretary?'

'Yes, sir, if your secretary was in her office, it would, otherwise whatever was said would be recorded on the system?'

'I am most grateful to you Duncan...'

'Should I check others on the system?'

'No, not yet I need some time to see how this could be used, so I will let you know as soon as I have made my decision on what action we should take. In the meantime, you must not under any circumstances report this to your senior manager, nor discuss it with anyone else. It must remain between the two of us for the moment, do I make myself clear?'

'Of course, sir, just give me a call when you need me to right the situation. Obviously, I did not change anything because of the sensitivity of the problem.'

'Good man,' said Adrian, as he stood up and shook Duncan's hand warmly, 'and thank you.'

Duncan picked up his small metal case and left the room.

After listening to the messages, Adrian pulled the plug out of the intercom and then used his mobile phone to contact Jeremy who at that time was driving down the M5 towards their destination.

Jeremy turned on the hands-free phone in his car. 'It's Adrian, Jeremy. Have you reached your destination yet?'

'Negative Adrian we are about 40 minutes way.'

'Okay can you confirm your plans?'

'We are keeping to our original plan and heading to Gidleigh Park Hotel, where we are to spend a night, then travel north to pick up the children from near Bristol and then...'

Adrian interjected. 'Right, now you should know that the Russians have notice of your destination.'

Ladvia leaned over to the speaker, 'but how, you are the only person we have told in the message we left you earlier today?'

'Yes, and by good fortune, I have now uncovered the leak, it has come from within this building. I expect the Russians to react, as it is clear they now know that the Muslim Fund have no interest in Ladvia. However, with your help, I would like to devise a plan and as I have not blown the whistle yet, we could lead the ungodly into a trap. Let me explain...' It took Adrian just over five minutes to tell them his intentions, and both Ladvia and Jeremy agreed to take part.

They arrived at the hotel in the early evening, booked in and after showering, went down for a drink. It was after dinner when they were walking outside. They turned left from the main entrance, and as they walked down the road, they noticed two people who were also staying at the hotel. Jeremy and Ladvia recognised them and gave a casual greeting as they passed by. The young couple smiled, and the man turned suddenly approaching Jeremy, who was caught off guard.

COLONEL JOHN DESMOND

Chapter 23

Scott-Jones telephoned Jeremy on the secure mobile system. 'Ah, Adrian, further to our discussion I have arranged for Colonel John Desmond to call you within the next hour. This is the man I referred to when we had lunch yesterday. He is very experienced and due to his exploits; he is currently the youngest Colonel in the British Army. I suggest you spend some more of that huge budget of yours and buy him a lunch in an appropriate place.'

'Thank you, John. I prefer to call him if you give me his number.'

Scott Jones gave a War Office number and rang off. Adrian then telephoned the number he had received and was surprised as John Desmond answered it himself. A lunch was arranged at Simpson's on the Strand for the next day. Adrian walked through to his secretary's office and asked her to book a table for two, with a special request for a table to be in a quiet corner of the restaurant. He gave her the time for the arranged lunch.

His secretary looked up from her notes. 'The PM's aide has just called, He asked that you call him as soon as possible, it's urgent,' she said. 'It might be a good idea for you to look at the file on your desk, before doing so, there is a panic regarding Covid-19.'

Adrian walked back to his office and picked a file up from his desk and as he was walking out, he shouted to Mary to get a car and driver ready, just in case.

He telephoned the number given to him as he was taking the elevator down to the garage area in the basement. But became annoyed when he realised there was no signal. Reaching the bottom, he picked up a wall phone and dialled the number. He was put straight through.

'Ah, Mr Bradley, thank you for phoning, the PM wants to see you straight away, he is currently with the Foreign Secretary, how long will it take you to get here?'

'I thought it may be something unusually urgent, so I'm already in the basement and I see my driver is waiting, so I'll be about 10 minutes.'

'That's great, I'll let the PM know.' The phone clicked off.

His driver opened the rear door, and Adrian climbed in. He shouted to his driver, 'Johnson, Number 10 Downing Street, and use your flashing lights, we're in a hurry.'

It took only eight minutes and Adrian was in the Cabinet office within two minutes of his arrival. As the door opened the Prime Minister got up and strode towards him, his hand outstretched.

'Are you sure you want to shake my hand Prime Minister?' Smiled Adrian. 'Bugger Covid-19,' he said, grabbing Adrian's hand, 'you've met our new Foreign Minister, of course....'

Adrian laughed, 'a few times, I think, Hi Charlie.'

Before Charlie Grimes could answer, the PM broke in. 'Adrian, have you seen the report just received from the CIA? it's dynamite.' he said, as he threw himself into a large chair.

'I agree Prime Minister,' Adrian did not admit that he had only just read the report in the back of the car.

'So, what are you going to do about it?' Asked the PM.

Adrian's brain was working fast, 'I have a plan,' he smiled. He then told them what his idea was and how he would implement it. Both the Prime Minister and Foreign Secretary were impressed. 'Now,' said Adrian, 'I need to put matters in place, so if you'll forgive me...' He turned towards the door, looking at his watch. He opened the door and was gone before anyone could ask any more questions.

Riding back in the car he telephoned his secretary and gave her explicit instructions.

He then called Jeremy.

THE LONG TRIP

Chapter 24

As Jeremy took a step back, he noticed the man smiling and holding his hand out. At that moment Jeremy's mobile rang. Ladvia had moved in front of Jeremy keeping her eye on the girl behind. It quickly became obvious that these two people meant them no harm and that was confirmed when the man held up his security card.

'Jeremy, it's Adrian. Look, I am sorry I am late in calling you, but there is a flap on now regarding Covid-19.'

Ladvia was now talking to the young couple, but still had her left hand on the butt of her automatic tucked into the rear of her jeans. Jeremy, seeing that there was no danger, turned away with the phone to his ear.

Adrian was talking. 'Okay, I have sent two people to meet you, they are staying in the same hotel, but will only make themselves known to you when you go out on your evening walk. Which I happen to know you do most days.'

Jeremy smiled, *a bit late he thought*. 'Yes, we have just met them. Anyway, they are here, and they are talking to Ladvia as we speak.'

'Yes, I am sorry I was late in calling you, but I was hijacked by 10 Downing Street, where there is a hell of a flap on, I'll explain in a minute.

'Before I do, Archie and Belinda will put you in the picture as to what you should do tomorrow morning. We now know that there are two Russians on their way down to you, and they have booked into the hotel you are staying in, obviously under assumed names. We have assessed the immediate danger to you and believe that it is highly unlikely that they are carrying any sort of biological or nerve agent as in the case of Sergei and his daughter.'

'Why do you think that?' Asked Jeremy.

'Two reasons, we now have a friend of Peter Validich who is attached to the GRU, and he has given us an indication of their plan. Secondly, in Sergei's case, they wanted to ensure the world knew about his death to put off others thinking of defecting, showing it would be a death sentence if they did. In this case they are planning some sort a car accident, which will be carried out on the M5 North. Archie Glover, the guy we have sent down to you is an explosives expert, and he will check your car before you move off in the morning. The reason they reached you so quickly, is that Belinda Carter, who is with him, flew a helicopter down and parked it at one of our safe houses close to your hotel. They used a company car to reach you, but they will not show that you are known to them. Once you set off, Belinda and Archie will be flying overhead watching over you as you drive.'

Jeremy frowned, 'well you know our plan is to collect the girls from school and bring them down here, where we will spend the next two weeks before flying to the States. So, what is the plan regarding the Russians?'

'They won't hang about because they will want to scuttle back to Russia via Scotland ASAP. I'll let you know what they intend to do in Scotland.'

'I can guess,' answered Jeremy.

'Yes, I am sure you can, we need to deal with them, and Archie will give you, his ideas. Now, we have another problem and need your urgent help. I am afraid we will have to postpone your trip to Washington as I have just received information that President Trump is cancelling all flights from the UK due to the virus. In a way, which is quite helpful as we have an even more urgent matter, we want you to complete before you go there.'

'Oh, and what about the children?'

'You will have time to see them tomorrow on your way up. My suggestion is that you pick them up from the school as planned and meet my wife at the airport, she will look after them again, until you return.'

Jeremy knew that the two girls would be disappointed, but as they had stayed with Adrian and his wife before, they would be happy enough, assuming the new situation did not take too long.

'I don't understand Adrian, where do you want us to go?

'Hong Kong.'

'WHAT, why Hong Kong?' he turned and looked at Ladvia who had raised her eyebrows.

'The virus the Chinese appear to have created is highly dangerous, you must have read about in the papers or seen a report on television.'

'Yes, of course,' answered Jeremy, 'but it has not created much of a problem in the UK, so...'

'I have had the Minister of Health call me and put me in the picture. It is highly infectious and will spread to the UK within a matter of weeks. Lombardy in Northern Italy have just announced that they have major problems, and their hospitals are already full. They expect a high death rate. We have had a secret message from our people in Hong Kong and they told us about a doctor who worked for the Wuhan Biological weapons facility and that he was murdered because he refused to spread the virus in a local market. Before his demise, he recognised that the powers that would be unhappy at his refusal, he took a vial of the vaccine and sent it to his sister. The next day, he was hit by a police car as he was walking his dog and pronounced dead when taken to the local hospital. The report on his death indicated that he died from the virus. As luck would have it, the sister was a senior stenographer who took minutes at the meeting of Ministers in Beijing. It was during that meeting that a decision to spread the virus was taken, to bring the economy in the Western World to its knees. The main target being the US President who is carrying out a trade war with China. But of course, it will have huge implications for the whole world. We understand that the news of the spread of the virus was not made public for over six weeks in China, thus giving them a chance to surmount the problem before it hit the rest of the world.

'The sister was told she should cancel her notes and take leave to isolate herself. She cancelled the minutes, but on arriving at her house in Wuhan she re wrote them from memory. Once she received the vaccine, and heard of her brother's death, she took off for Hong Kong where the Umbrella group is hiding her. She chose Hong Kong because she was born there, and she considered it to be the one place where she could contact people in the West.

'The tested vaccine was apparently made to safeguard the top echelon of the party apparatus. which means we can quickly recreate it and save thousands of people under threat. What we need is for you and Ladvia to fly to Hong Kong as tourists. We have you booked onto a flight the day after tomorrow, but the booking will show it was made two months ago. You are both booked into the Mandarin Hotel; you will stay there until contacted. Your passports are in the name of Mr and Mrs Brown, which is the name that you will use in USA, so we have passports and travel documents already made up for you. I realise this is an ask but remember your success may save many lives.'

'So, no pressure?' said Jeremy. 'How do we get back if flights are being cancelled?'

'British Airways are still flying to Hong Kong, but we have a better way of getting you out, so don't worry. Frankly, we could not think of better people to achieve success and time is essential as the Chinese now know that the stenographer has disappeared. You can be sure that they will be combing Hong Kong for our lady, as that is an obvious place for her to hide.

'I'll talk to Ladvia and get back to you.' Jeremy rang off and turned to meet his visitors who were still in conversation with Ladvia. "That was a long call,' she looked at him quizzically.

Jeremy smiled, 'wait until you hear what is being asked of us.'

'The answer is no,' said Ladvia firmly.

'It's not as easy as that, I'm afraid, we'll talk later.'

Ladvia nodded, 'well this is Archie and Belinda, and they are our guardian angels for tomorrow, and despite the fact they look like a couple of teenagers, I'm satisfied they know what they are doing.' Jeremy introduced himself and they had a brief chat, Archie said he would ring Jeremy in the morning with a final plan before they left the hotel.

They both disappeared into the trees, and Jeremy and Ladvia turned back towards the hotel. Jeremy recounted what Adrian had asked them to do. She agreed that in the circumstances they could not refuse. 'I have one question though, how do we get this person out?' Asked Ladvia.

'Good question, no doubt, Adrian will have a plan, which we'll learn about when we meet.' answered Jeremy. 'Now you tell me what the "youngsters" have in mind?

Ladvia smiled, 'they expect a tracking device will be added under our car sometime during the night, and maybe other items such as a listening device and even explosives. Our guardian angels will assess what they have done, if anything, and deal with it. If there is a tracking device and or a listening device, they will leave those in place, so we may have to be careful what we say in the car. If an explosive is found, they will remove it. At 09.30 precisely, we should set off from the hotel at a normal speed. We are to drive to the coordinates N50.663388 and W-3.748667. it is about 7.3 miles from the hotel and depending on speed, should take us about 21 minutes down narrow Devon lanes. About half a mile from the destination we should speed up until we reach a right-hand bend, and once round it we should stop diagonally across the road. At that point, we should remove our luggage and go through the trees to a farm gate on the left, put the luggage the other side of the gate and quickly remove ourselves from the area towards the farm building which is set well back from the road. Once we are at least 500 yards away, we should take cover'.

Jeremy frowned, 'what the hell are these people up to?'

194

'Don't know, but I suspect that the followers might be in for a surprise. Whatever, the helicopter will be nearby, and they will call us. The farm is an MI6 safe house, which is where the helicopter is overnighting. I understand that the road will be blocked in front of us, and as soon as the Russians have turned into the lane, and out of sight, the rear will be blocked too.' Ladvia shrugged, 'let's get to bed, we have a busy day tomorrow.'

The next morning, Ladvia told the receptionist that unfortunately they had to leave as they had an emergency to deal with in London.

Half an hour earlier, Jeremy had received a text from Archie indicating that the car was safe. There were only two cases to put in the car and Jeremy told Ladvia to stand well back just in case Archie had not found all the explosive material. Jeremy opened both the boot and the driver's door and started the engine before he waved to Ladvia to join him. 'So far, so good,' he said. He could see no signs of the Russians, and the car they had arrived in was nowhere to be seen. Jeremy set off and drove at a normal speed. Ladvia looked out of the window, but could not see the helicopter, which made her feel a little apprehensive. As planned. After about half a mile from the stopping point, Jeremy put his foot down, and knowing that the road was blocked at the other end, he sped down the narrow lane, as they reached the spot immediately after the bend, he swung the car sideways, blocking the road. They quickly got out, ensuring they gathered their luggage, and half ran through the trees to the gate. After running into the field, they kept near the tree line. Ladvia saw the helicopter first, it was at about 500 feet and well to the rear of any vehicle that had been following them.

Suddenly they heard a squeal of brakes and a bang as a car hit theirs at speed. There was a brief pause and Jeremy heard a car door slamming, immediately afterwards there was a huge explosion. The trees were quite high but one of the occupants was seen well above the foliage before falling back to the ground.

'Jesus,' Jeremy shouted, 'that was a hell of a bang.'

Just as he had finished speaking, the helicopter landed about thirty yards away and Archie jumped out. 'Where are your bags?' he shouted. Jeremy pointed to where they had left them. Archie pointed to the aircraft, telling them to get in the back and he would get the luggage and secure it in the compartment behind the rear seats. Within three minutes they were in the air flying towards Bristol.

Helicopters are quite noisy aircraft, so the conversation was muted on the trip, and it was not until they had landed on the school grounds and the jet engine switched off that they were able to converse.

Jeremy asked Ladvia to get the two girls and bring them back as soon as possible, as he knew that Adrian and his wife would be waiting for them at Heathrow. For the first time Jeremy noticed the helicopter they had flown in, it was an Agusta AW109S Grand. This helicopter had six seats, which was just as well, as six of them were to travel in it to London.

He turned to Archie who had climbed out of the aircraft ready to take the children's luggage. 'So, what happened back there?'

Archie smiled, 'when we checked your car after midnight, we found not only a tracking device placed under the petrol tank but a small explosive device behind the front passengers side wheel. There was no listening device,' he added. 'It was quite clever, as it would have been exploded by a radio signal from the car, they were in. I strongly suspect that they would have detonated the explosive when you were on the M5, perhaps when you were passing a heavily loaded articulated truck. Just when you had the rear of your car level with the front of a truck, it would have ensured your car swerved directly in front of it. These heavy trucks are usually travelling at speed, and the driver would have no hope in avoiding you. The corresponding crash on the motorway would have been catastrophic and assuming the Russians were far enough behind, they would not get caught up in the melee. Of course, it would have delayed them in getting up to Scotland.

'I must admit that I nearly missed the explosive device because it was quite small, but I didn't. After removing it, I put my own under the petrol tank. We saw that you had vacated the car as planned and removed yourselves to a safe distance; we only had to wait for them to catch up. Because you had increased your speed, the driver was surprised. He drove far too fast around the final corner and could not stop before running into the side of your car. I saw the man get out and I pressed my radio control button. They were vaporised. Of course, Our ground team had already closed off the road in front and as soon as they went through, they closed the other end so that we could be sure that no one else would be involved. I've just had a call from the clean-up team, saying that anyone driving in the lane now, would not know there had been an incident.'

'So, our Russian friends have simply disappeared?' said Jeremy.

'Yes, and as the only house nearby was one of our safe houses, no one will be recording their demise, the Russians will be extremely worried, as they were on their way to assassinate the First Minister of Scotland and now their headquarters in Russia may be worried that they've been caught.' Said Archie.

Jeremy smiled, 'so a fitting response to the Salisbury affair where two GRU guys tried to kill Sergei.'

Archie nodded and indicated that Ladvia was returning with the girls.

After everyone was in the aircraft, it took off, landing at Heathrow forty-five minutes later. Adrian and his wife were there to meet them on the tarmac, and after tearful farewells she took the girls back to the waiting car, where they were to be driven to Adrian's house in Hampstead. Adrian gave Ladvia and Jeremy their passports and travel documents and then took them to the first-class lounge, where they had lunch and a long discussion on their task in Hong Kong.

'No one from the British Embassy will meet you because you are normal tourists, so after going through immigration, you will get a taxi to the Mandarin Hotel. For the first two days, you will act as normal tourists. On the third day you will take a taxi to Wan Chai Park, where you will walk. Whilst in the park, a Mrs Carpenter will meet you. If she sees that you are being followed, she will not approach you, and if that happens you will walk around for not more than an hour and then return to the hotel. Frankly, it is unlikely you will be followed, but if Mrs Carpenter does not contact you in the park, she will call you that evening and say she is sorry she got the wrong number and ask what your number is. She will then say the number she intended to call; it will have one number different. Here is a map of Hong Kong Island where you will be and there are several numbers on it, which any tourist might have pencilled in as to what sight they wanted to see. You will go to the place shown. It will be another park to coincide with a number given to you on the phone. Here is the map,' Adrian handed it over.

'Now, when you leave the Mandarin, take anything you may need, as everything in the hotel must be left behind.

After meeting our whistle blower, you will not be able to return there. Mrs Carpenter will organise the meeting and you can trust her absolutely. Once you have met the Chinese woman; she does not speak English by the way, and you have studied what she has in her possession, you can give the green light for an extraction. If you are not satisfied, you should pretend that you are planning to get her out. There is just a chance that this is a trap for their security service to find out how and where many of their wanted people have disappeared to. In the latter case, we will extract you both immediately. If it were just documents, we would not need to go to all this trouble, but if she has a vaccine, we must get that back here, and the only safe way to do that is by you guys.'

'How will we know that the vaccine is pucker?' asked Jeremy.

'You won't,' Adrian shook his head. 'We are informed that it was tested over there, by exposing people to Covid-19 after they had been injected, they did not fall ill. The correspondence indicates that the vaccine was produced initially for those in official positions.'

'But that suggests that the virus was spread deliberately,' said Ladvia.

'Yes, it does,' said Adrian, 'but we will know more once we get the documentation.'

'So, how are you going to get us out?' Ladvia asked.

'By submarine,' answered Adrian. 'But there is some danger in that the depth of the water there is only about 230 feet even in the channel between Hong Kong and Taiwan, which makes tracking a sub much easier, whereas in the Pacific, and once past Taiwan or in the Indian Ocean, the depth is over 8,000 feet. However, we have a plan that should work. The South China Sea is one of the busiest in the world, so that means one can cloak a sub that is near to a large vessel such as an oil tanker or a large container ship. I have a great deal of faith in my friend John Scott-Jones who is Chief of Staff of our forces at this time, and he has organised your escape plan.'

Jeremy nodded, 'Well we know how important this trip is, and we'll do our best.' He went to shake Adrian's hand, but Adrian told him that was the quickest way to pass on the virus. Adrian slapped him on the back and wished them both god speed.

The plane did not leave until early evening, so they both bought some books from the newsagent nearby. Jeremy picked the Shanghai Incident by James Dalby, Ladvia picked the Gorazde Incident, which was a story about her early life, written by the same author. She said later that she never grew tired of reading the book.

First class was comfortable, and there was enough space to ensure the passengers were not too near each other, a matter that was now becoming more important.

THE SCOTTISH PREROGATIVE

Incorporating

THE WUHAN AFFAIR

THE IDEA

Chapter 25

The next day Adrian was driven to Simpsons on the Strand, and he told his driver that he would walk back to his office, one of the good things about being head of MI6, very few people knew his face.

John Desmond had already arrived, and he stood up as Adrian approached the table. 'I won't shake your hand,' he smiled as he sat down, 'but my name is Adrian.'

'And mine is John,' he said.

'I see you've come in mufti,' (civilian clothes) said Adrian smiling.

John Desmond nodded, 'Yes, I believe that you are meeting someone in uniform might cause a stir.'

'I doubt it,' answered Adrian, laughing, 'I am the most unrecognisable man in London.'

The waiter came to the table and Adrian ordered a bottle of a red Shiraz. 'I hope that meets with your approval?'

John shook his head, 'Believe it or not, I don't drink alcohol, I prefer to stick to water, far safer.'

Adrian had had time to study John Desmond, he was a tall man and he exuded confidence, had an easy manner, obviously a good leader, but not a man to cross, he decided. John looked superbly fit.

After chatting about the problems of the day, particularly the Covid-19 virus, and ordering their meal, John said, 'The Chief of Staff asked me to meet with you, and that you had a proposal to put,' he looked at Adrian enquiringly.

Adrian told him about Jeremy and Ladvia and what they had been doing in Scotland but because they had been compromised, they were being reassigned to Washington DC to act as the British liaison between MI6 and the CIA, he didn't mention that they had been sent to Hong Kong.

'The fact is John, the world is changing, as is the way we are fighting our battles.'

'Cyber war?' queried John.

'Yes, but that is only one thing we have to contend with, we believe that Covid-19 may have been a deliberate plant, but that is not why I am talking to you now.' The food came and there was a brief interlude as both started eating.

'The PM has been on to me about the Iranian situation, where a number of our citizens are imprisoned. Without causing a major war, we are helpless in doing anything about it.' Adrian put a succulent piece of steak into his mouth.

'Hmm, so you want the equivalent of a gun boat diplomacy?'

Adrian laughed, 'yes, but with deny-ability. Any way that is just one problem we are facing at this time, I am concerned about a situation nearer to home and that is the danger of Scottish independence.' Adrian went on to give John a clear brief of what was known so far on Angus Stuart and his closeness to Russia. 'We suspect that this earth moving company on the border is somehow implicated with a

Russian connection. We have sent inspectors in, but they did not produce anything untoward. Nevertheless, there are some matters that concern us, one is that they have a runway there that is larger than the original plan. Why? We also know that a huge basement was built but there appears to be no access to it from the factory. Why? Planes flying in with CKD parts tend to land well after HM Customs have left for the night. Why? The current work force must leave by 6pm. Why? Finally, there is a very heavy guard on the entrance, with electronic poles and the whole area which is over several acres appears totally secure, it is ringed with double closed fencing and every other stake has a CCTV camera and the top of the fencing has razor wire. Why?'

'Hmm, well it appears either they have something to hide, or the equipment they are building is expensive. The latter is the case of course, but no one is likely to pinch a large digger or earthmover that could easily be identified, and it is most unusual for a large enclosing fence to be used, so it looks as though they have something to hide, but what?' John finished his steak and took a drink of water.

Adrian nodded. 'Okay, John, let me give you the large picture. What we need is an operation headed by someone like yourself used to dealing with covert situations. Mossad have one, the CIA have one which they call SAD, I would like to set up a paramilitary organisation called SWORD, "Special War organisation for Research and Defence.' The team would be a small one, but with the power to request SAS personnel in numbers if required. If you accept the job, you will not lose any seniority, nor would the core members of your team, in fact you would be more likely to get further promotion more quickly, particularly if you were successful. So, although I would set up the parameters, you would still be in the regiment. Your pay and those of your men going on special missions would increase. However, the downside would be that if you were caught, there would be a denial and you would be on your own. If you and your men accept, the first job would be to find out what is going on in that factory. One more thing, we have a large budget, which means the sort of equipment you need to do a job would be available, no questions asked.'

The lunch finished, John thanked Adrian for the offer, and said he would talk to his non-commissioned officers to see if they would be interested. I would need another couple of men, on the team, one a junior officer who is a language buff and the other an engineer.'

It was a week later that John Desmond contacted Adrian and said that it was a go.

THE SCOTTISH PREROGATIVE

Incorporating

THE WUHAN AFFAIR

HONG KONG

Chapter 26

Jeremy and Ladvia had a good flight but nevertheless were quite tired by the time they reached Hong Kong, after spending twelve hours in the aeroplane. Once disembarked they cleared immigration and customs. Once outside, they noticed that there was still a lot of damage in and around the airport from the recent riots, but it seemed noticeably quiet for a major airport despite it being 08.00 hours.

They took a taxi to the hotel, and as they had eaten breakfast on the plane, they fell into bed and slept until the late afternoon.

They did not go out that evening but ate in one of the hotel's excellent restaurants. For the following two days, they did the tourist thing. The amount of damage in the area was considerable, but both Jeremy and Ladvia enjoyed the specially laid on tours. Had anyone been watching, they would in no way have created suspicion. On the third day, they walked to Wan Chai Park. They were only ten minutes into their walk when they noticed a tall, good-looking, and well-dressed woman coming towards them, her blond hair gathered into a ponytail. It appeared that she was going to pass them by, but she suddenly turned. 'Mr and Mrs Brown, I assume?' Jeremy was cautious, but when she produced a photograph taken of them at Gidleigh Park, he relaxed.

Obviously, Belinda or Archie, had taken the shot without them knowing. However, Ladvia was not satisfied, as she pointed out later that the authorities could have hacked such a photo. 'As you know, our real name is not Brown.'

'Yes, it is Kirkham, and your original name was Silonovic, but you used the name Lavinia Johnson at one stage of your career.'

Ladvia laughed, 'well perhaps you know too much, perhaps I should kill you.'

Mrs Carpenter smiled, 'my name is Gloria, and you had better not kill me yet, as we have some important business to conduct. You were of interest to the local security groups here, but after day one they found other fish to fry. As we are in an open space, we can talk freely. The person concerned is under our protection and perfectly safe. The problem comes when we move her.'

'Is she to be trusted?' Asked Ladvia.

'Yes, she worked for the Beijing government as a translator, stenographer, and secretary to one of the ministers, and she was the one who took notes from a recent high-level meeting. She has received a vaccination from the Covid-19 virus, but as she said she felt unwell, they gave her a week's leave. It was her doctor brother working in the Wuhan facility who received an order to spread the virus. He refused but before he left the facility, he managed to conceal a vial holding the vaccine. He knew if he opened it, it may become contaminated, so he sent it under special cover to his sister. Shortly afterwards, he died under suspicious circumstances, which persuaded Mei-lieu Wong; that's her name, to try to get the vaccine out and to atone for her brother's death. It just so happened that a relation of hers lived in Hong Kong and was involved in the Pro-Democracy Movement.

'So, when do we move, and how...'

'Tonight, we need to get her out before the goons find her, the security apparatus has already twigged that she disappeared from her home and somehow got out of Wuhan, which is currently a closed city. They have been active in trying to find her here, so there is no time to spare. For your interest, there is a move by the Chinese government to use the news of Covid-19 to crack down on the recent troubles in Hong Cong. The indication is that they are going to make it a treasonable offence to protest against the government. Treason here carries a death sentence. This shows the world what an appalling bunch of people run the Chinese government. They are attempting to do this under the cover of the virus scare.

'Now to give you your instructions. You should be outside the Mandarin at 20.00 hours. You should have no luggage with you, we will pick that up later and have it sent on to you. Someone will approach you and ask you to go with them to a nearby car. From there he will drive you to a departure point. The password is "shibboleth", the Chinese have difficulty in pronouncing it but the person who picks you up will be able to pronounce properly. I must go now, to ensure all the arrangements go according to plan. Just one other thing, if no one shows up, wait for ten minutes, then return to your room.' Gloria turned around and walked in the opposite direction.

Adrian and Ladvia had an early dinner and went back to their suite where Ladvia unpacked her handbag and filled it with requisites needed for a long journey. They were standing outside the front of the hotel at five minutes to eight but by 8.15, no one had come so they both returned to their rooms, where they hoped to get a telephone call. Suddenly there was a loud banging on their door. Ladvia opened it, and two Hong Kong police officers rushed in. A senior officer followed them. As they were being cuffed, the senior officer said: 'Mr Jeremy Kirkham and Mrs Patricia Kirkham, you are both under arrest for security breaches against the State of Hong Kong.' he turned to the two officers, 'put these people in my car, and I will take them to security headquarters, where they will be questioned.'

They were both bundled through the reception area, causing much consternation to other visitors, and put roughly in the back of the senior policeman's car. The two policemen then climbed into a Jeep and drove off. Several things were going through both Jeremy's and Ladvia's mind; was Gloria Carpenter a spy, or had she too been arrested. If so, would she give them away. They had nothing to incriminate them, but were they in fact being watched all the time? Would Adrian somehow intervene? The idea of spending years in a Hong Kong institution did not appeal, and Ladvia was now thinking how she could overpower the senior policeman who was driving the car. Certainly, he was going too fast to contemplate any rough stuff until the car stopped and then she realised that they may be going straight into to a police facility. She took a deep breath, both she and Jeremy had rehearsed their story in case of things going wrong and both knew that they would be separated during any interrogation, one or the other would be told that one of them had confessed. Of course, both knew that neither would, but that did not stop their minds from racing. Their position did not look good.

THE SCOTTISH PREROGATIVE

Incorporating

THE WUHAN AFFAIR

THE TEAM

Chapter 27

Several days before John Desmond's call to Adrian he had a meeting with his men and told them of his earlier discussion that week. He was careful to say that if they accepted, some of the roles may be highly dangerous and if caught, the British government would not lift a hand to help them.

Kieran McCauley, the second in command of the small team was from an Irish family who had moved to Liverpool before he was born, he was tough and looked it. He had short ginger hair and a muscular frame, which he kept in trim being a regular visitor to the gym when not on duty. A stranger looking at him would get the definite impression he was not a man to mess with. He reminded people of the English cricketer, Ben Stokes. He was a Senior Warrant Officer.

Josh Beeton was the great, great grandson of Mrs Beeton, the famous cook. He had transferred from signals to the SAS about three years previously. He was a small man with a ready smile, and nothing fazed him. He was not the smartest of soldiers from a dress point of view and wore his hair longer than the regiment required, but he was extremely intelligent, an absolute wizard on a computer and any type of signals equipment.

Carl Ronson was constantly ribbed about his name because his speciality concerned explosives, he was the quietest of the team and the deepest thinker. As his profession required, he had a cautious nature. A man of average height, he looked and spoke like the Yorkshire man he was, his ruddy complexion could have been mistaken for a Dales farmer, which is what his father was.

The last member of the team was Andrew Johnson who had joined the SAS from the engineers, the same set up that John Desmond came from, which is how they knew each other. Andrew: a slim individual with blond hair, blue eyes, fair skin, and well educated at a well-known public school. He had originally studied architecture at Leeds University, but much to the consternation of his parents threw it up to join the army to train as an engineer. Andrew was gay, but not overtly so. He had shown himself to be an excellent member of the team during the recent operation in Nigeria.

A new member to the team was Lieutenant George Maskell, he was young but showed real promise. George's ability was languages, German, French, Arabic, Mandarin, Farsi and Russian. While being technically senior to Kieran, it was accepted that Kieran was the number two.

After explaining the problem of the factory in Scotland, John then suggested a method of tackling it. 'My first call will be to the Chief of Police in the area concerned, to see if he has any worthwhile information. Andrew it will be your job to contact the factory inspectors who have investigated the plant.

'Josh you should carry out a complete reconnaissance of the outside of the area on computer, using Google Earth and any information held by our friends at GCHQ. Also trawl the social media and see if there is anything there to give any clues.'

'Yeah, I will get a Google map of the area, and Andrew can get a basic schematic of the plant, including the airfield. You have said that it is secure, so I will look for the best method of getting inside without causing the guys there to be aware of any insertion. Once in, we will need to build a hide so we can carry out an in-depth investigation. Obviously, we will not do this until you give the order.'

'Good, okay, Carl, I want you to go with Kieran, we need to know what arms they have, if any and whether the ground around the inside of the area is mined. I personally doubt it, but their security is most unusual for the type of vehicles they are building there. You should take some radar kit with you, so if we decide to go in, you can use it to determine how large their alleged basement area is. Look for obvious entry points and areas where we could set up an LUP (Lay-up Point) either outside or inside the factory area.

'George, I want you to go in with Andrew and get access with the factory inspectors. Your job will be to simply listen to the chat, apparently there are some Latvian's guards there, and they speak Russian.

'Okay, you will all be in clothes appropriate for the job. You can take arms but be careful how you use them. Now this is an external surveillance operation. Be careful not to raise any alarm. You have until tomorrow night to report back to me, and I will be staying at a safe house that was rented by a Mr Jeremy Kirkham, I will give you the coordinates and you all have my secure telephone number. It is nearby, so if you need a bed for the night, there is plenty of room.'

There were a few questions, but after that they all left to make their individual preparations. John Desmond picked up the phone to the Chief of Police in the area and they agreed to meet the next day.

THE SCOTTISH PREROGATIVE

Incorporating

THE WUHAN AFFAIR

THE ARREST

Chapter 28

The car driven by the senior policemen was going fast, with flashing lights blazing. Both Ladvia and Jeremy were in the back still handcuffed, but surprisingly the cuffs were not attached to anything but their wrists.

Ladvia leaned over to Jeremy, she whispered, 'there is only one man driving to deal with, when he slows down, we could overpower him between us.'

'My thoughts exactly, but he is going too fast now, deliberately so. My thoughts are why? Why did the two policemen not join him? Why are we going in the opposite direction from the police headquarters and finally if we have been compromised by Gloria or another, where would we go?'

It was at that moment the senior policeman looked in his mirror, 'I know exactly what you two are thinking' he laughed. 'You'll just have to trust me for the next ten minutes, and then you'll be free. I am afraid it was necessary to do what we did for public consumption. My name is Chen Wang, and I am a senior superintendent In the Hong Kong Police force. As you will shortly learn from Mrs Carpenter, I have been supporting the British democratic view for many years, but now I am due for retirement and the British have promised me an advisory position in the UK. I have already sent my wife and two children over there on "holiday",' he added.

The car came to a skidding stop just near Pier 9, deserted apart from a fast police launch tied alongside. Chen got out and with his key undid the cuffs. 'That feels better,' said Jeremy, rubbing his wrists. Ladvia however was still suspicious, until she saw Gloria on the boat. Chen led them to the side of the craft and told them to jump on board. Gloria stepped forward and gave both Ladvia and Jeremy a hug and then withdrew stating that hugs were no longer acceptable because of the virus. 'I am sorry I couldn't forewarn you, Chen learned you had been compromised, so we had to act fast. There were members of the security force from the mainland watching the hotel entrances.' Jeremy's eyes narrowed, 'but how?'

'I don't think you were compromised by anyone here; it is just that there are secret police from the mainland because of the riots, and they have infiltrated those causing the troubles and are helping to accelerate matters, in order to have an excuse to crack down harder. You are arriving in the middle of a pandemic, and that would have made them suspicious, and frankly I am surprised it took them so long to put a watch on you, perhaps they thought the local police were handling immigration suspects. Anyway, you will find Mei-lieu Wong, below, she has been in hiding here. She has some important documents and a vial holding the vaccine. I must go and leave you with Chen, who will be accompanying you and Mei-lieu to the UK.' She was up and over the side before Jeremy could ask how they would get there. Obviously, the boat they were on, was not fit for such a long journey. He then remembered Adrian saying that they would take them off by submarine, but he knew the risk could be high, as the Chinese were patrolling the area in force.

They heard a rumble as the engine as it started up, and Gloria on the pier released the aft line from the pier, the bow line was taken in by a young man who seemingly appeared from nowhere, and he jumped back onto the pier as the launch was pulling away. Jeremy took in the aft line. Within minutes they were moving quickly out towards the sea, with the red-light blinking on top of the cabin, showing it was a police launch.

Once away from the Hong Kong area, the throttle was pushed forward and the launch surged at full speed, about 35 knots, away from Hong Kong Island, heading in the direction of Taiwan. It was only then that Mei-lieu Wong, came out from the cabin and introduced herself, but she spoke little English. She was a slight woman and looked a little frightened as well she might, had she been caught, she would certainly have faced the death penalty. They had been going about 30 minutes when they received a call from a Chinese destroyer. They could see its mast light in the distance.

'Calling police launch heading North east, this is destroyer X one two zero what is your destination?' The language was in Chinese. Chen handed the wheel to Jeremy showing the direction he should steer. He picked up the microphone, 'Calling destroyer X one two zero, we are police launch 56 Alpha, we have been alerted to an unauthorised fishing vessel heading from Taiwan which we suspect is a smuggler, do you copy on your radar?'

There was a brief interlude, and then, 'Negative 56 alpha, how large is the vessel?'

'We understand around 20 metres,'

'Okay, it will not show up on our radar until it is closer, we will keep watch and advise. We do have a large Cargo vessel travelling south at 192 degrees at around 20 knots at this time.'

'Roger, we'll keep an eye on that, thank you, X one two zero, out.'

After around ten minutes, the cargo vessel loomed into sight, its lights showed it was about two miles away. Chen reckoned that they would reach it in about another ten minutes. He then called his base. 'This is police launch 56 Alpha, we are...'

A voice broke into the transmission, 'please switch to 16, this is an emergency.' Chen switched to 16 the emergency channel for all shipping. '56 Alpha, state your position please.'

Chen gave his rough co-ordinates. '56 Alpha, you were not authorised to take the police launch, but we have an urgent message from the Pro-Democracy Movement, one of their more militant units have placed a bomb on board your vessel, it is on a time switch. You must return at once, do you copy?'

'Copy base, do you know the time set for it to blow?'

'Negative 56 Alpha, you must return at once.' The voice at the other end sounded stressed.

'Thank you base, we are now searching for the item, and may have to...' Chen switched off. Jeremy who had been listening, raised his eyebrows, just visible in the half light.

Chen kept the launch heading towards the cargo vessel. They reached it quickly to find a submarine tower partly submerged on the blind side of the huge ship within about twenty yards of it. Chen turned his boat round to travel at the same speed and closed in. Two sailors appeared on deck and the four people on the launch transferred to the Submarine, which immediately submerged. The empty launch was left wallowing well behind, suddenly it blew up. Chen had pressed the button that created the demise of 56 Alpha. He explained later that they wanted to ensure that it appeared that everyone on board had died. The two policemen who had helped on shore were to disappear in Hong Kong and help the Pro-Democracy Party. It would be assumed that they were on the boat and that they had been blown up by militants.

It did not work entirely as planned. A Chinese air force plane flew over the British Cargo ship several times taking photographs but did not try to interrupt its passage. Several hours later Jeremy and Ladvia received an invitation to meet the Captain in his cabin. 'Phew that was close' he said when he offered them a seat and a drink. 'My name is Stephen Castle, and I run this old tub. To be honest with you we were concerned that they would stop the cargo ship, which would have left us exposed.'

Jeremy looked surprised, 'but we were submerged, how could they...'

Stephen laughed, 'we relied on the cargo ship to hide us from the destroyer's radar, because of the depth of the water where we were, we could have been picked up. We travelled down from Japan, where we were holding exercises, so we just joined up with the British cargo ship and used their bulk to hide under. I must say the Captain of the vessel was not pleased, particularly so when we surfaced to get you guys in. Fortunately, it took only seven minutes to get you aboard, but the Chinese were suspicious. The destroyer radioed the cargo ship and said they were going to board; this was the same destroyer that was aft of us. The Captain refused permission and said if they did interfere with his journey, it would cause an International incident. He then called our Ambassador in Taiwan and complained. Nevertheless, the destroyer followed us for over fifty miles before turning back. They believe the South China Sea belongs to them, but it is one of the busiest channels in the world, over \$5 trillion goes through annually, so it wouldn't be just Britain who would be cross if they started an Iran type incursion.

'Anyway, I called you in to tell you the plan from here. We are meeting the Queen Elizabeth just south of Sri Lanka and you will be transferred onto that ship. Our sailing time is approximately 6.6 days, and we will be going north up the Malacca Strait into the Indian Ocean. From there we will be heading West.'

'Isn't that our new Aircraft Carrier?' Asked Jeremy.

'Indeed, it is, and I expect a lot more comfortable than this old tub. I do not know what you are carrying, but it must be important because they are going to fly whatever you have straight to Cyprus, where we have a base. From there another plane will take it to the UK.'

'What about us?' Jeremy asked.

'Well, it's slow boat through the Suez, and then to the NATO base in Crete. You will spend a couple of days there and fly out to the UK on a regular C130 via Gibraltar. Should be home well before Christmas,' he exaggerated the situation and smiled.

'Well, we were on holiday when we were called in, so I suppose we should just sit back and enjoy it, at least the weather is good.' Jeremy wondered if there was any specific news from the UK, he was thinking about the Scottish situation.

'It's all about the Covid-19 virus, it's causing havoc over there, and the USA have stopped flights from the UK and most of Europe, so the best place for you to be is here.'

'Ah, the USA was our next stop, so I hope they sort things out before we get back,' said Jeremy, as he got up to leave the

Captain's cabin. He and Ladvia thanked Stephen Castle for the drink and went back to tell the others the news.

As they vacated the cabin, Stephen Castle asked them to apologise to the other two passengers, stating that there simply was not room in his cabin for more than three people.

THE SCOTTISH PREROGATIVE

Incorporating

THE WUHAN AFFAIR

THE START

Chapter 29

The next day, John Desmond called in to the police station in Berwick. Although in England, he did not want to alert the Scottish authorities that they were investigating the locality around the factory just north of the border. Superintendent Hamish McDonald welcomed him. After ordering coffee, Hamish asked what he could do to help. 'I know from my superiors in the south, that the new factory just over the border is of interest,' he said. 'In fact, we were involved in a missing person case, which took us to the factory, and we carried out a search of the land around it but found nothing. We were however hampered by the people running the company, they were very protective of the area. It is strange because it was a whole family, man, wife and two small children. They just disappeared. Their dog was found wandering around outside the fence. We know that the family were very keen on camping, but...' he shrugged his shoulders. 'I have a gut feeling that the factory and the family were connected, but I have absolutely nothing to go on.'

John nodded, 'Have you heard any stories or rumours about the factory in the locality?'

Hamish smiled. 'There are a number, a farmer who complains about aeroplanes landing on their strip in the middle of the night, a woman out walking in the evening who swears she saw a tank, the man and his son who were flying a drone nearby was shot down by security people inside the grounds, the two lovers who were attacked by dogs belonging to the factory, I could go on.'

'So, they are not popular with the locals?'

'That's an understatement, but on the other hand, they provide good employment in an area where there was none, so the Scottish Office tend to ignore complaints, as do the local police.'

'When you searched the area, did you come across anything unusual?'

Hamish thought for a few seconds, 'we noticed a lot of caterpillar type tracks on the area, and we were told that the earth moving equipment was tested there, which is why they needed such a large space. That seemed plausible enough. The thing I could not understand was why they were so security conscious, as if they had something to hide. It is the problem with being a policeman, you are always looking for...' he paused, 'for reasons, when the story given does not seem to fit with the circumstances. Quite honestly, I thought that it was a covert government establishment, manufacturing things other than earth moving equipment and this thought was supported by the obtuse way the Scottish Government Office answered questions.'

'The Scottish Government Office?'

'Hmm, we were always put through to Angus Stuart personally, apparently it is his baby.'

'Do you know who looks after the security?'

'They employ their own people, they are from Latvia, but their papers were correct as we understand each one had been checked carefully. Most of the workers are local except for the very highly skilled, but their shift finishes at 18.00 and the factory closes down overnight.'

John thanked Hamish and went to the rented farmhouse to await his team in the evening. He had bought several pizzas and beer to enable them all to have enough sustenance.

George and Andrew were the first to arrive and John told them of his visit to the policeman in Berwick.

Andrew confirmed that the chief Factory inspector was a Scot with a broad accent. Andrew reported, 'the inspectors had recently been at the factory and had not come across anything untoward. But they did let slip that the Scottish Government Office was not really interested in their findings, and so, like the police Superintendent you mentioned,' he looked up at John, 'he felt that there was something hush hush going on there and they were not encouraged to find fault. After leaving the inspector's office we decided to walk around the site on the outside of the security fence. We noticed that some trees near the fence had been cut down and a 3-metre area was devoid of vegetation. This was the same around the two miles or so of the boundary, and Andrew had made sketches of certain parts of the area.

Josh came back next with some interesting information from his computer searches and finally Kieran and Carl. John Desmond suggested they eat first and then talk afterwards.

George told the team what they had found, and Andrew pulled out his drawings of the site which they all studied. 'One of the things we noticed was that they had set up another fence to screen the runway, but there was a lot of activity there, suggesting that there was perhaps an aircraft due in tonight or tomorrow.'

221

'I can check if a flight plan has been filed.' Said John.

Kieran and Carl were late in arriving and they had much more information. Kieran told Carl to start off. 'Okay,' he sat down and stretched his legs out. 'I'm a bit stiff as I was holed up in a small hollow by the exterior fence. There is something illegal going on there, not only do they have complete security in their fencing, but they have spotlights that react to movement, I set one off as I was moving away, and within two minutes there was a Jeep type vehicle with armed guards on the other side of the fence where I had been. The CCTV cameras could not have caught me, because I was too low, and I had used periscope type equipment to study the ground the other side of the fence. From what I could see, they have planted IED's around the perimeter. Not only is that illegal, but it's fucking lethal for anyone getting over the fence. There are no warning signs either.'

'So, are our specially made ladders capable of adjusting?' asked John.

'Yes, they can be altered to fit, but we have more than enough evidence to force our way in there,' said Kieran.

'What time was it...?' asked John.

'Just after 19.00 hours.'

'So, it was dark?' said Josh from the back of the room.

'There's more,' added Kieran.

'Go on,' John looked on as Kieran took a swig of beer from the bottle.

'Well, while Carl was in his hollow, I spotted about 30 guys coming out of nowhere, and exercising near the trees away from the fence area. When they disappeared, another, different bunch appeared. They were not guarding; they were soldiers and special types of soldiers at that. I reckon they were Spetsnaz. You remember we came up against these guys in Crete, I recognised the way they train. The thing was that some were obviously sick.' Kieran wiped his lips with the back of his hand.

'So, these guys must be living below ground, which answers the problem of the large basement area that no one appears to have found an entrance to.'

'So where do we go from here?' Asked Josh.

John Desmond grimaced. 'We have to get in there and find the evidence, the question is how?'

'We create a diversion,' answered Carl. 'One thing I noticed was that they appear to be on the electricity grid, they may have their own generators, but they probably won't switch them on immediately in case of a failure and even if they do, they'll only light up the essential areas. With the specialist ladders we brought up with us, we could be over their fence in less than 20 seconds.'

'What about the IED's?' asked Andrew.

'We'll carry out a heat search with some equipment I've got. With the cold weather we have up here now, the ground will be warmer than the IED's.' said Carl.

'Well, that's true,' answered George, 'but how are you to use that equipment without setting off all the alarms?'

'Okay, the ladders we have create a bridge, so you have the first part which takes you above the fence, the second part bends to bridge across the top of the fence and the last part goes down the other side, this is run by a small electric motor and air pressure as it would be too difficult for an individual to manipulate it by hand alone. What we must do, is lengthen the last connected ladder so that it lands a good three metres from the fence. We can do that and then utilise our heat gadget to create a pathway.' said Carl.

'What if the other end of the ladder lands on an IED?' Josh asked.

'We're fucked,' answered Carl, 'but it's a chance we have to take, at least no one would get hurt, and we could withdraw the ladder before anyone could reach us.'

'Do you reckon three metres is enough?' Josh asked.

'Yeah, I reckon any IED's would be buried well within the three-meter area, anything outside would be picked up by my heat seeker gadget. So, I would be the first over the fence, and...' Carl was interrupted by Josh.

'There may be a better way.'

'Oh?' Carl looked at him with eyebrows raised.

'I'll have a word with my Friends at GCHQ, I think we could organise for them to do a heat seek by satellite, they've got some really sensitive equipment there, so, I'll ask the question.'

'Good, that's what we'll do,' said John Desmond after reiterating the groups reports, so the team was fully in the picture. John Continued, 'First thing in the morning you can call them on the satellite phone, which is secure and see what they can find. If that is a go, we can organise the lights to go out, and that is your job, Andrew. You will have to find the substation that deals with this area and disable it in the same way we did in Greece. I think it would take a repair team a little longer to simply find out the switch had blown, particularly if the padlock had been changed.'

Andrew nodded, 'Yes, in a country area at night, I reckon it would give us at least three hours if not longer. In fact, it might be better to blow the fucker up.'

'Good, now who goes in?' John Desmond asked. Hands shot up. 'No, it's got to be Carl, Kieran and George. Kieran will lead,' John turned to George, 'sorry George, but Kieran is by the best man in a fire-fight, Carl knows his explosives and you could be useful if you come across an inmate, because of your Russian. Josh, Andrew, and I will stay this side of the fence. Once Andrew has completed his job, Josh and I will manoeuvre the ladder and once the inside crew are over, we will pull it back in case the ungodly get their lights on quickly. Carl, you can give Andrew whatever explosives he needs. I will arrange for a company of SAS to be on hand if there is real trouble, so we will be the cavalry if things go wrong. Now what about dogs?' John looked at Kieran.

'Yeah, well we have the dog dazer...'

'Yes, but you'll remember in Nigeria, it kept the brutes at bay, but they still stood well back and kept barking with their snouts pointing in your direction.' John smiled.

'Yeah, we'll take a heap of aniseed, and spread it around the IED's, that'll give 'em something to yell about.' said Carl grimly.

'I didn't realise that Carl was an animal lover,' teased Andrew.

'Okay, now the main purpose of your surveillance is threefold. 1. find out where the opening is to the basement area, and if you can get a peek inside, all the better to see what is going on in below. 2. By then I will know if they have filed a flight plan, and I will call if they have, so expect the plane any time after 02.00 hours. 3. If you have a chance of persuading any of the people from inside to "jump ship" and

225

bring them back for questioning, so much the better. Stay connected at all times.' John got up, 'I don't know about you guys, but we have a busy day tomorrow, so I'm going to my bed, good night.' With that he walked out of the room.

The next morning when they had gathered for breakfast, Kieran made three other requests. 'Further to our talks last night, we feel that we need more than one company of the SAS, as to surround the base will take more than a company. I suggest we need a flame thrower operator with equipment, so as soon as we have gone over the fence, that area should be blasted, thus giving the impression that some of their electrical equipment has shorted out. This would protect our escape route, should we have to get out quickly as that would deal with the lights and cameras. We also need to have a mobile missile launcher on standby, if they have heavy equipment in there, and we need to be able to blast the area to prevent it moving out. I am thinking about that woman who said she saw a tank. We need to take in a light ladder which we can hide once inside, this would be used for a quick exit.'

'Okay, Kieran,' said John. 'I have already dealt with your first point, by this afternoon we will have three companies active. I will ask them to bring a flame thrower with them and a body who knows how to use it.

'I agree with your point about the ladder, I'll make sure we have one suitable, you don't need anything special, unlike the one used for getting in. I will have to persuade the powers that be to produce a mobile missile launcher, but I agree you may need some heavy artillery there, even if we do not use it. It will have to be sent up from the Catterick Garrison. Okay, you all have your daily tasks, get to it and we meet tonight at 18.00 hours.'

As he was going out of the door, Kieran called back, 'Don't forget the aniseed Boss...'

John laughed, 'get the hell out of here, McCauley.' The door slammed behind him.

THE SCOTTISH PREROGATIVE

Incorporating

THE WUHAN AFFAIR

THE TRANSFER

Chapter 30

The submarine had reached the Indian Ocean when the Captain called for Jeremy. 'Good news for you guys, we are meeting up with HMS Queen Elizabeth tomorrow morning and you will be transferred to that ship.

'Now, because they are desperate for the vaccine, let alone the Chinese lady who has certain documentation, they have taken on board a Lockheed Martin F-35 Lightning II trainer jet, it is a trainer version F39C. This one will have extra fuel tanks and a second seat in the cockpit so will refuel at the NATO base in Crete. Between here and Crete, a flight plan is already agreed, avoiding sensitive areas. The pilot will change in Crete, so the package including the vaccine will arrive in Brize Norton in less than 3 hours. Mei-lieu will overnight in Crete, under heavy protection and then be flown in a military C130 via Gibraltar. The whole distance is around 5,429 miles from where we are here, so in theory it will take the jet about nine hours plus the stoppage time for refuelling.'

The next day the transfer was made by utilising one of the helicopters from the carrier, and the submarine submerged. Within two hours Mei-lieu was in the F39C trainer with her package, and the jet took off heading east.

'Let us hope the package gets there without incident,' said Ladvia watching the jet trail as it disappeared. 'What did you think of her?' asked Jeremy.

'A strange woman and very frightened. She did not appear out of her cabin once while we were sailing. But I suppose she has led a very sheltered life in Beijing and the shock of her doctor brother being killed by the state, must have been traumatic for her.'

Yes, you are right, I hope she is treated well when she reaches the UK, and more importantly, given a secure environment in which to live, but it will be difficult for her to fit in. On the other hand, the Foreign Office will be delighted to get hold of someone who obviously knows a lot of secrets from within the senior party apparatus. The other person, the one who saved us, is our policeman friend, I understand he has been seasick for most of the journey.' Jeremy took a book down from the shelf in the officer's cabin where they had slept. It gave details of the aircraft carrier and how to get around it.

'He is a cleithrophobe, a fear of being trapped in a small space,' said Ladvia. 'It can have a marked effect on one.'

'Well at least he has plenty of room on this ship. I understand that we are invited to dinner tonight with the Captain, so we will meet our friend and hopefully find out when we can get off.'

They both enjoyed the sail, and, in the evening, they met up with the Superintendent of Police whose full name was Chen Baker-Wang. Chen was half British and half Chinese and proved to be an interesting dinner companion talking about the situation in Hong Kong. While chatting after dinner with an excellent brandy, not allowed to the officers while sailing, the Captain was handed an urgent message. 'Oh,' he said, 'I am very much afraid that we are not going to

229

Cyprus as originally intended. We have been ordered to the Gulf. Please keep that information to yourself, as I will not be letting our team know until tomorrow. My orders are to attach you to security Chen, and he turned to Jeremy, 'Adrian Bradley wants you to call him tomorrow. He says not to worry as the kids are fine.' He looked up from the message, 'kids?'

Ladvia laughed, 'we get the message.' She said.

THE SCOTTISH PREROGATIVE
Incorporating
THE WUHAN AFFAIR

SHEREPOV IS UNHAPPY

Chapter 31

General Sherepov arrived in his office early. He had not heard from Angus Stuart, and he was angry. He told his aide to get him on a secure line. It was about an hour later that Angus rang back.

'What the hell is going on over there,' Sherepov yelled, 'you have an excellent chance of proceeding with our plan now that Britain is caught up in the Corvid-19, You have two hundred and fifty Spetsnaz over there to see you through, the longer you wait the more our plan is compromised.'

Angus could feel a sweat building on his forehead, and it was not due to Covid-19. 'The problem I have, is that Britain have just given Scotland a huge boost to help to save the economy, for us to secede now would not be supported by the people.'

'To hell with the people, we have already given you large sums to set up the factory, and you have the people and the machinery to complete the plan, we have already offered you £7 billion annually, we can increase that if that is a problem, but I want action.'

'Well, the first minister...'

'If the first minister is a problem, we'll get rid of her. You can leave that to us. I am sending one of our senior officers to assess the situation, he will be on tonight's flight,' The phone slammed down.'

Sherepov shouted to his aide. 'Sergi, get me General Volkov on the phone'

His aide passed the phone to him and when Volkov had answered. Sherepov took the receiver, 'General Volkov, you are to take an immediate flight to Sweden, and you are to ride on the special aircraft from there to our site in Scotland. Find out what is going on and call me tomorrow morning. It appears that the GRU men we sent over may have been compromised. He explained the reason for his impatience and closed the call.

Volkov caught the next plane to Sweden.

THE SCOTTISH PREROGATIVE

Incorporating

THE WUHAN AFFAIR

THE FIRST LOOK

Chapter 32

Everyone was back by 18.00 hours and John Desmond asked for reports.

Josh was first. 'My GCHQ pals have carried out a scan of the area and they reckon that there are only IED's scattered inside the areas where there is cover outside the immediate area, so for instance, there is a substantial wood on the north side, and although it has been cut back by 3 meters, it would still give good cover for intruders. Other areas are free, and they e-mailed me a map which I have here. Because of the size it is in 8 pieces, and I have printed them all out and stuck them together with tape.' Josh walked over to a table in the room and opened the map, which was studied by all of them.

'I still think we should adhere to the original plan,' said Kieran. Getting in is not a problem providing there are no lights, it is getting out that could be particularly difficult, particularly if we cannot get out until daylight. Having a wood to disappear into would be helpful.'

'I agree with Kieran' said Carl, 'thanks to Josh we know what we are facing, and I can very quickly create a path once we are in, which would be used in any escape.'

'We were also lucky in that the satellite picked up the opening in the grounds, it's like a reverse drawbridge, and is quite large, big enough to drive a vehicle through. I have the coordinates of that, so we will keep our eye on it as it appears, which may happen when they are letting the guys out from underneath the factory.'

'Right' said John, 'let me have those coordinates and I'll pass them onto to the mobile missile truck that is on its way as we speak. We also need to find a spot where it cannot be observed.'

'The wood, would be ideal' said Kieran, 'Because it has thick foliage and now, we have co-ordinates, the guys running the missile launcher do not have to see what they are firing at.'

John nodded, 'okay Kieran, I don't have to tell you what to look for, you know the score. There is a bag of aniseed outside, which you can pick up. Anyone going inside should take arms with them. If you manage to get hold of any of the ungodly, let George handle them, they'll feel safer speaking in their own language.'

'Now Andrew...'

'Yes boss, I have found the substation that controls their power, I will need to take an acetylene torch as it has a heavy padlock on the door. I will not bother to replace as I intend to vaporise the whole substation. Unlike the Greek situation, where we wanted to buy time, in this case we want to destroy it, so Carl is going to give me something suitable with a time switch. I am aiming for a blow around 01.00 hours.'

'Right, Josh you're with me,' said John, 'we'll be in the wood behind the fence where you guys get in, so if you have problems and need to vacate quickly, we will be able to cover you. In any case the factory should be surrounded by the SAS by then. The password is TROUSERS. The reason for using this is that Russian speakers have difficulty in pronouncing the 'ou' syllable. When you have done, get out but do not forget the transport plane is due to fly in around 02.00 hours, and I need to know what is coming in and going out? 'To save you taking a ladder in, we will keep the exit ladder outside the fence awaiting your return. The operator with the flame thrower will be ready to blast the fence and surveillance equipment once the lights go out.'

THE SCOTTISH PREROGATIVE

Incorporating

THE WUHAN AFFAIR

GENERAL VOLKOV

Chapter 33

General Volkov was not a happy man, he had told his number 2 to meet him in Moscow, but he was held up because of protests in the centre of the city and Volkov was thus on his own, in a cold noisy C130 aircraft sitting in the third seat in the cockpit. He had been surprised to see the aeroplane was carrying 100 beds already made up, and four nurses and a doctor in the hold section of the plane. The pilot told him they were on a mercy mission to pick up sick soldiers from the factory site. No sign had come from Angus Stuart that there were health problems there. Volkov's orders were to ensure the secession of Scotland, and if necessary, to remove the First Minister permanently. He knew that he had the men on the base capable of such an act, but he had been relying on the two men sent to kill Jeremy and Ladvia. Nothing had been heard from either. There was now a worry that they had run into some sort of trouble. (The fact that they had died in the car explosion was not known.)

Volkov knew Angus Stuart, and did not like him, he felt that his superiors had been too trusting, and that Angus was incompetent, but that was above his pay grade. He resolved to ensure that he dealt with Stuart as soon as he could but would have to wait until the formation of the new republic. He then started to worry about the number of fit soldiers, there were only 250 on the base, 80 of those were tank crew which left only 170, if 100 were sick, he knew that the takeover would have to be postponed. Unless they could strike quickly, the plan may be permanently lost. He did not relish reporting back that there had been a failure. Sherepov would be looking for scapegoats.

He reached the factory in the early morning the next day and was surprised at the throng that met him on the tarmac. Some were walking, some were on stretchers and the rest in body bags. Angus Stuart, who had arrived by car earlier, met the General off the plane. He did not shake his hand.

'How many are left?' snarled Volkov.

'Thirty-five, a lot were taken on a flight yesterday...'

'You mean out of 250 men you only have 35 remaining, why were we not told about this?'

The C130 took off with a roar drowning out Angus's reply. Volkov repeated his question.

Angus cowered, 'It all happened so quickly, the problem was exacerbated by them all being underground in an enclosed space. We had no medical kit nor doctors; we couldn't take them to hospital because they were all illegal.' He looked at General Volkov defiantly. 'We could still manage with thirty-five...'

'You stupid fool, who is going to man the tanks, who is going to man the covered low loaders, who is going to defend the bases on the roads where we planned to station the blocking areas? We have 12 T14 Armata's and twelve low loaders. Each tank has a compliment of 3. That is 36 to start. The men of the first Guards division are specially trained on these vehicles, you cannot just put three men in a modern tank and expect it to be battle ready. Then there are the covered low loaders which need a minimum of 24 men and after that the Spetsnaz who would form protection squadrons. The plan is dead Mr Stuart, the tanks must not fall into the hands of the British.'

Now, Angus Stuart realised that with the plan dead, he needed to save his own skin. To do that, he decided to contact the British authorities and tell them of the plot before it was enacted. If he could hand over the tanks to the British Army, he may be deemed a hero. His confidence came back to him. He turned to return to the factory with ideas buzzing in his head as to his next move. It was the last thing he did. Volkov pulled out his MD-446 Viking 9 mm semi-automatic and fired. He then walked over to the body and kicked it. He turned to a soldier by his side. 'Who has been left in command?'

'Major Korsky sir.'

'Right take me to him and then dispose of this body.'

Major Korsky stood to attention as General Volkov approached the basement area. 'Korsky, the plan is dead, get the men together and put charges on all the tanks, ensure that any paperwork regarding the design and maintenance is destroyed. The time is now 03.00 hours, all work must be completed by 05.00. when I expect another plane to arrive to extract us.'

It was only half an hour later that Volkov received a call, it was General Sherepov. 'Volkov, what is the situation?'

'I was about to call you sir; We have only...'

Sherepov interrupted, 'I have just had a call from the Kremlin to abort the mission, the decision by the Saudi's to drastically increase their oil production has crippled our cash availability, and what we have must be now used to ensure we remain politically secure.' (*Which means to keep President Putin in power, thought Volkov*). 'Whatever happens the British must not get hold of our tanks; you understand Volkov?'

'That's fine sir, I had already come to the same conclusion but for a different reason, the number of troops have been reduced to only 35, the rest have been repatriated because of the damned virus. I will ensure that we fix charges to all the equipment immediately.' He did not say that he had already taken the decision to do so.

'How many tanks can be fitted into a C130?' Sherepov asked.

'Only 2 sir we will have to destroy the rest of them.'

'Make sure you do Volkov, or don't come back.' The phone slammed down.

Volkov turned to Korsky, 'how are things going?'

'We are fine sir, we had a blackout at around 01.00 hours, but we fired up our generators, so it only took about fifteen minutes from our time. I had already had orders from Colonel Trostky to fit charges, as he realised that we could not go ahead with the plan...'

'Where is the Colonel...?'

'He was one of the casualties taken on the last plane, he was extremely ill, and may not survive.'

'Damn this virus,' said Volkov, 'Why were we not told...?'

'I understand that we had strict orders to only contact Mr Stuart, we did that over a week ago.'

Volkov compressed his lips, 'what stupidity,' he paused, 'You say you had a blackout?'

'Yes sir, we immediately searched the grounds and found the problem, there had been a major short on the lights on section C1 on the perimeter.'

Volkov frowned, 'show me the map of the perimeter fencing.'

Korsky went into an office and brought out a large map and unrolled it on a nearby table. He put his finger on the area of the fence that had been damaged.

'Is that a wood behind the fence?'

'Yes sir, but we have a clearance of three meters...'

'Has it occurred to you Korsky, that such a burn could have been deliberate to allow people to get over the fence?'

'It's doubtful sir because we have IED's in that area and...'

'Hmm, it is too much of a coincidence Korsky, send an armed squad of six men, do you have dogs?'

'Yes sir, the men guarding the entrance have 2 Rottwiellers.'

'Okay, get them and search the area, make it quick, I feel we could be expecting visitors.' As Korsky went off to get a squad together, Volkov started making plans for escape.

THE SCOTTISH PREROGATIVE

Incorporating

THE WUHAN AFFAIR

THE NIGHT SURVIELANCE

Chapter 34

Everything was in place and on time. The substation blew up, but as it was some distance away, the sound was muffled. Immediately the soldier with the flame thrower aimed it at the nearby lights and cameras and so fierce was it that part of the top of the fence melted too. Kieran, Carl, and George were over the fence quickly and Carl stuck small night lights to identify the IED's, when shining a torch in the area. Then they ran down towards the small wood with the river running through it. They had a good sighting of the runway from where they were situated. Kieran was looking around for a place to build a hide, when he found a small teddy bear in the long grass. Shortly afterwards he found earth had been dug in a copse, and he realised that it could be a grave. Ignoring that, he set up a night camera and night glasses. He had just finished when Carl returned from spreading aniseed near the area they had climbed over. He trusted that the dogs would smell the aniseed over anything else. They had been there for some time when they noted the C130 land, and they saw Volkov get off. Kieran took a picture of him with the night camera. He had seen pictures of Angus Stewart which Ladvia had taken surreptitiously when she was in the office in Edinburgh. He was shocked to see him gunned down by Volkov. 'It appears our enemies are falling out' he said grimly. Carl had been searching the area further north and he examined the tracks that criss-crossed the area. When he reached Kieran, he told him that the tracks were made by T14 Armata tanks. 'If they have those things underground, we have a problem. They are believed to be the one of the most advanced in world at this time.'

'What, better than the US Abraham?'

Carl nodded. 'If they have more than one, we may be able to take the first one out with a missile, but more than one, and they could create havoc. I need to get hold of John and inform him.'

'Okay,' answered Kieran, 'I'll do that, while you skirt around. Where the hell is George?' There was a sudden rustle through the trees. Kieran swivelled round, his gun at the ready. An unarmed man appeared followed by George. 'Hi Kieran, this is Gorgi, he is a Captain and part of the armoured division of the Russian Army. He cannot speak a word of English, but he decided to leave his compatriots who were taken back on the plane. A lot of them were ill with Covid-19. He believes he has had a mild form of it, so he is no longer a threat to others. He is knowledgeable about the plans that were to have been put into action this weekend. He also knows the position of the hydraulic "drawbridge" which is the only way in and out of the basement area. It is on the other side, quite close to the main entrance.'

'Okay', said Kieran, 'I don't see we can do much more from here, the best thing is to get Gorgi out and discuss further actions with the boss, I'll call him now to get the ladder ready.' Just as they were about to move, they heard the barking of the dogs approaching the area where John and Josh were waiting. It appeared that they were extremely excited having found the aniseed. Suddenly, there was an explosion, and shouts from the handlers. Obviously, there were casualties, but how many Kieran could not assess from his position. They moved slowly to the fringes of the small wood to see four people carrying another away from the scene. As soon as they were out of sight, Kieran, Carl, George and Gorgi ran for the fence. As they passed the area where the dogs had been, there was a human body lying motionless, there was no sign of the dogs.

A few minutes later, after exiting over the fence, John joined them. Josh had received a call from GCHQ that they had noted the opening to the base area. As a result, he had moved the Rapier Field Standard C mobile missile launcher to a more advantageous position.

George introduced Gorgi. 'He has told me that they have 12 Armata's underground, and they are all fitted with ground to air missiles. They have a speed of over 70 kph but due to there being only about 35 guys left and only enough skilled crews to drive three or four, they should not provide too many difficulties. He also told me that a senior officer came in on the last plane, and he stayed behind.'

'Okay,' said John, 'Thanks for that information, George, I'll pass all that on to MI6 in the morning, and we'll get Gorgi down to London as soon as we have wrapped up here. It is time I spoke to the commander of the base, so I will tie a white flag to the aerial on the Range Rover and drive to the entrance. You better all come with me, as there is nothing to do here. Andrew is on his way back, so I'll inform him what's happening.'

John drove back to the road and round to the site entrance, which took only about ten minutes. He stopped the vehicle and stepped out onto the road walking towards the entrance.

Two heavily armed men, called out for him to stop, that the site was a prohibited area. George had followed John and called out in Russian. 'We are members of the SAS who now surround this site. My commander wishes to speak to the commandant.'

'The commandant is not available,' one spat out.

'In that case we will order our missile crew to wipe out the site, we know what you have been up to, and if you wish to save your own lives and those of your colleagues, you have ten minutes to reply.' shouted John. George repeated what he had said in Russian.

George shouted into his phone, which had not switched on, and said that the missiles should be loaded and ready to fire. They were anyway, but the shout had the right effect.

One of the guards was on the phone.

'My commandant is coming to talk to you.'

The drawbridge opened slightly allowing a tall man in uniform along with two others, who were to come out heavily armed. They stayed the other side of the closed gate. John smiled, as he recognised Volkov. 'Good Morning General Volkov, I see you have received promotion; may I congratulate you.'

Volkov taken off guard, moved closer to the gate area as the bright lights did not entirely cover where John was standing.'

'May I know who I am speaking to?' Volkov asked.

John moved closer to the gate. 'Ah, Colonel, I believe we have met before, in Crete, no?

'And on the Greek Albanian border, you will remember that you tried to kill us there. However, we have you surrounded, we know the numbers that you have underground, and that some are sick. The reason for you being here is known to us, but the plot has failed. We suggest

244

you surrender, and we will send you and your men back to where you came from.'

Volkov laughed. 'You know that the Spetsnaz do not surrender Colonel, I told you that once before, we are heavily armed and are well capable of breaking out.'

'This is not Crete, General, you cannot disappear into the countryside or into the sea, as you tried to do over there. You would be hounded and captured, and the world would know of your plot to rule Scotland by proxy.'

Volkov smiled, 'and do you have an alternative, Colonel?'

'Yes, bring your men out without arms, and we will move them into the factory area. We will then bring in a C130 and transport you all back to Russia or Latvia where you came from, they are all illegal immigrants, and we have no wish for them to remain in our country.'

'I will return to my men and discuss your terms with them.'

With that he turned abruptly and went back through the small opening afforded to him by the slight raising of the reverse drawbridge.

John turned to George. 'Okay alert the missile crew, my guess is that Volkov may try to break out.' He called to Kieran. 'Kieran, get anyone with tank destroying weapons over here quickly and Josh get onto air control who are on standby and put them on full alert.'

Twenty minutes went by, and nothing happened, then suddenly the drawbridge opened wide to show an unarmed soldier in full uniform walking with a white flag, followed by a column of apparently unarmed men also in full uniform.

Kieran looked at John, 'well boss it looks as though you were wro...'

There was a sudden mechanical noise and a T14 Tank raced up the slope and headed straight for the entrance where they were standing. It had reached 50 mph when it hit the sentry box behind the gate crushing it like a matchbox and scattering the guards. Following it was a second tank. The operators on the missile launcher hesitated until a forward spotter shouted that the first tank was rotating its turret to aim at them. They had already computed the aim for the opening, and they fired. The first missile hit the third tank, the force of the explosion forcing it back down the slope. The second missile went into the bowels of the basement and there was a massive explosion as it obviously hit some armaments deep inside. The driver of the mobile launcher then started his motor, but he was far too late, and the first round from the lead tank hit it fair and square, creating another huge explosion. Then the two tanks started to fire their KORD 12.7 mm and PKTH 7u.62 mm machine guns. Fortunately, most SAS soldiers were under cover, but it was noticed that the ones behind the white flagged soldier had armaments strapped to their backs, and they were now running in the direction of the airstrip, firing as they went. The two tanks turned and covered their retreat.

As they reached the runway, a C130 was just landing and the men who were not wounded scrambled in the back of the plane as it was still moving turning as it moved to be able to take off. Most of the ordinance from the SAS simply bounced off the T14's but one lucky round found a vulnerable spot, and it came to a halt. The first tank drove straight into the C130 and the back door started to close leaving the tank crew of the other exposed as well as most of the guards who threw down their arms. The C130, was hit several times but was saved by its protective armour and it took off the as rear door closed.

John stood up and made sure his men were okay, before phoning the Royal Air Force at Lossiemouth in Moray, north east Scotland. They had previously been alerted by Josh. They scrambled 2 TGR4 Typhoons. John then phoned RAF Marham in East Anglia who scrambled 2 F35B's that also took off to ensure that Russian fighters could not intervene. The pilots knew that there were Russian fighters outside the three-mile zone, but they did not cross over into Scottish air space. The typhoons caught up with the C130, and radioed that it should turn around, but with the call ignored, the TGR4 released a missile that destroyed it. Just before the British fighter pilot unleashed his missile, he noticed a parachute floating down near the sea. Taking avoiding tactics after releasing the missile, he searched the sea and thought he saw a submarine that had just submerged, but he could not be certain. He radioed to the Coastguard who in turn radioed the nearest RNLI station, but nothing was found.

Back at the site, the three-man crew on the missile launcher had been killed, and some SAS soldiers had wounds, but fortunately not severe. The medics were on the scene and the local hospital were sending ambulances. The Russians left behind were either dead, wounded or had surrendered, three escaped but were caught later that day. After interrogation, they were all repatriated to Sweden and from there to Latvia.

THE SCOTTISH PREROGATIVE

Incorporating

THE WUHAN AFFAIR

THE AFTERMATH

Chapter 35

John Desmond returned to London, and some weeks later over lunch, Adrian told him the MOD were delighted with the result in Scotland, as apart from the damaged tank near the runway, they had found two T14 Armata tanks virtually untouched in the underground area. Surprisingly, there were no explosives found on them. They were also delighted at the capturing of Gorgi. Being a Captain, he was able give a very clear view of how the Russian Armoured Divisions worked, exactly where they were based and their tactics and strategy.

He also told John that the head of personnel, whose office was linked to his intercom had shot himself leaving a letter apologising for passing secrets to the Russians. His excuse was that his daughter had gone to Moscow as a Ballerina, and the FSB had threatened her with years of imprisonment for some misdemeanour. However, it was found that he had set up a separate bank account in the Isle of Mann where they found over £100,000 paid there through an account traced to the Russian Embassy.

Adrian continued. 'The Russian plan for Scotland was for the elimination of the political head of the country by the two GRU men sent to first to deal with Ladvia. Angus Stuart, who would be by then the Deputy First Minister, was to take control and at once secede from the Union. The night before the declaration, the tanks were to be taken in covered low loaders to strategic spots near the border. There are very few roads leading into Scotland from England, and their job was to capture a house or farm next to a road crossing the border and hold the inhabitants as hostage. In each case, the tanks and the Spetsnaz attached to them would block all traffic from travelling north. While this was going on, Angus Stuart was to call in the Russian Army claiming he had the right to do so as a new sovereign nation, thus negating NATO. The Russians would have quickly taken over all the UK's naval assets and RAF bases in Scotland and from then on Russia would have complete control of the North Sea, Irish Sea, and the Baltic. It was realised that the scheme had originally been set up based on a different government being in power in the UK. Although the Russians had used their fake news apparatus to try and ensure Brexit, which proved successful, it was Ironic, that it was partly the success of Brexit that complicated the plans for Angus Stuart. What, of course the Russians could not have foreseen was the Covid-19 virus. Keeping around 250 people underground meant that if only one person became infected from the outside, it ensured the rest would be susceptible to the disease, and that is what happened.

'It was fortunate that Jeremy and Ladvia were free at just the right moment to enable them to go to Hong Kong as tourists and bring out Mei-lieu Wong. Not only was she a stenographer, but also a secretary to a Minister. Wang, a senior police officer there, who had been helpful to British interests in the past, had decided to take up the offer from the Foreign Office to get him out, and he had sent his family to the UK on holiday some weeks before.

'The vaccine was sent to Porton Down and as testing had been done in China, it was simply a matter of trialling it to ensure its safety and ensuring that it could be replicated quickly. Of course, the fact that it came from China will not made public, a university in England will be given the credit and the patent. Hopefully, vaccinating NHS staff and the most vulnerable people should start by September/October of 2020. manufacture will be via pharmaceutical companies in the United Kingdom.'

The data noted that no top official of the Chinese government have caught Covid-19.

The fact that the minutes of the meeting in China indicated that the virus was spread deliberately will not be made public either, as the stenographer did not have the original document, it was replicated from her memory. Nevertheless, it shows the measures that China will go to, to damage the western economies, and those countries affected will take their own action in due course.

The Chinese reckoned they would bring down the Western economies, and they have been successful. What they did not cater for was that the Western World would find out who was responsible.

The Western World will hold China to account, putting heavy tariffs on their goods, while at the same time rebuilding their own manufacturing assets, with the help of government capital. The whole of the Western World will not forgive China. The Democracies will now create punitive commercial and financial retribution that will eventually bring down the closed state and free the Chinese people. Until that happens people in Europe and the USA will not be encouraged to purchase Chinese goods.

As far as the Russian business is concerned, it never happened. The news will eventually filter out that there was a major fire at the factory, closing it down.

Covid-19 helped to ensure Scotland stayed in the Union, the Russian plan had ironically been defeated by the Chinese, and it has shown that the people who run China are just as bad as Mao Zedong in suits and their treatment of the people in Hong Kong will further sour the Western World.

THE SCOTTISH PREROGATIVE

Incorporating

THE WUHAN AFFAIR

THE VICTORS

The Chairman entered the room smiling and all his ministers stood up and clapped. A lackey pulled out a chair for him to be seated.

He waved the ministers to sit adjusting the brief of papers he had brought with him and looked up. 'Well gentlemen, a job well done, I think. By the decision we took to ensure the virus was spread widely has achieved for us almost all our expectations. Because we had already developed a vaccine, the Chinese deaths were minimal. To belay criticism, we had to pretend that there was a resurgence of the spread, but that was easily contained. In the meantime, we were able to deal with the Hong Kong question. Of course, the Western countries will huff and puff, but our powerful economic situation will bring them back to the table, particularly now they require goods that they have lost the means to manufacture.

'Our second target was to make sure Mr Trump did not win the next election in the USA, and I feel confident that will now be achieved. Because of his desire to win, he has been responsible for over 3 million cases of Covid-19 and the US voters will not forgive him for that.

'So, we now have complete control of Hong Kong, we have brought the economies of the Western world to their knees, we will see Trump be thrown out of power, allowing us to become the power house of the world going forward.'

'We do have an immediate problem with the UK over Hong Kong,' said the Deputy Chairman.

The Chairman looked around the 30 ministers seated in front of him, he sneered. 'Our Ambassador in the UK has already threatened to punish that little country, now out on its own. There is nothing they can do to hurt China, we already own most of their water, we have investments in their transport system and farming, their power stations, their railways, steel, pubs, sport and much more. with Huawei we will completely control their telecommunications.' He laughed, 'with a snap of my fingers, we can bring down their economy again, which is already weak due to Covid-19.

'Of course, due to American interference we may temporarily lose the deal with Huawei. but we can apply sanctions on their motor industry but remember my friends the capitalist system is built on greed. It is what drives their economies. They cannot afford to lose China's business.'

'I would mention that our method of spreading fake news is working well. We have put out that the virus could have come from Spain, another story that is growing credence is that Covid-19 has been found previously in sewerage in many countries. The minister for social and media affairs should be congratulated.' The minister opposite him bowed and felt a warm glow at the Chairman's comment.

An important looking individual who was a senior minister, raised his hand.

The chairman looked mildly annoyed at the interruption He raised his eyebrows. 'Yes Wong?' He asked impatiently.

'Chairman, as our industry minister I am concerned about reports coming out of Xinjiang regarding the Uighurs, how is this news getting out into the free world? I fully understand that the release of the Covid-19 virus has brought the Western countries to their economic knees and dealt a killing blow to the President of the United States, but it has done China much harm and could be damaging to our future trade relations. I am also concerned about Hong Kong, as by breaking a treaty we...'

'Sit down Wong, we have covered all the possibilities and whatever result China will come out on top.'

The minister scowled but sat down without his questions being answered.

'Well gentlemen, you should all be well pleased with our progress, the time has come for China to come out behind our shield and deal with our outstanding problems in the South China Sea and Taiwan and while our enemies are in disarray, we will strike. At the same time, our glorious Peoples Republic Army will finally deal with the border problems with India and her allies.' He raised his voice, 'Now is the time for China to regain its rightful place in the world, and to pay back the Western powers that for so long plundered our country and massacred our people. LONG LIVE CHINA.' The ministers rose in unison, clapping the chairman as he moved from his seat and exited through the double doors at the end of the room where there stood two armed guards. He spoke to the senior officer who was also standing by. 'Captain, arrest Minister Wong for subversion' he snarled, 'and I do not wish to see him again. This will send an appropriate message to the others.' He turned and left with the sound of cheering behind him.

There were many in the room who agreed with Wong, perhaps coming to the view that a strong man in office for life was not necessarily a good idea. The attitude of present-day China has opened the eyes of the world to their appalling abuses and while the Chairman claimed a victory, it may well prove to be pyrrhic. We shall see.

NOTES

Jeremy and Ladvia collected a substantial amount of data about Iran before being air lifted from HMS Queen Elizabeth by helicopter and returned to the UK from Kuwait. They then flew with their children to the US on a military plane and now live in the British Embassy in Washington DC, pending the end of the Covid-19 pandemic.

British citizenship was granted to Mei-lieu, and she received an English name. She now lives in London working for the government.

The Chinese policeman also returned to the UK on the same flight as Jeremy and Ladvia, and now lives in London with his family. He is working for MI6 in the China section.

The grave found by Kieran was found to contain four bodies which turned out to belong to the family that had disappeared all those months before.

The vaccination file was handed to Oxford University for trials to be carried out.

The last bit of this story is that weeks later, one of our ambassadorial staff happened to spot General Volkov walking across the Bolshoy Moskvoretsky Bridge in Moscow in full uniform, indicating that he parachuted from the C130, leaving his men to die.

No doubt John Desmond and his team will meet up with both Sherepov and Volkov again in the future.

The next story will be about IRAN, and it will be called 'BREAK OUT'.

APPENDIX

CHINA – A REPORT

As the most populous country in the world and third largest in area, China also has the largest number of land neighbours (fourteen) sharing its twenty-two-thousand-kilometre land borders - north: North Korea, Russia, Mongolia, Kazakhstan, Kyrgyzstan, Tajikistan, Afghanistan, and now to the south, Pakistan, India, Nepal, Bhutan, Myanmar (Burma), Laos, and Vietnam. As I noted before, China still has border issues with some of its neighbours, manly its maritime neighbours. The biggest outstanding border issue is with Japan. These papers review the origins of China's border disputes with its neighbours and the current state of development.

Kazakhstan

China and Kazakhstan share a border of 1.7 thousand kilometres in China's vast North Western province of Xin Jiang. Border disputes date back to Soviet times. With the collapse of the Soviet Union in 1990, the new Central Asian countries including Kazakhstan took over these border disputes with China. In 1998, a treaty was signed between China and Kazakhstan, which settled a disputed area of 680 square kilometres near the Baimurz pass and another 380 square kilometres near the Sary-Charndy River. When the treaty was signed, China offered a lucrative economic package including investment in one of Kazakhstan's biggest oil fields, a 3 thousand kilometres gas pipeline across Kazakhstan, and a 15-year economic co-operation programme. A close relationship with Kazakhstan serves

China's long-term interests in the region, both economically and strategically. Not only does it release China from relying excessively on imported oil from the Middle East through a lengthy and risky shipping route but also it serves as a buffer zone between China and Russia. Kazakhstan is increasingly important for China in terms of security cooperation, especially combating Uighur separatism. Of course, the oil from this region is in no way sufficient for China's needs.'

The Uighurs are a Turkic-speaking people of interior Asia. Uighurs live-in north-western China in the Uygur Autonomous Region of Xinjiang; a small number also live in the Central Asian republics. There were 9 million Uighurs in China and about 300,000 in Uzbekistan, Kazakhstan, and Kyrgyzstan in the early 21st century. They are Sunni Muslims and there is some considerable friction between the Uighurs and the Chinese Han, who live in the same region. The Han makes up 92% of the people in China but are still a minority in Xinjiang Province, but the Chinese are actively encouraging more Han to move into the area (ethnic cleansing). In fact, one of the stories the Chinese put out was it might have been dissident Uighurs who brought down MH370. Of course, some on Social Media have also suggested that the CIA were involved, both theories are equally ridiculous.

Comment: this area is one that could create major problems for China going forward as there are religious (Sunni Muslims) and ethnic connections with the Uighur and when the chips are down one might assume that 'blood is thicker than water'.

India
The borders between the Indian subcontinent and China have been peaceful for thousands of years and India was

among the first nations to grant diplomatic recognition to the PRC in 1950. However, there have been disputes over competing historical claims, partly fuelled by the British penchant for drawing administratively convenient borders during the colonial period. Two territories currently in dispute are Aksai Chin and Arunachal Pradesh. China claims Aksai Chin as part of Hotan County in the Hotan prefecture of Xinjiang, autonomous Region and by India as a part of the Ladakh district of the state of Jammu and Kashmir. Despite being an uninhabitable area with no resources, Aksai Chin has strategic importance for China as it connects Tibet and Xinjiang. In 1957, China completed building a road in Aksai Chin, which India did not know about until China published a map in 1958.

Arunachal Predesh situated in India's north-eastern border has been a separate state since 1986 and is claimed by China as "Southern Tibet". British Administrator, Sir Henry McMahon drew up the 890 kilometres "McMahon Line" that defined the border between British India and Outer Tibet at the Simla conference in 1913-14. While the British and Tibetans signed the resulting Accord, the Chinese did not.

Today, India still recognises the McMahon Line as the border, but the Chinese disagree, citing Arunachal Predesh as being geographically and culturally part of Tibet since ancient times. After tensions built up following the Dalai Lama's exile during the Tibetan uprising in 1959, a Sino-Indian war erupted in 1962 over this disputed Himalayan border. China swiftly declared victory but voluntarily withdrew back to the McMahon Line. Aksai Chin and Arunachal Pradesh remain sources of tensions between China and India and neither side has managed to negotiate an agreement as to the precise border. Despite this dispute, trade and economic ties between China and India have developed in recent years.

Comment: India is almost certainly going to be the biggest competitor to the growth of China and the latter are extremely worried that the idea of a democratic state, encompassing free speech, free press and human rights could seep into their autocratic system. Certainly, there is little doubt that a democratic India must surpass China in economic might if the latter continue to suppress most of its people. That the Dali Lama received political asylum in India created considerable amount of bad feeling in China. It has done its best to punish countries that support him, including France and Britain because they invited the Dalai Lama to visit their countries.

Bhutan

Another buffer state between China and India and a traditional ally with the latter, Bhutan has not established official ties with China, thus relations have been frosty. Both sides share a border of 470 kilometres with a disputed territory of 495 square kilometres. Although there have been negotiations on border settlement in the last two decades, their competing claims have not been reconciled.

Myanmar

Burma established official ties with the PRC in 1950, the first non-Communist state to recognise Communist China. Today, China and Burma share a 2.19-thousand-kilometre border based on the border agreement of 1960. Relations between both sides were volatile throughout the Cold War, due to alleged discrimination of ethnic Chinese within Burma. Since China started supporting the military junta in 1986, the Burmese regime has become highly dependent on the Chinese both financially and militarily, especially after the crackdown on the pro-democracy movement in 1988 in Burma.

Today China is the largest trade partner for Burma. Whilst China has been helping Burma build its infrastructure and develop its industries, Burma in return offers China oil, gas, and other natural resources. The economic relations between the countries have strong political connotations. China had for years sheltered the Burmese military junta from UN sanctions and ensured its domestic stability. Burma, on the other hand, is important for China, not just for its natural resources, but its strategic location in South Asia.

Comment: a growing number of problems on both sides, evidenced by the sudden halt of the Myitisone dam project and incidents on the Mekong River, have shown the limitations of their relationship. In 2009, violent clashes between the Burmese government and the Kokang, a group of armed rebels in northern Burma, resulted in Chinese casualties and Burmese refugees flooding into the Chinese province of Yunan. Fearing the escalating violence would threaten China's border security and economic interests in Burma, China repeatedly called for a ceasefire.

Vietnam
China shares a land border of 1.3 thousand kilometres with Vietnam. For centuries, Vietnam was subject to Chinese domination resulting in conflicts and invasions. During the Vietnam War (1954-1975), China was the ally of North Vietnam against South Vietnam and its ally, the United States.

'Following the Vietnamese invasion and occupation of Cambodia in 1976, relations with Beijing deteriorated, in 1979 China invaded, and fought a short but bloody war with Vietnam. While both sides claimed victory, each suffered heavy casualties. A border agreement was eventually signed in 1999 following border skirmishes throughout the 1980's. In 2007, the building of the Hanoi-Kunming highway was announced that marked a significant improvement in Sino-Vietnamese relations. While China has now become the second-largest trading partner and the largest source of imports for Vietnam, tensions over territorial issues were recently rekindled over the Spratly Islands, an oil rich area in the South China Sea.

Comment: The tensions over the Spratly Islands are becoming more serious and are not likely to be settled without conflict of some sort, as potential large oil reserves are under the sea in this area.

Maritime Borders

Besides the obvious difficult cross-strait relations with Taiwan, China shares maritime borders with four countries, Japan and South Korea in the East China Sea, the Philippines, and Vietnam in the South China Sea.

These borders are not agreed and the subject of continuing disputes. In the East China Sea (1.2 million square kilometres), China is currently in dispute with Japan and South Korea over the extent of their respective exclusive economic zones, each resorting to different parts of the UN Conventions on the Law of the Sea.

In the South China Sea (3.5 million square kilometres), one of the world's busiest waterways with huge potential oil and gas fields to be exploited, China claims most of the water "based on historical facts and international law", a position that is disputed by all its neighbours, particularly Vietnam and the Philippines. ASEAN has attempted to resolve the disputes through multi-lateral talks, but China prefers to deal with each country on a bilateral basis, no doubt as it will be easier to use the "muscle factor" if they don't get their way.

Another factor is the presence of the US in the Pacific and its determination to uphold freedom of navigation. China has expressed concern at the American plans to increase its military presence in the region.

Comment: to give you an idea of the complexity of the problem, the Paracel Islands in the North West, are occupied by China but claimed by Vietnam and Taiwan. The Pratas Islands in the North East are occupied by Taiwan but claimed by China.

The Spratly Islands in the South East are occupied in part by China, Taiwan, Vietnam, Malaysia, and the Philippines, but claimed in their entirety by China, Taiwan, and Vietnam and in part, by Malaysia, the Philippines, and Brunei.

The Macclesfield Bank and Scarborough Reef are claimed by China and Taiwan, whilst the Philippines also claims the Scarborough Reef.

Comment: We are going to need more than a Solomon to sort that lot out.

North Korea

North Korea (DRPK), China's closest ally, shares a 1.4-Thousand-kilometre-long border, which has been mainly defined by two rivers, the Yalu, and the Tumen, as agreed between both sides in the 1962, Sino-Korean border treaty. There are, however, still disputes concerning the demarcation line in the middle of the rivers, ownership of islands and particularly Mount Paektu, which is the highest peak in the region and the source of the two rivers. Another source of tension is access to the Sea of Japan. Since the last part of the Tumen River defines the border between the DRPK and Russia, China has no access to the Sea of Japan, which has further implications on its military strategy in the region. In the Yellow Sea, an economic and fishing zone has been drawn unilaterally by the North Koreans 200 miles off the Chinese coast. Unlike the border demarcation between the DPRK and Russia, which was renegotiated in the early

1990's, the territorial and maritime disputes between North Korea and China haven't been effectively resolved, largely due to China's unwillingness to negotiate and the DPRK's dependence on China, both politically and economically.

Comment: China is hugely embarrassed by the actions of North Korea and the state of their economy is a drain on China's resources. It is my view that China was behind the recent putsch by the current leader's uncle, as they would like much more control over the region and access to the Sea of Japan. They are also concerned that the present leader will go too far by either invading South Korea or creating a serious "incident" with the USA, thus bringing the former into another conflict with US forces.

They know that North Korea, despite their grandstanding of military might, is poorly defended and their military hardware not fit for use. Although North Korea has nuclear weapons, they would be destroyed before any damage could be done to the free world.

Russia

China shares its second longest border of 4.3 thousand kilometres with Russia. The disputed area on the eastern border concerns Zhenbao Island (Damansky in Russian) on the Usuri River and some islands on the Amur and Argun rivers situated on China's northern tip. China claims historical ownership over these disputed territories arguing that unfair treaties were signed between the Qing Empire and Tsarist Russia in the 19th century. The USSR refused to accept this interpretation and insisted on its ownership. Although both sides reached, a preliminary agreement in the early 1960's that Zhenbao Island would be under Chinese sovereignty, border clashes took place that lasted for seven months in 1969. Later that year, there were further conflicts in the Pamir Mountains that lay on the western border of China's Xinjiang Uighur Autonomous Region and Tajikistan. Consequently, Sino-Soviet relations soured after the 1969 conflict.

Serious border negotiations did not take place until the fall of the Soviet Union in 1991. The question of control over

Zhenbao Island, and three other islands in the Amur and Argun rivers were finally settled in 1995 and 2004 respectively, whilst the demarcation of the western border was completed in 2008. In 2011, Heixiazi Island (Bolshoy Ussurysky Island), once a cause of disagreement at the confluence of the Amur and Ussurui rivers, was officially opened as an eco-tourism zone after Russia had ceded half of the 335 square kilometre island to China in 2004. Both sides now refer to each other as strategic partners and are fellow members of the BRICS.'

Comment: 'BRICS is an acronym for Brazil, Russia, India, China, and South Africa. In face of economic turbulences, the BRICS countries are pushing forward structural reforms to promote growth and reduce dependence on external markets. They are also increasing domestic demand, upgrading infrastructure, boosting regional connectivity, and promoting trade and financial cooperation. It is a loose confederation, which China is hoping will create a greater influence in world affairs in their favour.

Both Russia and China keep exceptionally large forces facing each other along the strategic parts of the border area and tourists are forbidden to enter these areas. Putin is no fool and he knows his biggest potential enemy is China at the end of the day, which is no doubt, why he is concerning himself with shoring up his western defences. Russia would be better concentrating on entering solid treaties with the western world which would do much more to create peace in the Russian European area so he could concentrate on 'his back door'. Of course, China is delighted that Russia is being brought to its knees economically by the west, the weaker Russia becomes, the more China benefits.

Mongolia

Having been taken over by China in the Yuan Dynasty (1271-1364) and gained international recognition of its independence in 1946, Mongolia shares a border of 4.7 thousand kilometres with China, the longest for both countries. The Sino-Mongolian border treaty was signed in 1962, and a final agreement on the exact demarcation of the border was reached in 2005. China increasingly turns to Mongolia to meet its energy needs. Interestingly, when in 2008 both China and Russia offered to build a railway from the Tavan Tolgoi mine, one of the world's largest unexploited coal deposits, the Mongolians used different sized tracks in opposite directions. The Mongolian government decided to "synchronise" the opening of two export railways, adopting a middle-way approach to please both sides. Having been effectively a Soviet colony until 1991, Mongolia has since developed closer ties with China, not just in trade and natural resources but also on security issues.

Comment: One cannot help wondering which country Mongolia would side with in the event of a conflict. The bet would be Russia, so from Russia's point of view, Mongolia is a handy buffer between the two major powers.

Kyrgyzstan

As with Kazakhstan, the border dispute between China and Kyrgyzstan is the legacy of Soviet times. An agreement was reached in 1999, which defines 900 out of 1.1 thousand kilometres of the Kyrgyz Chinese border. Accordingly, Kyrgyzstan received 70% of the disputed territory including the 7,000-metre peak of Khan-Tengri in Tien Shan, whilst China received nine square kilometres of mountainous area of the Uzengi-Kush located south of the Issyk Kul Region. The signing of the agreement provoked some heated reaction in the Kyrgyz parliament as the then-President Akayev was considered "traitorous" and ousted. The demarcation of the boundary was finally completed in 2009. Because of ethnic tensions in Kyrgyzstan, China temporarily closed its border in 2010. China has offered to help Kyrgyzstan build a power grid in the South, which would be the largest inter-governmental project between the two countries.

Comment, here is yet another way the Chinese settle its disputes, "the stick and carrot method."

Tajikistan

After reaching border agreements with Kyryzstan and Kazakhstan, China's border negotiations with Tajikistan lagged due to the civil war in Tajikistan. In 1999 an agreement was reached in which China would gain sovereignty over an area of 1 thousand square kilometres in the Pamir Mountains, lying on the Tajik border with China and Afghanistan, less than 5.5 percent of what China had originally claimed. China's substantial concession in this border settlement is believed to be closely associated with the surge of violence in Xinjiang province since the early 1990's. China looks to Central Asian governments to crackdown on Islamic fundamentalism and Uighur separatism.'

Comment: The problem is not going to go away, China re-established control in 1949 after crushing the short-lived state of East Turkestan, since then, there has been large-scale immigration of Han Chinese, but the Uighurs are still the majority. They are a different ethnic group, they've a different religion, they speak a different language, and the Chinese government has brutally cracked down of their way of life. There are now over ten million Uighurs and despite the deal made with Tajikistan a land locked country of only eight million, they have more in common with the Tajiks as both are Sunni Muslim, something China fears. Neither have any ethnic connection with China, the Uighurs being of Turkish descent (although further back, Mongol, and the Tajiks originally Persian (Iran). The Chinese answer to the Uighurs is to lock them up in re-education facilities, the equivalent of concentration camps. This is a growing problem for the Chinese, who try to pretend to the world that they are a free society.

Afghanistan
China and Afghanistan share the 210-kilometre border known as the Wakhan Corridor, situated between Badakhashan Province in Afghanistan and the Xinjiang Uighur Autonomous Region. Historically, a caravan trade of fruit and tea flourished in the Wakhan corridor for centuries. Border disputes in the area were settled as early

267

as 1963. During most of the Cold War period, China had very friendly relations with Afghanistan. However, relations with the Taliban regime were very hostile as the Taliban was a staunch supporter of the Uighur separatists and the "East Turkestan Islamic Movement". In 2009, the Afghan government proposed to open the border as an alternative supply route to help combat the Taliban. To co-operate with Afghanistan, China adopted "an earnest and positive attitude" over transport, trade, and economy. In December 2011, the Afghan government signed a deal with China's National Petroleum Corporation (CNPC) allowing the CNPC to exploit natural gas and oil in the country's northeast that could earn Afghanistan $7 billion over the next 25 years.

Comment: Afghanistan is also Sunni Muslim, so one wonders how long this cosy relationship will last, especially as the western troops pull out. Afghans are Pashtun, Tajiks, and Uzbeks, the first two being originally connected to Persia (Iran) and the Uzbeks to Turkey.

Pakistan

Four years on from its independence in 1947, Pakistan established diplomatic relations with China, one year after India. At the time, there were unresolved border issues to which neither side paid serious attention. After the Sino-Indian war in 1962, China and Pakistan became aligned with each other, even though they clearly did not share the same political or religious values. Because of a border agreement in 1963, China ceded 1.9 thousand square kilometres to Pakistan in exchange for Pakistan's recognition of Chinese sovereignty over parts of North Kashmir and Ladakh. This agreement is considered economically beneficial for Pakistan and bilateral relations between Pakistan and China have since improved significantly. Currently, China and Pakistan share a 523-kilometre-long border, ending near the Karakoram Pass. There are no border disputes between them. China has sided with Pakistan in the dispute that Kashmir does not belong to India. When the Kashmir dispute is resolved there will need to be an additional agreement between Pakistan and China.

Comment: Of course, it suited Pakistan to give part of Kashmir away, particularly as they did not own it anyway. This was in the hope that it would put more pressure on India. Again, money keeps the unlikeliest partners together, but how long this lasts with the emergence of India, as a superpower is uncertain.

Nepal

China and Nepal share a border of 1.4 thousand kilometres, which was demarcated according to a 1961 treaty. There has been no major border dispute since and China's relations with Nepal have been smooth and friendly.

Comment: Nepal considers China a major source of investment, development aid, and economic support, whereas China sees Nepal as a strategic buffer state against India regarding Tibet. Although Nepal stopped accepting Tibetan refugees in the 1980's, they can cross Nepal on their way to India, an informal agreement, which does not seriously antagonise China. They would be delighted if all the indigenous Tibetans left what was their country.

Laos

China shares a border of 505 kilometres with Laos based on a border treaty signed in 1991. Although Sino-Laos relations were strained during the Cold War due to China's involvement in Cambodia and Vietnam, diplomatic relations have been normalised since the early 1990's and China has become the largest foreign investor in Laos.

Tibet

Representatives of Great Britain, China, and Tibet met in 1914 to negotiate a treaty marking out the boundary lines between India and its northern neighbours.

The Simla Convention granted China secular control over "Inner Tibet", (also known as Qinghai Province) while recognizing the autonomy of "Outer Tibet" under the Dalai Lama's rule. Both China and Britain promised to "respect the territorial integrity of Tibet and abstain from interference in the administration of Outer Tibet".

China walked out of the conference without signing the treaty after Britain laid claim to the Tawang area of southern Tibet, which is now part of the Indian state of Arunachal Pradesh. Tibet and Britain both signed the treaty.

As a result, China has never agreed to India's rights in northern Arunachal Pradesh (Tawang), and the two nations went to war over the area in 1962. The boundary dispute still has not been resolved.

China also claims sovereignty over all of Tibet, while the Tibetan government-in-exile points to the Chinese failure to sign the Simla Convention as proof that both Inner and Outer Tibet legally remain under the Dalai Lama's jurisdiction.

At the beginning of the twentieth century, China would be too distracted to concern itself with the issue of Tibet, as Japan had invaded Manchuria in 1910, and would advance south and east across large swaths of Chinese territory through 1945.

In 1950, with stability re-established in Beijing for the first time in decades, the People's Liberation Army (PLA) of the newly formed People's Republic of China invaded Tibet as Mao Zedong sought to assert China's right to rule over the country.

'The PLA inflicted a swift and total defeat on Tibet's small army, and China drafted the "Seventeen Point Agreement" incorporating Tibet as an autonomous region of the People's Republic of China. Representatives of the Dalai Lama's government signed the agreement under protest, and the Tibetans repudiated the agreement nine years later.

Comment: Reverting to the post World War2 era, the new government of the Republic of China would hold nominal power over most of the Chinese territory for only four years before war broke out between numerous armed factions. Indeed, the span of Chinese history from 1916 to 1938 came to be called the "Warlord Era", as the different military factions sought to fill the power vacuum left by the collapse of the Qing Dynasty. China would see near continuous civil war up to the Communist victory in 1949, and the Japanese Occupation, World War II exacerbated this era of conflict. Under such circumstances, the Chinese showed little interest in Tibet.

The 13th Dalai Lama ruled independent Tibet in peace until his death in 1933. Following Thubten Gyatso's death, the new reincarnation of the Dalai Lama was born in Amdo in 1935. Tenzin Gyatso, the current Dalai Lama, was taken to Lhasa in 1937 to begin training for his duties as the leader of Tibet. He would remain there until 1959, when the Chinese forced him into exile in India.

The Mao government of the PRC immediately initiated land redistribution in Tibet. Landholdings of the monasteries and nobility were seized for redistribution to the peasants. The communist forces hoped to destroy the power base of the wealthy and of Buddhism within Tibetan society.

In reaction, an uprising led by the monks broke out in June of 1956 and continued through 1959. The poorly armed Tibetans used guerrilla war tactics to drive out the Chinese. The PLA responded by razing entire villages and monasteries to the ground. The Chinese even threatened to blow up the Potala Palace and kill the Dalai Lama, but this threat was not carried out.

Three years of bitter fighting left 86,000 Tibetans dead, according to the Dalai Lama's government in exile.

On March 1, 1959, the Dalai Lama received an odd invitation to attend a theatre performance at PLA headquarters near Lhasa.

The Dalai Lama demurred, and the performance date was postponed until March 10. On March 9, PLA officers notified the Dalai Lama's bodyguards that they could not accompany the Tibetan leader to the performance, nor were they to notify the Tibetan people that he was leaving the palace. (Ordinarily, the people of Lhasa would line the streets to greet the Dalai Lama each time he ventured out.) The guards immediately publicised this ham-handed attempted abduction, and the following day an estimated crowd of 300,000 Tibetans surrounded Potala Palace to protect their leader.

The PLA moved artillery into range of major monasteries and the Dalai Lama's summer palace, Norbulingka. Both sides began to dig in although the Tibetan army was much smaller than its adversary and it was poorly armed.

Tibetan troops were able to secure a route for the Dalai Lama to escape into India on March 17. Actual fighting began on March 19 and lasted only two days before the Tibetan troops were defeated.'

Conclusion

China has clearly been successful in resolving border disputes with most of its smaller neighbours in a "win-win" situation since the 1990's. The Central Asian borders were the easiest to resolve with China being willing to make concessions to enlist the support of these governments in combating a perceived security threat.

The borders with the two fellow members of the UNSC were more difficult. It took a decade to reach agreement with Russia and the border with India remains unresolved. However, the maritime borders have caused most trouble in the past two years with China being accused of increasingly belligerent behaviour towards its neighbours.

It may be useful for China to revert to the diplomatic language it used during its "peaceful rise" to assure its neighbours that it is not a bully. Whether China can regain the respect of its neighbours that it had during the era of the "Middle Kingdom" remains to be seen. It will be a difficult balancing act for China – on the one hand demonstrating that it's back as a major power after the century of humiliation, and on the other wishing to be regarded as an important but peaceful neighbour.

The last thing that China needs in its current situation is an armed conflict with any of its neighbours. In an era of growing political and economic interdependence such a development could only impact negatively on China.'

Comment: Conflict, if they cannot bribe their way out, so they will use the only other method they know, "the stick" but they will not move until they are ready.

Although Tibet is now part of China by force, it's an area that may well prove to continue to be contentious.'

Comment: That completes the assessment of the current situation as far as China and its neighbours are concerned. Regarding the maritime problem, there are five main areas of contention, three of which in certain circumstances could blow up very quickly, Tibet, Hong Kong, Taiwan, Japan, and South Korea, the last three being the most contentious. Since the death of Chairman Mao, China has spent a lot of time and effort in peaceably dealing with border disputes by using the stick and carrot method. This has worked well with small countries, particularly those that are land locked whose interest was based on the financial influence that was offered by the Chinese and the sober alternative to toe the line. This has not worked with the larger economies such as India, Japan, South Korea and Vietnam, the latter who fought fiercely to maintain their independence. The Tibetan situation was precipitated by Chairman Mao and is still an outstanding sore in world politics maintaining the impression that China is quite happy to subjugate not only its own people if they step out of line, but also sovereign countries with adjacent borders as is shown with Tibet. When General MacArthur pushed his troops into what is now North Korea, Chairman Mao received a promise from the Russians that if he used Chinese troops to stem the defeat of the North Korean army, they would provide air cover. They ratted on that promise and Mao had to use resources that had been earmarked for the invasion of Taiwan. The Chinese still claim Taiwan as their territory and it is interesting that now China has secured most of its inland borders, it is looking for further expansion in the east. The problem they have is that the countries they are dealing with are not so susceptible to bribery, coercion, or threats because they have extremely strong economies themselves, i.e., Japan, Taiwan, The Philippines, South Korea, and India. India is a nuclear power, and the rest are protected by treaty with the United States. While China is keeping the pressure on these disputed areas, it is gradually expanding its economic power and its military might, particularly its navy and air force. If one looks at the figures of China's military expenditure compared say, with United States, it appears that China is way below. The latest statistics from SIPRI show the USA annual expenditure at $711 billion against China of $143 billion this based on relative exchange rates. However, this is a false assumption as one must use a PPP conversion factor (GDP) to market exchange rate ratio.

The PPP conversion factor (GDP) to market exchange rate ratio in China was last measured at 0.67 in 2012, according to the World Bank. Purchasing power parity conversion factor is the number of units of a country's currency required to buy the same amount of goods and services in the domestic market as a U.S. dollar would buy in the United States. On this basis China's published military expenditure is nearer $214 billion, but not only are they increasing their military expenditure by over $12 billion per annum, year on year, it's estimated that their real expenditure is running at 140% higher than stated (The Economist), making the true figure nearer to $300 million. If the United States maintains its present expenditure, it is likely that the Chinese will pass the USA within 8 years and possibly earlier.

One must remember that the USA has many other areas in the world to keep peace, whereas China need only concentrate its military assets in a small area.

Now the Chinese military are concentrating on widening their presence on their eastern seaboard, particularly in the Taiwan Straits and the East China and South China Sea.

Taiwan is their first target, and it is thought that the political changes in Hong Kong are to this end. An attack on Taiwan would make Hong Kong an ideal place to use as a launching area for an invading force, but first China must be sure that their man is in charge there. The other reason is a concern that the idea of a "free" Hong Kong may spill over into their tight hold over the rest of the country and loosen their autocratic power hold.'

Comment: They are spending large amounts on cryptology and laser beam technology too. According to the Economist, something similar may be happening with the new high-tech military hardware China is deploying. Over the past decade, the country has striven to bring once obsolete forces up to the point where they would make a regional intervention by America on behalf of an ally (above all, Taiwan) too dangerous to undertake lightly. To that end, it has invested heavily in cost-effective technologies that target weaknesses in the platforms on which America depends for projecting power in the Western Pacific, such as strike carrier groups, nearby bases, and military satellites. A large part of China's military budget goes on increasingly long-range anti-ship, air-defence, and land-attack missiles launched from shore-based batteries, land-based aircraft, guided-missile destroyers, fast patrol boats, and submarines.

Naval modernisation has been especially vigorous. The PLA Navy (PLAN) now has around 190 "major combatants", vessels mostly designed and built in China. In terms of size, it is on course to overtake the American navy by 2020—though it will have at most only a couple of the small new aircraft-carriers by then, compared with America's 11 much larger ones. The aim is for the PLAN to dominate in contested territorial waters and to be able to push any hostile forces well beyond the "first island chain"—that is, beyond the Philippines, Taiwan, and the Japanese archipelago.

However, the more China commits itself to sophisticated weapons systems, the more it dissipates the cost advantages of buying (and sometimes stealing) mature foreign technologies. Christopher Johnson at the Centre for Strategic and International Studies in Washington, DC, says that while China's different bits of hardware are now good, the tricky bit is developing the software to make them all work together. The country has, so far struggled to develop the targeting infrastructure to turn an anti-ship ballistic missile called the DF-21D into a real threat to American carriers. In addition, while China is testing home-grown stealth fighters, replicating the communication, sensor, and information systems that make America's F-35 so potent is another matter.

In one of the biggest military reforms for years, announced in January, China is now attempting to create a Western-style structure of joint command. However, that may prove a long and painful undertaking, because Chinese forces suffer from a lack of any recent operational experience. And as China seeks to project power, Andrew Erickson of the US Naval War College and Adam Liff of Harvard's Belfer Centre predict it will find itself getting ever less bang for the buck. Developing the ability to wage war beyond its "immediate vicinity", they write, would require much bigger increases in military spending and "heavy investment in new platforms, weapons and related systems".

'China appears to have recently committed to creating a large new naval base on Hainan Island which is south of

Hong Kong. This would give them a further naval presence in the South China Sea area and could act as an important back up to any future invasion of Taiwan. This is surprising as they already have three naval bases on Hainan, so that may just be a diversionary tactic.

Then there is the tyranny of demography. While China may for some time be able to sustain the current rises in defence spending, before long its military ambitions will be curbed by a slowing economy and the demands of a rapidly ageing society for better pensions and health care, none of which means that neighbours are wrong to be worried.

China has relatively weak command and control; it has senior commanders who lack experience of war but who are spoiling to show what their shiny new stuff can do; it chafes at unresolved claims and resents what it sees as encirclement by an American-led alliance. Hubris coupled with insecurity, is a scary mix. It is worth pointing out that some Chinese Nationalists envisage fighting Russia sometime in the future to take control of Eastern Russia, which at one point was paying tribute to the Qing Emperor.

To help them control the seas around China; they need submarines, particularly ones that fire underwater missiles. In addition, China's moves reflect its determination to beef up its presence in both the South China Sea and the Indian Ocean, through which four-fifths of its oil imports pass. This coincides with escalating tension in the disputed South China Sea, where Beijing's naval superiority has rattled its neighbours. It is likely that they will be sending their underwater craft much further afield in the future, even to Europe, the Middle East, and the Pacific coast of the United States.

It is surprising that the South China Sea carries more than half the world's merchant fleet tonnage and a third of all maritime traffic. About $5.3 trillion flows through the region of the South China Sea each year, with one fifth of this being U.S. commerce. 80% of China's crude oil imports, 60% of Japan's and Taiwan and 66% of South Korea's arrive via this sea and as most of this comes from the Middle East you only need to look at a map to see how important the Indian Ocean is to this trade. The reason China is so interested in the various islands around the South China Sea, some of them hardly islands, more atolls, rocks, and reefs, is that there are hydrocarbons in the area, which could help to release China from the dependency of Middle East Oil. Interestingly they are now creating artificial islands to expand their maritime control.'

China has a problem as already indicated. They have picked a capitalist way to enlarge their power and influence, but by being a Communist state, they control their citizens by force. If you consider that Al Capone was a dangerous and ruthless gangster with no thought for human life then both Stalin and Mao Zedong were similar types, they ruled by force of arms and killed far more people than any external force. Today we have men who control world crime, they are just as ruthless, just as uncaring about human life, but they are smart, they use modern technology to carry out their appalling policies and they control the people who work for them absolutely. Meet the modern men, and they are mostly men, who rule China.

The western democracies have their faults, but the big difference between them and China is that those in power are accountable to the electorate, and they must consider public opinion otherwise they will lose their jobs. A free press and human rights are as important as is democracy. In China, the law is what is dictated by the PNC (Peoples National Congress); the people have no choice as to what party they may vote for. Human rights are not considered, and the press is controlled by the State. However, there is a significant dissident population in China who are looking for change. As capitalist policies create a greater middle class, so there will be more pressure on the leaders to give up their dictatorial stance, you cannot possibly keep over a billion people in subjugation without something breaking.'

The best way to extend that is to have an enemy, as this not only enforces discipline from the masses, but allows those at the top to keep control, Hitler, Stalin, Chairman Mao, the previous Argentinean President Gualtieri, have all used this method to retain power and arguably, President Putin is currently following the same policy. All the evidence points to China using her economic might to build up an unassailable military machine to subjugate those that do not kowtow, to use a Chinese expression. The present concern regarding ISIL and other Islamic militants is annoying and serious, but it's a sideshow, the challenge to the western world is China and to a lesser extent Russia, it's essential that it's not allowed to become the largest economic power, because there may be no stopping it once it reaches a paramount position.

China fears India more than any other nation. It is a nuclear power, its land mass is next to China, land border disputes are unresolved and if India decided to move into what was Tibet, those in the International community would silently applaud the move. If the opposite were the case, the International community would certainly go to India's aid. To do battle with Japan, without the cover of the USA, may in many eyes be justified because of the horrible atrocities Japan forced on China in the 30's and 40's.

Their claim in Taiwan is reasonable in the circumstances if one looks at the geography and history of China. If only John Foster Dulles had continued to recommend the backing of Nationalist China, we would not be facing the problem we have today. China believes its destiny is to rule the world, and it would have done so if one of their Emperors had not closed the country down to outsiders in the 15th century. The Chinese believe they are a Master race, where have we heard that before?' Professor Chu smiled. 'They believe that the Americans are a polyglot of inferior races, what they don't understand, is that is what makes America strong.'

The Communist Party has made strenuous efforts to keep signs of its enduring power out of sight to the Chinese public and the rest of the world. Richard McGregor writes on the secrets of the world's largest political machine and its role in Beijing's growing influence.

On the desks of the heads of China's 50-odd biggest state companies, amid the clutter of computers, family photos and other fixtures of the modern CEO's office life, sits a red phone. The executives and their staff who jump to attention when it rings, know it as "the red machine", perhaps because to call it a mere phone does not do it justice. "When the 'red machine' rings", a senior executive of a state bank, told me, "you had better make sure you answer it".

The red machine is like no ordinary phone. Each one has just a four-digit number. It connects only to similar phones with four-digit numbers within the same encrypted system. They are much coveted, nonetheless. For the chairmen and chairwomen of the top state companies, who have every modern communications device at their fingertips, the red machine is a sign they have arrived, not just at the top of the company, but in the senior ranks of the Party and the government. The phones are the ultimate status symbol, as they are only given out under the orders of the Party and government to people in jobs with the rank of vice minister and above.

The phones are encrypted, not just to secure party and government communications from foreign intelligence agencies. They also provide protection against snooping by anyone in China outside the Party governing system. Possession of the red machine means you have qualified for membership of the tight-knit club that runs the country, a small group of about 300 people, mainly men, with responsibility for about one-fifth of humanity.

The modern world is replete with examples of elite networks that wield behind-the-scenes power beyond their mere numerical strength.

None can hold a candle to the Chinese Communist Party, which takes ruling-class networking to an entirely new level. The red machine gives the party apparatus a hotline into multiple arms of the state, including the government-owned companies that China promotes around the world these days as independent commercial entities. As a political machine alone, the Party is a phenomenon of awesome and unique dimensions. By mid-2009, its membership stood at 76 million, equal to about one in 12 adult Chinese.

China's post-Maoist governing model, launched by Deng Xiaoping in the late 1970's, has endured many attempts to explain it. Is it a benevolent, Singapore-style autocracy? A capitalist development state, as many described Japan. Neo-Confucianism mixed with market economics, a slow-motion version of post-Soviet Russia in which the elite grabbed productive public assets for private gain, robber-baron socialism, or is it something different altogether, an entirely new model, a "Beijing Consensus", according to the fashionable phrase, built around practical, problem-solving policies and technological innovation?

'Few describe the model as communist anymore, often not even the ruling Chinese Communist Party itself.

How communism came to be airbrushed out of the rise of the world's greatest communist state is no mystery on one level. The multiple, head-spinning contradictions about modern China can divert anyone. What was once a revolutionary party is now firmly the establishment, the communists rode to power on a popular revulsion against corruption, but it appears they have succumbed to the same cancer themselves. Top leaders adhere to Marxism in their public statements, even as they depend on a ruthless private sector to create jobs. The Party preaches equality, while presiding over incomes as unequal as anywhere in Asia.

The gap between the fiction of the Party's rhetoric ("China is a socialist country") and the reality of everyday life grows larger every year. However, the Party must defend the fiction nonetheless because it represents the political status quo.

The Party's defence of power is also, by extension, a defence of the existing system. In the words of Dai Bingguo, China's most senior foreign policy official, China's "number one core interest is to maintain its fundamental system and state security." State sovereignty, territorial integrity and economic development, the priorities of any state, all are subordinate to the need to keep the Party in power.

The Party has made strenuous efforts to keep the sinews of its enduring power off the front stage of public life in China and out of sight of the rest of the world. A decade into the 21st century, the Beijing headquarters of the big Party departments, whose power far outstrips that of mere ministries, still have no signs outside indicating the business inside and no listed phone numbers. For many in the West, it has been convenient to keep the Party backstage too and pretend that China has an evolving governmental system with strengths and weaknesses, quirks, and foibles, like any other country. China's flourishing commercial life embracing globalisation is enough for many to dismiss the idea that communism still has traction, as if a Starbucks on every corner is a marker of political progress

Peek under the hood of the Chinese model, however, and China looks much more communist than it does on the open road. Vladimir Lenin, who designed the prototype used to run communist countries around the world, would recognise the model immediately. The Chinese Communist Party's enduring grip on power is based on a simple formula straight out of the Leninist play book. For all the reforms of the past three decades, the Party has made sure it keeps a lock-hold on the state and three pillars of its survival strategy: control of personnel, propaganda, and the People's Liberation Army.

Since installing itself as the sole legitimate governing authority of a unified China in 1949, the Party and its leaders have placed its members in key positions in every arm, and at each level, of the state. All the Chinese media come under the control of the propaganda department, even if its denizens have had to gallop to keep up in the Internet age. In addition, if anyone decides to challenge the system, the Party has kept ample power in reserve, making sure it maintains a tight grip on the military and the security services, the ultimate guarantors of its rule. The police forces at every level of government, from large cities to small villages, have within them a "domestic security department," the role of which is to protect the Party's rule and weed out dissenting political voices before they can gain a broad audience.

China long ago dispensed with old-style communist central planning for a sleeker hybrid market economy, the Party's greatest innovation. However, measure China against a definitional checklist written by Robert Service, the veteran historian of Soviet Russia, and Beijing retains a surprising number of the qualities that characterised communist regimes of the 20th century.

Like communism in its heyday elsewhere, the Party in China has eradicated or emasculated political rivals; eliminated the autonomy of the courts and press; restricted religion and civil society; denigrated rival versions of nationhood; centralized political power; established extensive networks of security police; and dispatched dissidents to labour camps. A good example of this was the British businessman Neil Hayward who was poisoned after he threatened to expose a plan by a Chinese leader's wife to move money abroad.

The Party in China has teetered on the verge of self-destruction numerous times, in the wake of Mao Zedong's brutal campaigns over three decades from the 1950's, and then again in 1989, after the army's suppression of demonstrations in Beijing and elsewhere. The Party itself

283

suffered an existential crisis after the collapse of the Soviet Union and its satellite states in 1992, an event that resonates to this day, in the corridors of power in Beijing. After each catastrophe, the Party has picked itself off the ground, reconstituted its armour and reinforced its flanks. Somehow, it has outlasted, outsmarted, outperformed, or simply outlawed its critics.

Few events symbolised the advance of China and the retreat of the West during the financial crisis more than the touchdown in Beijing of Secretary of State Hillary Clinton in February 2009. Previous U.S. administrations, under Bill Clinton and George W. Bush, had arrived in office with an aggressive, competitive posture towards China. Before she landed, Ms. Clinton publicly downplayed the importance of human rights. At a press conference before leaving, she beamingly implored the Chinese government to keep buying U.S. debt, like a travelling saleswoman hawking a bill of goods.

Deng Xiaoping's crafty stratagem, laid down two decades earlier, about how China should advance stealthily into the world, "hide your brightness; bide your time"—had been honoured in the breach long before Ms. Clinton's arrival. China's high-profile tours through Africa, South America, and Australia in search of resources, the billion-dollar listings of its state companies (including Petro China and the Industrial & Commercial Bank of China) on overseas stock markets. Its rising profile in the United Nations and its sheer economic firepower had made China the new focus of global business and finance since the turn of the century. China's star was shining more brightly than ever before, even as its diplomats protested, they were battling to be heard on behalf of a poor, developing economy.

The implosion of the Western financial system, along with an evaporation of confidence in the U.S. Europe and Japan, overnight pushed China's global standing several notches higher. In the space of a few months in early 2009, the Chinese state committed $50 billion in extra funding for the International Monetary Fund and $38 billion with Hong Kong for an Asian monetary fund. It extended a $25 billion loan to cash-strapped Russian oil companies; set aside $30 billion for Australian resource companies; offered tens of billions more to various countries or companies in South America, central and South-east Asia, to lock up commodities and lay down its marker for future purchases. In September, China readied lines of credit of up to $60 to $70 billion, for resource and infrastructure deals in Nigeria, Ghana, and Kenya.

Beijing's ambition and influence were being lit up in ways that would have been unthinkable a few years previously. The Chinese central bank called for an alternative to the U.S. dollar as a global reserve currency in early 2009 and reiterated its policy as the year went on. France obediently recommitted to Chinese sovereignty over Tibet to placate Beijing's anger over the issue, after Beijing had cancelled an E.U. summit in protest at Paris's welcome for the Dalai Lama. On its navy's 60th anniversary, China invited the world to view its new fleet of nuclear-powered submarines off the port of Qingdao.

The giant Chinese market had become more important than ever. Just ahead of the Shanghai auto show in April 2009, monthly passenger car sales in China were the highest of any market in the world, surpassing the U.S. A month later, Wang Qishan and a team of Chinese ministers met Catherine Ashton, then the E.U. trade commissioner, and about 15 of Europe's most senior business executives in Brussels to hear their complaints about Chinese market access. Sure, Wang conceded after listening to their problems over a working lunch, there are "irregularities" in the market. "I know you have complaints," he replied. "But the charm of the Chinese market is irresistible." In other words, according to astonished executives in the meeting, whatever your complaints, the market is so big, you are going to come anyway. Even worse, many of the executives realised that Mr. Wang was right.

285

The rise of China is a genuine mega-trend, a phenomenon with the ability to remake the world economy, sector by sector. That it is presided over by a communist party makes it even more jarring for a Western world, which, only a few years previously, was feasting on notions of the end of history and the triumph of liberal democracy.

'In just a single generation, the party elite has been transformed from a mirthless band of Mao-suited, ideological thugs to a wealthy, business-friendly ruling class. Today's Party is all about joining the highways of globalisation, which in turn translates into greater economic efficiencies, higher rates of return and greater political security.

In the absence of democratic elections and open debate, it is impossible to judge popular support for the Party. However, it is indisputable that support for the Party has grown with reform since Mao's death. The Chinese Communist Party and its leaders have never wanted to be the West when they grow up. For the foreseeable future, it looks like their wishes will all come true.'

AUTHORS NOTES

I stated in this book that the one thing that brought a country together was a common enemy. Covid-19 has done that. But what happens after the Covid-19 defeat?

If Donald Trump is wise, he will coalesce the Western Democracies against the appalling gang that subjugate 1.35 billion people in China.

It matters not whether China created the virus in their Wuhan facility for biological weapons and deliberately spread it, the fact is, it started in Wuhan where China has a biological weapons facility, financed by the Peoples Liberation Army.

The Chinese government hid the fact that there was the possibility of a pandemic for a period of several weeks or more. There is little doubt that the economies of the Western World have suffered and the country that will benefit most is China unless we take punitive measures against that country.

Will Donald Trump become the Winston Churchill of the 21st century? The opportunity is there for the taking.

Characters: Jeremy Kirkham and Ladvia appeared in the Gorazde Incident.

John Desmond and his team appeared in Moscow Assassin, and the Castrators.

Printed in Great Britain
by Amazon

66554915R00163